THE NEGLIGENT MAGICK TRILOGY

LOCKDREST

soul trap

ADORA MICHAELS

120

THE NEGLIGENT MAGICK TRILOGY
LOCKREST

ADORA MICHAELS

Lockdrest

Copyright Adora Michaels 2024

Cover by Maja K

Title page by Alana Tedmon

Key designs by Eli Quaycong

Lockdrest landscape by Julija Gumbryte

School layout, schedules, and hall cutaway by Austin Michaels

Book formatted by Samantha Pico

ISBN 978-1-961830-05-9 (hardcover)

ISBN 978-1-961830-04-2 (paperback)

ISBN 978-1-961830-06-6 (ebook)

ISBN 978-1-961830-07-3 (ebook, SE)

Printed in USA

Moonshade Press

For those who died for all the wrong reasons,
I wish I could have made the world better for you.

For the children who were not protected when their differences showed, I
wish I could have shown you just how much you bring bright colors to this
dull world.

Dust Eater by Austin Michaels

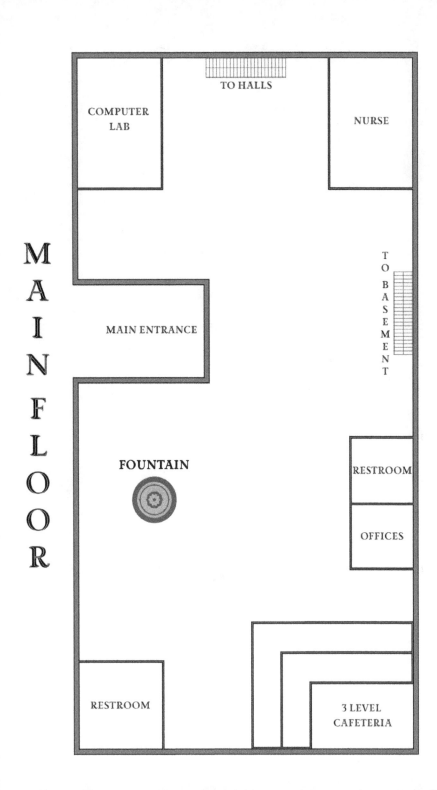

LIBRARY

LIBRARY OFFICE

CLASSROOM

CLASSROOM

CLASSROOM

CLASSROOM

CLASSROOM

CLASSROOM

CLASSROOM

CLASSROOM

CLASSROOM

CLASSROOM

CLASSROOM

CLASSROOM

CLASSROOM

CLASSROOM

CLASSROOM

CLASSROOM

B
A
S
E
M
E
N
T

WATER TUNNEL

KEY
GIVER

LOCKDREST

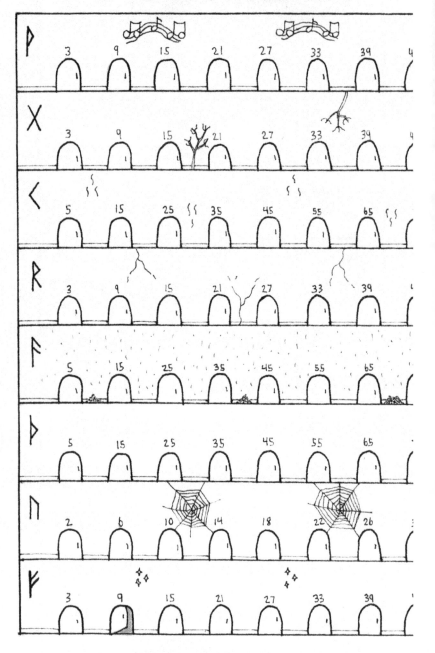

HALLS

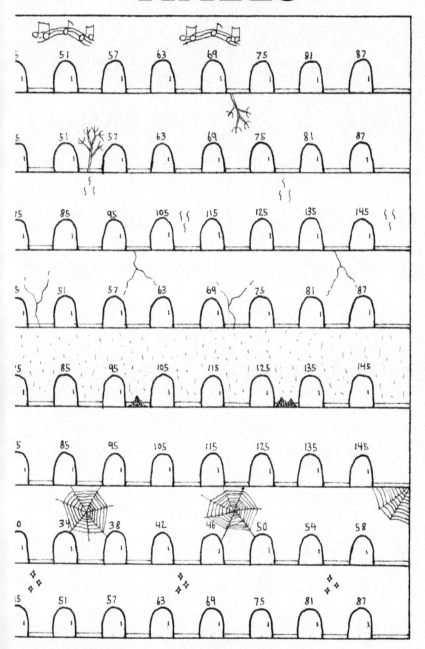

ROOM ASSIGNMENTS

MOLLY REESE	KENAZ 260
NAMU FERNELL	RAIDO 114
OVA FROY	URUZ 150
KOZ CEYRES	URUZ 76
REM TIFFLET	THURISAZ 225
LILY PATHON	FEHU 9
DERRIN NIMPER	RAIDO 96
MR. VERO	KENAZ 190
CELTA HEARD	WUNJO 147
MRS. YITTER	WUNJO 147

STAFF

Mr. Vero	Spirit Magick 4
Mr. Bell	Key Giver
Mr. Dreft	Spirit Magick 3
Murs. Eddl	Divinations and Sensing 1
Mrs. Heard	Religious Coordinator
Mrs. Sleck	Spirit Magick 1
Mrs. Yitter	Librarian
Mr. Young	Transformation Magick
Miss Weelt	History and Transformation of the Magickal World
Mr. Ferrer	Transformation Drinks & Remedies 1
Mrs. Fissh	Techno-Magick
Miss Gilt	Symbols 1
Mx. Focus	Runes 1
Mrs. Jilish	Visionary Magick
Mrs. Refra	Projection and Memory Magick

MOLLY · NAMU · KOZ · REM

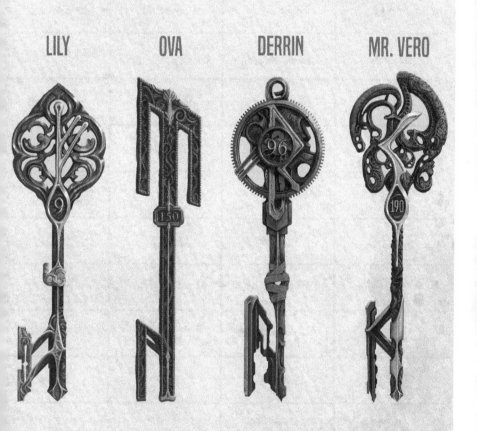

LILY   OVA   DERRIN   MR. VERO

CLASS

	MOLLY	OVA	NAMU
7:30	BREAKFAST	BREAKFAST	BREAKFAST
8:15	Divinations & Sensing Magick 1	Divinations & Sensing Magick 1	Spirit Magick 3
9:15	Symbols 1	Symbols 2	Runes 2
10:15	BREAK	BREAK	BREAK
11:15	History & Transformation of the Magickal World	Runes 2	Private Lessons with Mr. Vero
12:30	LUNCH	LUNCH	LUNCH
1:30	Spirit Magick 1	Spirit Magick 1	Symbols 1
2:30	Techno-Magick	Religious Studies with Mrs. Heard	Visionary Magick
3:30	BREAK	BREAK	BREAK
4:30	Transformation Drinks & Remedies	Projection & Memory Magick	Transformation Magick
	Online Classes	Online Classes	Online Classes
6:00	DINNER	DINNER	DINNER

SCHEDULES

REM	KOZ	LILY	DERRIN
BREAKFAST	BREAKFAST	BREAKFAST	BREAKFAST
Techno-Magick	Spirit Magick 2	Spirit Magick 2	Projection & Memory Magick
Divinations & Sensing Magick 1	Symbols 2	Divinations & Sensing Magick 2	Divinations & Sensing Magick 1
BREAK	BREAK	BREAK	BREAK
Symbols 1	Divinations & Sensing Magick 1	Transformation Magick	History & Transformation of the Magickal World
LUNCH	LUNCH	LUNCH	LUNCH
Techno-Magick	Techno-Magick	Runes 2	Transformation Drinks & Remedies 1
Runes 1	Runes 2	Visionary Magick	Transformation Magick
BREAK	BREAK	BREAK	BREAK
History of Magickal Creatures	History of Magickal Creatures	Symbols 2	Symbols 1
Online Classes	Online Classes	Online Classes	Online Classes
DINNER	DINNER	DINNER	DINNER

Glossary

All-Seeing Time: when magick was discovered by the majority of the world because of technology

Alteress Powder: an altering golden powder that is hard to get and not commonly known as fairy dust

Cell Magick: new magick, also known as techno magick that is used on cell phones

Chalk-rising: a sport to practice symbols where the drawn symbols rise from the ground

Chaos Magick: the manipulation and use of god or goddess essence

Deep Magick Market: a market where things are sold and hidden from the Magickal Society

Druidry: the act and study of guiding people to their gods or goddesses

Dust Eaters: little creatures that come out at night and eat away all the dust and germs

Gnome Magick: a magick created by gnomes that uses very precise geometrics that mimic the hats they wear

Magickal Society: a society who has managed the perception of magick in the world throughout the years

Memory Magick: the act of taking or giving an essence and solidifying it into a place

Mini Trolls: (there are only two known) they are trolls that have been turned mini after encountering and bothering a witch who was from the Forbidden Tell

Nano-bits: the bit of essence in the techno world that work alongside of lincs, stacts, and revers

New Magick: magick created with technology or mixed with technology, the technology making it a magick of its own

Old Magick: magick that uses symbols and raw materials to create, transform, and fix things

Pathon Airlines: airlines made by Sernan Pathon using techno magick and memory magick where the planes can arrive instantly to where they have been before if it is cloudy enough by using water vapors in the clouds to access memory magick.

Spirit Sprites: little creatures with blue-slender, transparent bodies who like to steal and turn things of silver, gold, and bronze noncorporeal and hide those things away in walls, ceilings, and floors

Techno Magick: a new magick using technology

Trendy Drinks: magickal drinks that host trending magickal spells that people can drink and try out

Trolls: giant creatures with a life expectancy of about 300 to 400 years who are in many ways savages and not sophisticated at all

Vigilplunks: pink hairy creatures with big eyes and large lazy mouths containing sharp teeth that attack anyone who is bullying and not appreciating privacy

Trigger Warnings

Drowning, codependency, spiritual assault, bullying,
kidnapping

THE NEGLIGENT MAGICK TRILOGY
LOCKDREST

soul trap

Molly

Chapter One

The back of Molly's phone was warm in her palm, making her hand sweat. She had been using apps nonstop for the last hour with two of her fifteen-year-old freshmen friends, who were just like her, showing off spells they had learned the night before. The new magickal apps that had come out in the last month were so lively and compelling that Molly found herself unable to stop. She just had to try them. They sparked a desire that left her thirsty for more.

By how her friends were acting, she figured that they felt the same way.

"Look! This one's cool! Took me over an hour last night to get right!"

Molly turned her attention to her friend Rexa as the three of them walked down the bright street. Rexa snapped her fingers once before swiping across and down a deep blue app that Molly hadn't seen yet. Five burning white balls like stars rose from the screen and connected, making a constellation above Rexa's phone.

Rexa stopped and flashed her flawless white smile, her brown eyes glistening.

"Perfection!" She blew a kiss at the balls of light above her, the highlighter on her dark cheeks shimmering gold. One of the balls floated over to the non-magickal medical clinic across the street and vanished when it hit the red-and-white sign on the door, which read No Magick Allowed.

Rexa slapped her hand across her mouth to hold in a laugh, then shook her head, bouncing her black curls. "Oops. I should have aimed it that way." She looked over her shoulder to the magickal medical clinic with the letters MMC above its door glimmering the color of ocean waves in the hot summer sun.

"It's not your fault," Val said, smirking at the non-magickal clinic. Her straight blonde hair with purple highlights fell over her shoulder. "The world has been changing drastically since new magick was introduced. It's only going to keep going that way. They need to get over it. At some point, magick will be everywhere. Who our age isn't using it?"

She peered at Molly with sassy blue eyes. They narrowed until Molly nodded in agreement, although Molly didn't quite agree that people and companies needed to get over magick becoming a part of everyday life. But Val wasn't wrong about how things were changing even more now than when their parents were young.

Magick had been proven real only twenty-three years ago, thanks to the internet. In far-off countries in 2007, magick had been caught on video repeatedly, spreading everywhere over the web. It was horrifying to watch the past videos of non-magickal people capturing those who they assumed were magickal and forcing them to do spells. If those people failed to perform magick, they were then beaten on video. If they did perform magick, they were forced to create that magick over and over again. That magick, called old magick, had used symbols and raw materials to create, transform, and fix things. Now, years later, when the chaos had finally calmed, the world had "new" magick, spells one could do with technology.

"I don't know. There are a ton of annoying parents who still refuse to use any kind of magick, like um . . ." Rexa put her fist to her mouth and fake coughed. "Molly's parents . . . They were only in their early twenties when magick went mainstream."

The way Rexa eyed Molly degraded Molly to an ant on the sidewalk. Molly's parents were not a fan of magick, but that wasn't her fault.

"Yeah, that generation are weirdos. Why would they be upset at something that fixed the hellscape they lived on? Can you imagine school shootings every single day? Why would your parents want that, Molly?" Val sneered at her. "What's wrong with them?"

"I . . . I don't think they want that. My mom just liked how things were when she was younger."

"So, she liked being shot at?" Rexa said with a nod.

"No—I don't think she ever—"

Val put up her manicured hand, not giving Molly the chance to explain, which was fine. At least Molly wouldn't make a fool of herself by tripping over her words even more.

When magick had been deemed undeniably real, a massive spell had been cast that got rid of any weapon intended for harm. To this day, if any weapon is made, it disappears in a cloud of smoke.

Although, to Molly, it sounded petrifying the way her parents had lived as young children. Some adults still talked about it as if control had been taken away from them. Which was confusing. Wasn't there less control with countless weapons in the hands of almost everyone?

Molly's parents didn't talk about it like that. They never liked weapons. But they were vastly different than Rexa's and Val's. Although Molly's were around more, they hated magick—well, at least her mom did.

Rexa's leftover glowing stars from her app, which were still suspended above them, flickered out with the odd smell of burning timber.

Val rolled her eyes and pursed her pink lips. "Look at this one."

Val shook her phone and touched the screen to her nose before closing her eyes. Molly watched as her friend hummed a few syllables Molly couldn't comprehend before she pulled her phone away. A long string of droplets rested between Val's nose and the screen, becoming level with Val's eyes. They then splattered to the ground.

"Snot. That's snot!" Rexa said with a shake of her head.

"No. That's real water," Val defended.

"Not possible. Cell magick can't make real things like that. I don't care how many pixels of your soul you give up," Rexa said.

Molly sighed. Her friends had been fighting a lot more lately since they started using cell magick. She wondered how many pixels of her soul Val had given to the app to be able to make something that looked so real.

"Your turn, Molly," Val said, bumping into her and scratching the top of Molly's curly head with her long pink nails.

"I'm . . . I'm a little over it. My phone's burning up."

"Oh, come on! One more. Impress me," Val pushed.

Molly looked down at the magickal apps she had downloaded and flicked past the first page on her screen to the next. Her favorite was one that made sounds come to life. Sometimes, when she couldn't fall asleep, she would lie in bed and listen to the drops of rain from the magick she created and feel them touching and tapping her skin, even through her clothes. It was comforting, like having a night-light in the dark.

Molly didn't want to share this part of her with her friends, but it was the only app she had that could measure up to theirs.

Molly opened the app, prepared to give it one pixel of her soul. Out of all her friends, Molly had been the most reluctant to become a cell witch. She had only tried it when her friends convinced her by explaining how little a pixel really was and that she could do thousands of spells and still have most of her soul to herself.

The problem was that none of them knew how small a pixel really was. No one knew how cell magick really worked. Everything was new. But it was easy to use, and no one had any problems yet, so everybody was trying the apps.

Molly pressed her thumb into the screen, giving her phone her identity. At first, something trickled through her veins like a shot of caffeine before a heaviness rested right behind her eyes. Even though a pixel was small, she swore she felt a little part of herself leave her body when she swirled her thumb to the top left of the screen and then to the bottom of the yellow glare coming through the glass. Her soul and body felt as if they were cement for a moment before whatever had ahold of her let her loose.

It was all just part of the magick.

Molly whistled a tune in her head, calling to what she wanted to come. Hushed whispers blew and wisped around her. She swore it was shaking Val's dangling blue earrings.

She wanted a cold wind in this heat.

The wind started slowly, but the cold bite on her skin was harsh once it picked up. The red flush she had from the sun beating down on her arm was starting to fade.

"Oh, okay—enough!" Val yelled, grabbing the phone from her hand.

Molly hadn't realized that Val had been shaking. Rexa was, too, her arms crossed over herself. She was biting her lips, which were beginning to turn blue.

"It affects you guys, too?"

"Yeah." Rexa rubbed her arms, which were covered in goose bumps. "What kind of spell was that?"

"I don't know. I thought it only worked on me."

"Well, don't do it again. Or at least, next time, could you call something more pleasant?" Val shook her head.

Val gave Molly back her phone and pointed to the place she wanted to go: a shop with a big green sign that read Trennly's Drinks: Where You Can Get Your Trendy Drinks in cursive. It had an outdoor serving window and Trennly himself, the mini-troll who owned the place in the front. His was one of the most popular shops on this street.

Molly let her eyes travel over the shops next to it.

Right next door sat a tanning salon called Aged To Bronze, where people went to get their skin tone changed for a while. They had packages where a customer could get a tan or lighter undertones layered into their skin by a magickal mist. Molly had seen some kids come to school with a hint of a tinted violet orchid to their skin. It all depended on how much one was willing to spend. Val had tried it but complained that the orchid coloring had stung her too much. Her skin had smelled like flowers for days.

There was also a small clothing boutique called Swipe For Change that catered to cell witches. The clothing could change its color and the textures of its frills with a specific app, but it lasted only a short time. Even the more expensive clothing lasted only three days before turning gray and dull, no flicker of color ever returning to them.

Lastly, there was a coffee shop owned by another mini-troll named Kren. The shop, called No-Jitters, sold boring drinks and concoctions that didn't do anything to you and that no one cared about. It wasn't like Trennly's Drinks, where you could always get the latest magickal trend, like glimmering eyes, bunny ears, and, even sometimes, a lion's tail.

Molly had always wondered how two mini-trolls had come to own two shops on the same street. She swore that mini-trolls were not common in any part of the world.

But ever since magick became known, more and more creatures and beasts of myths were finding their way into society; creatures that had been hidden before by spells and magickal specialists. There was a griffon that came to town quite often. Everyone left it alone, unsure what it would do to them with its thick eagle's beak and giant talons if they approached it.

Kren, with downturned lips, a stout body, and a stiff brown button-up above his creaseless black pants, watched them walk over to Trennly's Drinks. When he noticed Molly studying him, his lips formed a thin line before he turned his attention to the metal chairs in front of his small coffee shop. He straightened them as a breeze rustled his unkempt green hair.

Molly's steps were heavier than they were before. She looked back down at her phone, and a wave of lightheadedness had her blinking to steady herself. Had they been on the magickal apps too long?

She pocketed her phone.

"Don't you guys think we should try to learn old magick?" Rexa asked.

Molly had often considered it but had no one to teach her and didn't want to try any sketchy spells from unreliable sources. From what she had researched on the internet, old magick didn't require giving up parts of your soul.

"I don't care to. Who has time for that much work? Too much work and no time," Val said with a dismissive flip of her blonde hair.

"But I did hear there's this school—" Rexa stopped to dodge Val's hand, which almost hit her in the face.

Val was waving at someone, her pink nails glistening in the sun.

Trennly waved back with a sneer, his bright violet mohawk standing still in the breeze. He was short, the top of his head stopping at their waists. When they stood over him, the pleasant smell of his most-likely-magickal hair products wafted up into Molly's nose.

"Unicorn Surprise?" Trennly asked with a smile, running his hand through his mohawk, which stood straight back up after his fingers left it. He knew they always wanted whatever drink on the menu was trending.

"You know it!" Val said, leaning into a table to get closer to his hair. Molly could see her taking in his scent, which disturbed her. She knew it smelled good, but just like the refreshments he would give them, who knew what kind of magick he used on it.

Trennly turned, and Molly couldn't help but hold her breath. She didn't know why. He had never done anything bad to them in all the times he had served them. Besides, all her friends thought he was cool.

Soon, he returned with three tall glasses of sparkling purple-and-pink liquid with shimmering blue straws. Rexa reached for the first one, but Val ripped it away from her reach. When she did, Trennly gave Val a wink, which made her smile as she took in a big mouthful of the cold, frothy liquid.

At first ghostly and then ever-more solid, a twinkling unicorn horn about half a foot tall grew from Val's forehead.

Rexa took the next drink and beamed at her own twinkling purple horn.

Molly knew hers would be light blue, like it always was.

Trennly handed Molly her drink with another wink. His green eyes bronzed for a split second as Molly brought it to her lips. It was as if a silent scream were building up inside her head, with the pressure rising as she took a long sip. Then, all of a sudden, that scream dissipated into a relaxing chemical throughout her body that made her feel sluggish for a moment before her horn grew.

She knew it would last for three hours. Even though that wasn't long, she did it because it was the hip new thing. Some kids came to Trennly consistently in the summer to keep their horns, but Molly and her friends only came every few days. She heard one of the girls in her class say it made her feel more connected to magick. Molly didn't feel that way. If anything, she felt like, whenever she had any of the trendy drinks, it caused more problems for her than it was worth.

Like the problem coming toward her now.

Two spirits.

She sighed inwardly. Spirits always targeted her, for some reason, while leaving her friends and everyone else she was around alone. It had started when she was little, but now—ever since her first visit to Trennly's, she thought—they seemed to notice her more. As if they were drawn to her.

Her friends couldn't see them. But they knew that she did.

Rexa rolled her eyes, taking another sip of her drink. "How many?"

They must have noticed that her eyes had gone wide.

"Two," Molly answered. The spirits of two older men were running to her as if some musical horn were calling them. They were stumbling over their feet and bumping into each other.

"What do you mean how many?" Trennly asked behind her.

She had never had an encounter near him before. Usually, it happened when they were farther away from his shop after she had a drink. But Trennly's Drinks had opened only recently, last year.

"Ghosts. She sees ghosts," Val said, glaring where Molly's eyes were glued.

"Ahhhh," Trennly said, an amused inflection to his voice.

Molly set down her drink and took out her phone. She would have to give another pixel to fight them away. She hated it, but she had no other choice. Whenever one touched her, they tried to take over her body. In the past, before cell magick, she had almost been taken over multiple times. It wasn't pleasant . . . at all.

She opened the app. A source on the internet had said that it was "the new way to use old magick when it comes to spirit hunts." It was the closest thing she could find when she'd researched spirits and ghosts and how to get rid of them. In the black screen were lines upon white lines that had to be connected and pulled from one side of the screen to the other to form some kind of diagram with a symbol in the middle. The diagrams changed, but the symbol in the middle was always the same.

She began working and pulling. Trying to form the picture that was hinted at really small in the right corner. How the phone knew what kind of diagram she needed for the spirits, she didn't know. But this was a complicated one. Was it because there were two ghosts?

One spirit pushed the other. The second one grabbed the back of the first one's hair and dragged him down, giving her more time.

From the corner of her eye, she saw the green-haired troll coming over from his shop. He was studying her intensely. Her horn was warming in the sun, making her dizzy as she tried to work the lines.

But something was wrong. Her fingers would no longer glide over any of the strings. They didn't move as she swiped.

She hit the screen twice. Three times. Pounding it with her finger.

She looked up to see that the ghosts were closer now. Close enough to touch.

Molly scrambled out of her chair.

"Are you done yet?" Val asked.

But Rexa could tell that something wasn't right. "What's wrong?"

The next thing Molly knew, Trennly pushed her aside with a confident shrug to face the two ghosts himself. They stopped for a second, unsure of Trennly. Then, with a clap of Trennly's hands, they were gone, splattered across the sidewalk.

"How . . . how did you . . . ?" Molly gasped.

The troll went over to where the ghosts had been and laid his hands flat on the ground. The leftover transparent bits were sucked into his hands.

"Old magick," Rexa breathed.

"Well, duh." Val laughed. "How else do you think he makes our—"

Val stopped talking. Stopped moving. Molly realized she was paralyzed. Trennly held up his two hands, symbols glistening on his thick palms, as he trudged toward Molly. They were the same symbol that always appeared on her app.

"What are you doing?" Molly asked, stepping back and accidentally hitting the table behind her. Her drink splattered on the ground like those ghosts had been splattered moments before.

"I help you, you help me," Trennly winked.

What did those symbols on Trennly's palms mean?

Molly noticed that Rexa was also unmoving beside her.

But why? Why wasn't she frozen like Val and Rexa? She glanced across the street. The other mini-troll was approaching them.

Trennly's symbols disappeared, and her friends were moving again the moment Trennly reached his hand out toward her. Now, Molly froze when she saw a transparent bluish hand stretching through Trennly's solid one. It reached out for her like she had seen many spirits try to do without a physical body. It wanted to grab her and take her over. She tried to scream. She didn't want to go through, again, what happened when a spirit touched her.

She pulled her arm away but not before Trennly grasped it with that ghostly hand.

And then she was gone.

She was not with her friends anymore. She was under a dark-blue sky on a thin sheet of purple ice. A lake where she had been too many times. Every time a spirit tried to overtake her, she came here and fell through the ice.

She'd only ever been saved when an outside force disrupted whatever had ahold of her physical body. She had no control here.

She hated it. She hated herself. She just wanted to be normal. She wanted to do what her friends did. She wanted to drink magick drinks and follow magickal trends and fit in.

Not end up here.

The ice cracked, and she fell through.

But just as the water covered her head, something grabbed her and yanked her out.

She was standing on the street. Kren had his hand wrapped around her arm, his brown eyes boring into hers. With his other hand, he held Trennly by the hair, while Trennly yelled at him to stop.

Kren pulled Trennly's mohawk harder and then let go, making Trennly fall to the ground. Molly watched as Trennly opened his hand. He quickly hit his palm to the cement and then he was gone.

"Get your hands off her!" Rexa said, diving to tear Molly's hand away from Kren.

"Are you okay?" Val scrambled to her.

But then they stopped. The symbols that had once been on Trennly's palm were now on Kren's.

"What's going on?" Molly asked. Her heart was beating so fast she could barely breathe. She had almost just drowned and lost herself again to that nightmare. Then she came back to this? Trolls with powers? Trolls freezing her friends? Spirits splattered on the sidewalk?

Kren tsked and looked into her eyes again. "I saved you. You are lucky."

"Saved me from what? Trennly? The trendy drink troll?"

Kren bit his lip and shook his head, throwing away Molly's arm. "You not belong here and not belong using that kind of magick." He pointed to her phone. "You are going to get yourself killed."

"Everyone uses it," Molly said, looking to her friends, who had their phones still clutched in their hands.

He shook his head. "Pixels . . ." He tsked again, then grabbed her phone, threw it to the ground, and stomped on it with his thick brown shoes. The screen shattered as he crushed it to pieces. "You need to learn who to trust. You need to learn where those come from."

She didn't understand what he meant. Her friends knew who to trust. She trusted them. She trusted their judgment.

"You . . . empty vessel, see ghosts, spirits, yes? You go to place in mind when touched?"

How did he know?

"Trends." He pointed to her horn, then put down his finger and sighed. "You are going to get killed. Get new phone. One less tainted."

Her mom was going to be so angry with her. "Why would you . . . ? Why did you—what do you mean, less tainted?"

This time, he pointed at her face. "You need to learn. At Lockdrest."

"Lockdrest?"

"School. So can learn to survive."

"But . . . how? Wh-Why?" She didn't understand what he was talking about. She didn't know if she should be listening to him, even though he had saved her life. Even though he had grabbed her out of that place that was her prison. A place where, before, when she was younger, if she happened to escape, it was only out of luck.

She looked to her frozen friends again, desperate for their opinions, but their eyes were only glossy marbles gazing at her.

"To keep you from slipping into your mind. To keep you from being taken over by spirit magick. You will learn old magick." He waved his hand. "Better than giving pieces of soul to who you don't know."

"I can't. I already go to school. My parents . . ."

"You want to survive?"

Her friends unfroze when he squeezed his hand into a fist in front of her face. The horn on her head crumbled, and pieces of it fell to the ground as her friends gasped and jumped away.

"Yes, but . . ."

"Then, I will get you there. To your world, to them, you are now dead."

He snapped his fingers, and all went black as Molly heard a scream.

Namu

Chapter Two

Namu hated this world, this school, and magick. He could not stand the emptiness he felt every day as he walked the halls of Lockdrest as a sixteen-year-old second-year student. Especially the one he walked now, Raido Hall. It was five floors up from the main floor of the school and was the hall his room belonged to.

Raido meant journeys, pleasure, and healing.

He would probably laugh at the irony of it if he didn't have jagged, gaping holes in his soul given to him on this floor.

All thanks to a secret antechamber, which had to be in his room for some reason, that led to a tormenting door. He wondered if he would ever fully laugh again.

No. He would. One day, he would laugh. One day, he would feel whole again. He would fix this.

And Mr. Vero, the only teacher and person who knew about what had happened to him, was going to help him. He had promised.

Namu would hold him to that.

A flash of anger flared through Namu's mind at the thought of the professor. None of this should have happened. Mr. Vero should have been one of the teachers who had protected him. Even if the school had placed him there, Mr. Vero should never have allowed Namu to be in that room.

Although that door had ended the horrors of the outside world twenty-something years ago, it had created nightmares for anyone who had found themselves inside it, like him.

He still didn't understand why that door had to be placed in a student's room in a school full of kids. Why would they put the core of the spell that had gotten rid of all weapons here?

He was going to leave once he was healed. He would leave and go back to the normal life he had always wanted. He would never come back to this. He would work in construction like his dad and, hopefully, never have to think of the world beyond that door or Lockdrest again. Which was one of the reasons why he had never told his family what had happened. He never wanted to be faced with pity or fear in their eyes once it all passed and he had fixed this.

Inky black tendrils—probably the fingers of some kind of creature or beast—waved out of a stony crack between two doors in his hall. Namu wanted to ignore it. Wanted to roll his eyes at it and walk away. But he found he couldn't. It was hard to ignore things, especially something like this that was unique to his hall. Some people, especially Mr. Vero, didn't understand that. How was he expected to ignore something that had changed him forever? Something that through some kind of magick had forced metallic chaos through his veins. That had torn literal holes in his soul.

That metal was pulsing now to the beat of his heart. The holes gaped wider each and every day.

Lockdrest

The black fingers continued to crawl out down the wall until they could reach no farther. Then the smoke-like blackness retreated back into the wall, then completely disappeared.

Namu shook his head, letting his eyes travel down the endless cracks, where many other kinds of beings, monsters, and creatures had never been able to get through. Anyone brave enough to get close could see them through the cracks, if the creatures hadn't already gone. It was always as if they had accidentally found their way behind the wall and could never find their way back. He rarely saw the same creatures twice.

As if in answer, two deep-orbed eyes the color of the ocean stared at him until they blinked out and were gone.

He hated this school.

Namu gave a deep sigh, bit the inside of his cheek, and pulled out his phone to check the time. Bright green numbers illuminated the screen, telling him he would be late if he didn't rush. He had three minutes to get downstairs for his special session with Mr. Vero—one of many Namu was sure they would have together over the year to try to find a way for spirit magick to fill up the holes that the monstrous creatures behind the door in that nightmare world had torn into him.

He headed to the stairwell. He noticed the light scars on the dark skin of his hand from when he had helped his dad with construction work years ago. He wished his dad could come to the school and see how uniquely built it was. He knew his dad would especially love the stairwell, with its many stones embedded in the dark hardwood. Namu had tried taking pictures of it to send to his dad, but the images couldn't capture the extraordinary design.

When Namu reached Fehu Hall, the first hall off the stairs of the main floor, he had to blink his eyes to get them to stop watering from the glare. This was where Lily's room was. Lily was the friend he had followed to Lockdrest and the only reason he had come. Lily was lucky that their hall had gilded walls, doors, and no creatures coming in between any cracks.

Next was the main floor, which was deserted at this time, as most students were in their classes, which were held in the basement. Mr. Vero had set aside this hour, the class period before lunch, to work with Namu. It was hard to find any other time in the day, with all the other classes during school hours, and then online non-magickal schooling happening in the evening.

Namu pulled out his phone from the back pocket of his cargo shorts again; he was two minutes late. He ran down the wider grand staircase that led to the basement, annoyed at himself, then rushed to Mr. Vero's classroom.

But someone was in the basement, standing in the middle of the hall that held the classrooms. Anger swept through Namu's heart.

The older boy was practicing expelling some of his soul from his body right outside of the second-highest-level classroom for Spirit Magick Three. The older boy's ghostly purple spirit left his hand until he had two. A transparent one and his physical one.

The spirit part of him was whole and healthy. It had no holes.

The boy smiled, turned the handle to the classroom he had been standing in front of, and walked into the class.

Chipper, proud of himself, happy.

Something Namu may never be.

He was most likely trying to prove to the teacher where he should be placed. Perhaps he failed Spirit Magick Two last year and was desperate to get into Spirit Magick Three.

Namu shook his head and continued to where he needed to go.

Mr. Vero had left the door open and was sitting at his desk, looking bored, until he saw Namu. Then, his serious blue eyes lifted, and his thick lips stretched into a teasing smile.

"Look who's late for once."

Namu didn't say anything. This was why he didn't want to be late. He knew Mr. Vero would find fun in it.

"Namu, be careful. If you don't cheer up slightly, I might threaten not to start until you smile."

Namu contorted his mouth to a scowl in Mr. Vero's direction as the Spirit Magick Four teacher stood up and made his way around his large wooden desk. His black shirt clung to his muscular arms and hugged the small pudge of his stomach.

"Let's get started," Namu pressed, his jaw clenching. He hated how desperate he was. How empty.

Mr. Vero smiled, bending down only slightly to be at eye level with him.

Namu didn't understand why Mr. Vero didn't reflect any of the pain that Namu felt or why he was still at the school. About twenty years ago, during his time as a student, the door had formed in Mr. Vero's room, which was Namu's room now. Mr. Vero had gotten lost deep inside it, just like Namu had last year.

"Mr. Vero—"

"Once again, Namu, Mr. V. You can call me Mr. V. We went through this all of last year."

That wasn't true. They had only started going through it after Mr. Vero had saved him from beyond the door. That had been when half the year had already passed.

"Mr. Vero. I would like to get started so we can move on." So he could leave the school and never look back. Mr. Vero had told him just to ignore the door if that was what he wanted, and leaving was the easiest way to do that.

But he could only leave if he found out how to heal himself from what had happened in that dreadful place. And the only place that could help him do that was also the one place he didn't want to be: this school.

Mr. Vero sighed deeply, looking into Namu's eyes for a moment before straightening up and walking back to his desk. He pulled at the bands of his black shirt around his pasty biceps before picking up a pot containing a thin, twisted tree from the floor and putting it on his desk with a thud.

Namu walked around a couple of the desks, studying the potted tree that should have been outside. Last year, Mr. Vero and Namu had tried symbols, runes, transformation drinks, meditations, and even some of the magick that most students in the school were blocked from learning, like chaos magick. Now he wanted to try a tree?

"I'm surprised—pleasantly, of course—that you returned." Mr. Vero winked, which made Namu want to turn away, but he didn't. He just stared at the fragile-looking tree with the twisted stump that Namu could easily wrap his whole hand around. It had only four leaves sprouting from the top, which were a lively deep green.

"I delayed meeting with you these last couple days so I could prepare some suggestions and you could get settled for another year. I want to start slow this year with your healing."

"What were you doing all summer, then?" *While I've been suffering and trying to figure things out alone*, Namu thought. He had learned that it was impossible for him to do anything at home without the school and its resources. The internet had very little to say about any dimensional worlds, especially ones containing creatures that ate away at your soul.

"I have my own things to do, Namu. You know this."

"You live at this school, though, guarding that door. Why would the headmasters give you that job if you aren't that good at it? Why have they not tried to get rid of it? Why do they leave it for kids to find their way into?" *And die.*

Mr. Vero only nodded, ignoring Namu's questions like he always did. He smiled again, pushing the plant toward Namu. "We will try this first. An easy transfer, something you should be learning more about in class with Mr. Dreft this year, since I bumped you to Spirit Magick Three. I thought maybe if you try to take the spirit of a living thing like this tree—"

Namu backed away. He'd learned since Spirit Magick One that almost everything had a spirit, but stealing a spirit from something, like parts of his spirit had been stolen from him? He didn't want to do that.

"Namu, I know it sounds alarming, but the spirit may possibly live on inside of you. Like if a tree is cut down and made into a table or paper, part of its spirit still lives on in those things until it passes into the other life."

"Possibly?"

Mr. Vero bit his lip and ran his hand through his long black hair. "You said you were willing to do almost anything. It's just a tree."

"It still has a spirit."

"Which may continue to live on in you if you take it in. Then it may mend and mold with you. Since it's living, it may fill up the holes in your soul."

"But what happens if it doesn't work?"

"You know this is new, Namu. New for all of us. I don't know. I cannot answer that question. I figured you would at least want to try."

Namu shoved away from the desk and away from his teacher. He hated how new this all was. It shouldn't be new. The school should have figured this out.

Other students had gone through the door and had died before Namu had found his way inside. Namu was only one of two people who had survived. Mr. Vero was the first, back when he was a student. But Mr. Vero's soul came away barely eaten, with only one or two holes, not like the twenty or more that Namu had; he had given up counting long ago as tears overtook him each time he tried. He only let himself look at his spirit-self now when he expelled part of his soul from his body to check if anything they had been trying had worked, even though he could already feel that he wasn't healing.

It had been over half a year, and not one of the holes in his soul had gotten smaller or knitted back together. He had always heard of people losing pieces of themselves, but to *see* that he had lost parts of himself when he looked down at his arm or torso in spirit form, to not see his full self there—it burned inside.

"It isn't fair. I shouldn't be the one being experimented on."

"If you're not ready to try this, I understand," Mr. Vero said.

But what was Namu supposed to do if he wasn't willing to try these new things? Live incomplete forever? Never live out his dreams or, even if he did, never be satisfied because he had lost the part of himself that allowed him to be happy? Never find a wife because he only had bits of himself to give, which wasn't fair to anyone?

"Okay," he said, defeated. "Tell me what to do."

Mr. Vero slid the pot to the middle of the desk, then grabbed some marble slabs, clanking them against each other. "I know spirit magick is complicated. And I have briefly discussed before how spirits can be destroyed *if*—and only *if*—they have been out of a host for a long time, have no placement, and are not bonded to something."

Namu cringed. He remembered that from his readings. How a spirit from a human, creature, or other living things could, in a way, be sucked up and its magick used but that it was usually done by experts, and it was looked down upon.

Namu hated the idea of destroying someone else's soul, since the same kinds of spells relating to spirit magick could be used using one's own spirit. You could then replenish yourself by doing something you love, something that grants fulfillment and contentment. It would be hard to destroy one's own soul because spirit magick actively drains the person using it; before you caused too much damage to yourself, you would be too drained to continue. It was self-adjusting. What someone usually did was borrow a little bit of soul essence from something else, not taking the whole spirit, only the essence or energy of it. That mainly worked on objects that weren't alive, and it only gave a little boost to most spells, but at least a whole someone or something wasn't destroyed in the process.

Mr. Vero set the two slabs of pink-and-white-veined marble on the student desk closest to Namu. "The hope is that, if you can take the spirit from this tree and bond it to you, it will stay in you and not disintegrate into your own soul. Maybe then it will fill up the parts of you that are missing. Over time, we can work on different kinds of transformation magicks to get it to meld better with your soul so you feel more like yourself again."

"Leaving the tree to die?"

"The body of the tree . . . Well, yes. It isn't like taking a soul's essence. For this, we need an 'alive' thing and need to take in the whole. Last year, remember, taking the essence of unalive things did not work. The remaining parts of your soul used them up, saving the reserves for spirit-magickal use, while not touching the holes in your spirit."

"Yes." They had tried taking the essence of some of his books about construction, random statues that Mr. Vero assumed Namu found intriguing, and other things that Mr. Vero thought may give Namu any sense of delight when he saw them. Nothing had worked.

"That is why, hopefully, this essence will be drawn to your empty spaces and fill them up, since it might want a space of its

own to fill. Then maybe we can bond it there to stay until . . .
well, we can make those parts less tree-like, I guess."

Namu tilted his head back and looked up at the five small
chandeliers on the ceiling above them giving off hazy yellow
light. He didn't understand why the school had decided to
modernize some rooms, while leaving others untouched. Maybe
it depended on the teacher.

"Directions. So. Use this transfer symbol like I've shown
you before, but this time, you need to add these parts to it for
the Tree of Life."

Mr. Vero took a thick quartz wand from his pocket and drew
what looked like an "S" at first onto the marble plates. But then
it became a leaf at the end of an overturned tail, with two dots
at the top and bottom.

"You will draw the spirit of the tree out with your own,
making a connection like I taught you. Then draw this symbol
twice, once into the tree's spirit and then into your own hands.
When you connect with the tree, take it in. Then put your
spirit hands in the marble and concentrate to become one. That
simple. The hardest part will be concentrating—if you want it to
settle—and trying not to make yourself sick."

"Because I'm becoming one with a tree . . ."

Mr. Vero ignored him.

Namu sighed and went over to the tree to get to work. First,
he let himself go but not completely. He held onto himself, his
persona, as if on a string, but let freedom from the world around
him wash over him. It created a feeling of floating. He felt his
soul wanting to connect back with his body like two magnets,
but that force became weaker the farther he let his soul slip away
from what held it in place.

And then he saw them.

His hands, transparent blue. As the essence of his spirit was
leaving through his palms, a big empty circle became visible

in the middle of one. Then the spirit essence of his forearms started to escape. In them, he saw three more holes.

Holes that left him disconnected from the world and from himself.

He let his spirit call out to the tree, which was easy, compared to some of the spirits he'd had to call out to in classes before. Like called to like. He looked beyond the tree and took it in as if he knew it and let his subconscious guide his way. The tree was strong and was built for greater things, just like he was. He grasped onto those similarities and slowly pulled the spirit of the tree out of itself.

It came out like a wisp.

The wisp was white, unlike his blue. It was thin and new, yet the farther he pulled, there were layers of old, as if from the seeds and lives before it. He pulled just enough to not disconnect it or break it completely but enough so that he had room to write.

Without losing his concentration, he looked down at the marble slabs containing the symbols and lines to remind him what he needed to write. Then, using his spirit finger, guided by his corporeal one, he drew that symbol in two spots into the tree's spirit.

He withdrew his hand from the tree and traced that symbol onto the palms of his hands through his spirit form. The symbols began to glow a deep white and then blue.

Taking a deep breath, Namu looked for Mr. Vero's approval. The teacher nodded, then Namu placed both palms against the two symbols he had made on the tree's spirit and closed his eyes.

Like called to like.

He drew the spirit in.

He let it fill him up.

It filled his essence at first. The first layer of his soul.

Then the stronghold of the tree went deeper. The beauty, the future of many possibilities, and the roots dug so deep. He inhaled and took it all in.

He placed his hands on the cool surfaces of the smooth marble slabs.

The symbols lit up with a shocking fit of light before they dulled, like he knew the tree was doing behind him. Dying and dulling. Living the rest of its life through him, having given itself to him to use.

He tried to feel it fill him completely. Tried to take the firmness of the tree and collide it with his full self, enough to fill the holes, enough to heal all his aching.

But he still felt empty . . .

Until, for a moment, he didn't.

He felt it then. Every piece of himself held onto a feeling of strength, of stubborn desire.

He was whole.

He was one with himself. One with the earth. One with the world.

Until it began to wither.

He closed his eyes, biting his lip until he felt pain. He tried to keep the feeling of wholeness there for good, tried to make it stick, but it was slipping away. The metal from that nightmare world was stirring in him. Eating away at the gratification by reminding him of the mistake he had made and who he now was.

He passed out.

He was back in that place. A bruised purple sky above him. The sky that haunted him every night in his sleep. It was looking down at him. No matter how hard he tried to look away, he couldn't.

His eyes were frozen open. Petrified. Just as they were before.

Forced to look up into the otherworldly sky as purple starry dust sprinkled down, unable to move or blink. He was trapped inside a husk of black metal. Black metal that was burning his flesh.

He wanted to scream but could not. He wanted to cry out for being here again but could not. He wanted nothing more than to free his body, but those creatures were there again.

Those white creatures, who, at first, he had thought had come to save him. Small, no bigger than his hand, with three heads and three little toes. They began crawling all over his metal husk, leaving tiny tingles all around him.

He couldn't count them. He could only feel them.

Only because he had done this before, he knew what they would need.

He didn't want to live it all over again.

But, once again, he was forced to.

His hand was outstretched, reaching for the metal trees. That was the first place the creature bit as it dug its head into him and took a chunk from his soul.

The first bite was freezing. He was left cold and in shock.

Until, slowly, he was devoured. Creatures were crawling over his eyes and over his skin until they stopped and then dug in deep for another bite. One on his chest, one on his neck, one on his arm.

He couldn't breathe.

He was going to die. Completely lose himself all over again.

All because he went through that mysterious door. A door that no one had warned him about. Not the headmasters or Mr. Vero. When they knew.

He had to pull away.

It was then that he did, just like he had the first time. His soul tore away from his body. The threads that held him together pulled to their limit with a yank. He fell and then watched as the tiny creatures kept digging into his metal husk. There were so many of them.

With only bits of himself left, he ran. Stumbling, not knowing where to go or how to escape, he ran to the door that had closed behind him, locking him in, and found that he could pass right through it, which he did, leaving his body behind. After that, he passed through walls until he found himself outside Mr. Vero's door. The one teacher who had given brief clues that Namu hadn't put together until now. The one who then went back with him to save his body. The one who could not save him now.

Molly

Chapter Three

Molly's stomach dropped. She was falling. Eyes wide, limbs flailing, she tried to grab onto something, but her arm only brushed velvet as her stomach lurched. Then her head hit something hard and unforgiving.

She groaned, rolling onto all fours. She closed her eyes to retreat back into darkness, then rested her forehead against a soft fabric ground that smelled of fresh mint.

"Careful," someone said with no humor or care in their voice. She recognized that voice as everything rushed back to her. She remembered hanging out with her friends, the unicorn horn drinks, the spirits, the mini-trolls, being attacked, and dying . . .

Dying?

Molly lifted her head, only to have it hit something again. She grimaced.

Now a pounding pulse was swimming in her head.

From the area rug she found herself lying on, she tilted her head a little and saw that what she kept hitting was a sturdy wooden coffee table.

She kept her head away from it this time as she leaned against what she must have fallen off of earlier, which was a yellow-flowered couch, to stare at Kren, who had a drink in his large hands and was studying her. His brown eyes held no emotion, just like his voice hadn't. He was in a chair built just for him. A small wooden one, where he could set his feet on the ground.

Molly was hesitant to move. To make a sound. She had seen him do things that she had not known were possible.

She waited for him to say something. To explain himself. Explain why he had taken her away from her friends and her family.

The words slipped off her tongue. "You . . . killed me." She stared at him, waiting for him to blink. He did not. Then she forced herself to pat her chest with her palms and then her arms.

She couldn't be dead. She didn't think she was dead. But she had heard him say . . .

"Did not kill you. Friends only think that."

Her friends. What happened to them when everything had gone black? Had they run for help? Had they called the magickal police who worked for the Magickal Society? Did they even have the number for the Magickal Division of Officers? Were there magickal officers near her town, since they didn't live in a city? She had never needed to know before.

"What about my family?"

"I'm sure they too." Kren nodded, then took a sip from the deep violet mug he was holding. The slurp was noisy in the quiet room.

"But why? Why would you . . . How did you get me here?"

Molly tore her eyes away from him and looked around. Her brain was so frantic she didn't know if she was looking for an exit or just taking in her surroundings. Her heart was pounding so fast that her breathing couldn't keep up.

She glanced down. The rug under her was striped dark green and orange. She followed it with her eyes to the wooden floors and then up the walls, which were painted a cool green. There were shelves upon shelves on the walls filled with different kinds of mugs. There was a bookshelf, what looked like a small kitchen off the room they were in, and then . . . a handle on a wall where a door should have been. There was also a large glass window that looked like it should be a sliding glass door that led to a balcony outside. But there was no outline to it.

There was no way for her to escape.

"Transformation magick bring you here," Kren said, taking another sip as he watched her. Then he waved to the doors and said, "Transformation magick also," as if to explain those.

"But why?" Her heart was pounding harder. What was she supposed to do against someone who knew magick? Old magick? Her hands slid to the pockets of her pants in search of her phone, but then she remembered he had broken it.

"For you to live," Kren said and shook his head. He looked agitated. His green hair brushed across his large forehead as he set his mug down on the short side table next to him. "Stupid Trennly."

Trennly had attacked her. He tried to take her over like other spirits had tried to do, but why?

"You brought me here to protect me from Trennly?"

"Brought you here to protect you from self." Kren looked disgusted with her. "Cell magick, trends, spirits, Trennly. Need to learn to protect self."

"By making the world think that I'm dead?"

Kren shrugged. "Easiest way. You tell me. In this town. Are parents accepting of changes of magick? Would they let you go to Lockdrest?"

She didn't know what Lockdrest was.

This was a horrifying mess that Molly would have to clean up. This was embarrassing. Now her parents would never allow her to do anything relating to cell witches or cell magick . . . if she found her way back.

"But what about your shop? How are you supposed to go back to that if they think you killed me? Doesn't anyone know where you live?"

"Doesn't matter. No-Jitters doing bad anyway. I don't use magick like Trennly. Only magick for calming or energy. Not trends. Trennly's Drinks was ruining No-Jitters. Trennly . . . ACK! Trennly . . ." Kren seized his mug again, sloshing its contents.

"But why did . . . Why would he . . ." Trennly had never done anything to her before, and he had always seemed like a nice guy. She had trusted him because her friends had trusted him.

She felt the sudden urge to run away. Dizziness overtook her as she recalled how that spirit hand had reached for her and had come out of a physical body like her own. She felt sick. It had been someone she thought she knew. Someone she thought she trusted. But he had tried to take advantage of her.

"Sit," Kren commanded as he rose from his seat and disappeared into the kitchen.

She scrambled up and fell into the too-small couch. The yellow velvet with threaded flowers rubbed against her arm, making her skin feel all wrong.

Kren returned with a small green trash can that he set beside her foot, then pulled a box of tissues from it and handed it to her. From his other hand, he gave her a multi-shaded blue mug that reminded her of the ocean. It was heavy in her hands, even though it was empty.

"You are empty vessel," he stated as he turned and walked back to the kitchen.

This time, she watched the back of his brown button-up, which looked worn, like it had lost some color over time. It crinkled and released with each step as she sat there in shock.

What was an empty vessel? Did it mean that she was empty inside? That she did not have a soul?

"Wait! What does that mean?" she yelled after him.

He returned with a clear kettle of steaming light-blue liquid and motioned to her to hold out her cup. She did, and he poured carefully, then headed back to the kitchen to put it away.

Should she drink it? He had saved her. Now he was giving her a drink? What did that mean? Maybe he did want to help her. Maybe he did want to teach her to protect herself.

The steam from the liquid rose to her cheek, warming her face until she felt it turning damp. She shifted the mug in her lap so the aroma could rise straight to her nose instead. Even with panic muddling her senses, she could smell some kind of exotic flower in a mystic mist. Or maybe it was fruit trees growing bountifully in a fog.

The steam was calming, dazing, and guarding.

"Take sip."

Kren was back. She, instinctively, did what he said. She had the desire to trust him and please him, and she hated herself for it. She was always falling into those patterns with her friends, her teachers, and her family.

The hot blue liquid touched her lips first, and she took in a blooming feeling of wellness. It was like three liquid petals were set individually on her tongue before they dissolved into a foggy, candy-like vapor that steamed up through her nose, calming her nerves.

"Oh, wow."

Kren nodded, satisfied, and then asked, "You see spirits?"

Molly nodded. "Ever since I was little." At first, she thought that everyone did. When she was a baby, apparently, her parents took her to every non-magickal doctor they could think of, trying to figure out what was wrong with her since she screamed and cried all the time. The day she was finally old enough to yell out at a preschool—of all places—and say what was wrong with her was when she realized that no one else saw spirits. After that, she shut up about it and always kept it to herself, embarrassed. She did not want her parents to be disappointed in her or send her somewhere far away. It wasn't until she got older, after doing research and forming a bond with her friends, that she told her friends what she saw. They initially thought it was cool until they found it annoying, but that was better than them thinking she was weird when things happened to her that they could not see or understand.

"Not normal," Kren stated.

She nodded and looked out the window. She wished she could see the busy street. She could almost hear it below. She knew it wasn't normal to see spirits. It was one of the things she hated about it—besides having to be on guard all the time.

A question formed in her mind and snapped her attention back to him. "Can you see them? And Trennly? Can mini-trolls see them, too?" No. That couldn't be it either. She had done the research. More people had to have seen them. Otherwise, there would have been nothing on the subject.

He recoiled and motioned for her to take another drink. She could tell that her sudden outburst startled him. Folding his hands in his lap, he took a deep breath. "Beings who work with and have studied spirit magick can see them too."

Spirit magick? "But I haven't studied any magick. Well, not really. Especially not when I was a child."

He glanced at her mug and nodded to it. Annoyed, she took another sip and let the mystic fog fill her lungs and slow her heartbeat.

"Empty vessels. You are different."

"How?"

"Not much known. Not empty. Bad term. But rare. From what known, bodies easily ready to take magick or anything else. But spirit won't leave own body. You won't be able to astral project or do spirit expelling. Mind too ready to sink somewhere else and let others take over. Soul just wants to fall into self. Spirits see this, then want to take over. Want body because alive body better than dead. Spirit then can keep body alive."

Molly wished she had her phone to look up what some of those terms meant.

She took another long slurp of the liquid that Kren had given her. Why was her soul so different than others?

Kren cleared his throat and asked, "Where do you go when a spirit takes over? Or tries?"

She didn't want to think about that. She didn't want to go back to that place of ice. She didn't understand why she went there.

He noticed her hesitancy. "You don't fight back?"

Her voice broke. "I can't."

He nodded and took another sip of his own, looking out the sliding glass door. "You had bad incident?"

She did. When she was in middle school, she had been on a subway in the city with her parents one day. A spirit tried to take her. It was so crowded that she couldn't move or get away and then she had woken up in the hospital. Her parents had said she was having seizures on the subway. She imagined that the spirit had lost its hold on her during the commotion.

After that, she had tried to find some way to protect herself, while trying not to look weird, trying to keep up with her friends, and trying not to go against her parents' wishes and beliefs. It was exhausting.

Kren seemed to realize she wasn't going to tell him about the incident, so he moved on. "Tell me where you go. I tell you why Trennly tried."

She took a deep breath and put the mug on the coffee table. She didn't want to start shaking and spill its contents. "I go to someplace under a dark blue sky on a thin sheet of purple ice. Sometimes, the ice cracks, and I fall through."

With a nod, Kren put his mug down and went to the giant window that showed the balcony. She was thankful that he didn't ask any more about the place. "Trennly has had problem for long time since he was changed. He has been—is desperate to not be troll any longer."

Molly watched as Kren lifted his hand to the side of the window and closed his hand into a fist. The lines that were supposed to outline a sliding glass door came back. Her shoulders relaxed. She wasn't entirely trapped anymore. There was a way out if she wanted to take it. If she wanted to jump.

"Trennly wasn't always a troll?" she asked.

Kren shook his head as he headed to the main door and made his hand into a fist again. Dark lines grew around the door, forming its outline. "He was always a troll, not always a mini-troll."

"But why would he not want to be a troll? Wouldn't he want to go back to being a normal-sized troll?" After she and her friends had first run into Trennly and Kren when they opened their shops, they hit the internet to research trolls because they had never seen mini-trolls before. They could find nothing on mini-trolls but found that normal-sized trolls were huge— basically giants. Most lived in caves on Troulo, which was the island closest to where they lived, but desert trolls and ice trolls lived in other places.

"No. Trennly hates trolls. He hates self."

Lockdrest

Trennly hated trolls in general? He hated his own people? Why? Molly felt bad for him. She despised herself sometimes, but she didn't mind the body she was in. She couldn't imagine being trapped in a body she hated or hating being human in general. It wasn't fair that he did. "Why doesn't he use magick?" She pointed to the door as she said this. She also thought of the horns that could grow on their heads with a simple drink. The drinks that Trennly himself had made them numerous times.

"Trennly took all transformation classes could at Lockdrest. Even if transform briefly into something, still in same body. Not like trans humans, who can change bodies to fit genders in this world. Not enough study for creatures to change into other creatures. One day, something will be found for him." Kren had his hands behind his back and was staring out the window. She wondered if he felt as bad for Trennly as she did, even though he had attacked her. "But now, is trying magick. Trying to take your body. Become human."

Molly gasped. He had been trying to take her over? Become her? And then Kren had saved her . . . Why?

"How do you know him? And how are you both . . ." She couldn't bring herself to say it and hoped she didn't have to. She hoped he knew what she meant so she didn't sound rude.

"One day, kid-witch picking on me. I try to stop him. I moved foot to get him away and knocked kid-witch into tree. I was young. Mother of kid, mom-witch, saw and turned me to mini-troll. I went back to my parents. They tried to stomp and kill new me. Days later, found Trennly, mini-troll also," Kren said.

Molly's heart squeezed tight. He still wouldn't look at her.

So, Kren had been trying to protect himself and was turned into something different? Still a troll? But smaller? What kind of magick did that? And by trying to stomp and kill him, did

63

that mean that his parents didn't want him just because he was different?

"How was Trennly . . ." She wondered if Trennly was changed in the same way.

"Trennly did not want to be troll before mini-troll. When six, found mother beating father to his death, then eat him."

Molly didn't mean to gasp in horror, but when she did, Kren turned and looked at her with only one eye before waving her off. "Way of most trolls. But Trennly disgusted. Tried stealing magick from same witch. Witch cursed him into mini-troll. I then followed Trennly to school. Followed him every day since. Not trust him. Know will do something stupid." He looked at her fully this time, critically.

Did he blame her for causing his friend to do something stupid?

Kren plopped down in his short chair and started taking off his shoes and socks. His feet were huge, his toes misshapen and curved with bulbs at the end, and the middle of his foot was wide. She wondered where he found shoes and socks that fit him. He also had a swipe of a scar on the top of his left foot. She wondered where that was from.

Setting his shoes neatly beside his chair, Kren picked up his mug and took another slurp. "You can leave if want. But suggest stay. Learn."

"Learn what? And stay for how long?"

"Magick. Protection. *Sense.*" The last word was said as if he wanted to spit it in her face. "Stay for basics of school, then go home. After knowing how to protect self."

She had always wanted to know how to protect herself and had tried to learn how. If she could do that, would she be able to live a somewhat normal life? Would she be able to hide the fact that she was different from people and the fact that she could see ghosts from her friends?

To her, it might be worth it to take time away from her home, school, and social life to learn how to blend into society better.

But if she did, would she be able to jump right back in? Or would she fall behind in what was popular? Would her friends be willing to catch her up if she came back? Would they still even be her friends after she chose to leave them to go to another school? Even if it were to learn how to protect herself from the spirits that tried to take her over so often, she honestly didn't know if they would understand.

"Will I be allowed to talk to my family or friends while I'm away?"

"No."

Her heart sank. "But why can't I . . . why can't I just let them know that I'm—" Tears were forming in her eyes. She wanted to grab a tissue, but she couldn't move to get one because her emotions had locked her in place like their own kind of magick.

"Because what would world do if know kid was stolen. Taken. Forced to go to magick school. Problems." He paused, thinking. "If come back alive . . . Will be okay. Just learn fast."

But what if she was not able to learn fast? She had never done magick before. Not old magick. "But I don't know any magick. I don't know how to freeze people like you did or transform anything. I didn't even know transformation magick was a thing."

"Freezing is freezing souls. Spirit magick. Need symbols in own spirit. Anyone can do magick, if learn. I will teach you easiest spell. For amateurs, but will help."

He got up then, his large feet squishing into the carpet. He put his mug back on the table and strolled over to sit beside her. Sitting, his head was as high as her armpit, but his body was as wide as her shoulders.

He took her mug from her hands and held it in only one of his. He squinted, scrutinizing it, his brown eyes losing focus for a moment, before he straightened out his other hand.

She saw a thin purple film coming out of the mug like a snake toward Kren's hand. It swayed to the rhythm of its own essence and connected to a similar pink wisp that was coming from Kren's hand. Kren put his hand into his hair, scratched his thumbnail on one of his green strands, then returned his hand to swipe that same nail across the skin of his finger with a snap.

In an instant, the mug turned green.

And then the purple smoky veil was gone, returning into the mug.

"Transformation magick. Hard to do. Not hard to detransform." He handed the now-green mug to her. It still felt the same. It was just as heavy, with the same blue liquid inside, but it somehow made Molly nervous holding it. There was also a small glimmer to it if she looked closely enough. "Call to mug's essence. Everything has a soul. Like calls to like. Use your soul. Find how you are like mug. Call. It will come. Then, when connected, close hand in fist." He demonstrated, squeezing his hand tightly in front of her. "Crush bonds. Will fall away. Easy."

It didn't sound easy, but she was willing to try. She had always wanted to but had been scared to because none of her friends wanted anything to do with old magick.

At first, she tried to call or feel her soul like he had said but felt nothing. It was like nothing was there. Like she was empty.

Her heart raced again.

She heard Kren sigh. "Focus," he said as he got up. He left the room to let her be.

She tried again, but she only began to feel anything in herself when she thought of the place by the lake. It was then that her mind started slipping. She was not willing to go there. She pulled back.

If she wasn't able to de-transform the color of the mug, how was she supposed to learn how to protect herself against spirits wanting to take her over?

She decided to skip to the second step instead. He said that like calls to like. The mug . . . She didn't think she was heavy or dense like it was. She was blue sometimes, if that meant sad, but did that even matter now if the mug was green? Ugh! She was getting annoyed, which wasn't helping her focus.

She decided to take a sip from the mug instead, hoping it would calm her nerves. The gentle fog washed over her mind and did just that.

A gentle fog . . . It was almost like nothing, almost like her, in a sense. A follower. Except the mug wasn't a follower. What was she thinking? No. She looked to her hands, one holding the handle and the other wrapped around the smooth green surface of the mug where the warmth was dying out. She was the follower. She needed her friends to feel like she was something. She needed her friends to guide her and lift her up, just like the mug needed someone to guide it and lift it to their lips.

There. She felt a tiny spark of something within herself. A small part of her was reaching out, as if she had found something similar to her in the mug. It was calling to her soul.

Then she saw it. Her own essence of spirit. A small shimmer. The color of the body of water under that layer of purple ice. It was trying to reach for something.

Like called to like.

She thought again on how the mug needed her as much as she needed someone else. How functionality didn't exist without another set of hands or a mind.

That purple veil was coming out of the mug just like before. It was darker than hers, but it was searching for and reaching for her. She guided her hand to it until the two purples touched, then she closed her hand into a fist.

And watched as the mug turned back to blue.

"Good job."

Molly nearly dropped the mug when she flinched. Kren held out a plate of what looked like garlic bread. She could smell it on his breath. It reeked, curdling the emptiness of her stomach.

She shook her head.

He rolled his eyes. "Have strawberry strudel too. Will get phone and clothes tomorrow. Will take you to school. You sleep here." He motioned to the couch.

She smiled, looking to the mug again. She was almost tempted to ask him to turn it back to another color so she could do it once more.

"I'll take a strudel." She couldn't believe that she would finally learn how to protect herself. She couldn't believe that she could do old magick. And she couldn't believe that she had learned what was wrong with her, what made her different. She had a term to define herself now: an empty vessel. Although she still wasn't entirely sure what that meant.

She felt guilty for leaving her mom and dad, of course. But they never wanted anything to do with her problem anyway. This was a chance for her to fix it and get back to them and her life without having to worry about ghosts or magick.

The next morning had been a rush. Kren had used visionary magick on her mixed with transformation magick, which tickled her skin the entire time that she wore the persona of an extra-tall blonde woman, the opposite of her short and brunette stature. He said that there may be a slight glimmer to her since it was a more complicated transformation spell but that she wouldn't be in it for long. Kren took her to get a week's worth of clothes and then a new phone. He didn't let her drop the disguise until they had entered the airport. She felt bad that he was spending his money on her, especially since he was closing his shop, but then she remembered that he had kidnapped her and had smashed her phone in the first place.

The guilt came back, though, while they were waiting at the airport. After Kren had her input his phone number, she downloaded a few of the apps that she had liked from before. Not her social media—she knew that wouldn't have been allowed—but certain cell-witch apps.

She didn't plan to use them unless she needed them. She just figured that she shouldn't go into a magickal school without any type of knowledge or protection. And she was sure that other students would have the same apps too.

Over the years, the apps had become a comfort, especially in case she ran into another spirit, which the airport was surprisingly full of. Also, if she couldn't fall asleep, she usually needed the rain to drip on her all night. As her friends had said, a couple of pixels of her soul was nothing. And Kren hadn't elaborated anymore on that. He also seemed old with his mannerisms. She was sure he wouldn't understand. She pocketed the call card he'd gotten her that held only a certain number of minutes.

While Kren was getting their tickets, she tried to research empty vessels but couldn't find anything on the internet. So, maybe it was true that being an empty vessel was rare, or perhaps that wasn't the right term.

Kren was nice enough, though, to help her avoid the airport spirits. Trying not to make a scene, since magick wasn't allowed in airports, he steered her away from the spirits until they could find a magickal airline worker to report they were being harassed.

Another magickal worker then led them to their plane after Kren showed them their tickets and a fake magickal ID for Molly that no one seemed to care about. A big religious company that had sworn off magick had taken over and rebranded the non-magickal airlines. Ever since the change, thanks to technology and magick emerging, non-magickal people could travel on magickal airlines, but magickal people could not travel on non-magickal ones, which didn't seem to bother the magickal people that much.

Molly had traveled by plane a few times before on vacations, so she was thrilled to finally be allowed on a magickal airline to see how it was different. To her dismay, though, they were not heading to those airlines. They were going to another section where the private planes were held, past the TSA, straight to a smaller plane with golden letters glittering on the side that said "Lockdrest." Next to it were two other smaller planes with the words "Opendrest" and "Closedrest."

"Need certain ticket," Kren explained as they followed the worker. "Pathons owns it. Will take us to school. Used to have one plane to take to all schools. Then two. Now three. Use to have no names on sides."

Molly didn't know what Pathons were, but excitement was rushing through her, especially when they climbed up the stairs to what felt like a private jet. The seats were soft and gray, and there were far fewer seats than she had seen on most planes. And there were only three passengers on it, every single one of them kids. Two girls and a boy. They had to be students.

Kren walked down the aisle ahead of her, then sat near a boy with deep tan skin and straight black hair. The boy's brown eyes glanced away from a picture of a girl he was staring at to Kren. For a moment, he looked shocked but then composed himself and tucked the picture away in his bag as if he were trying to hide it. He stared straight ahead.

"Is everyone on this plane students who are going to Lockdrest?" Molly asked Kren as she sat down next to him.

Kren nodded, closing his eyes as if he wanted to sleep.

Lockdrest

She sighed and then turned to the boy they sat next to. She didn't want to go into the school completely unprepared.

"Hey," she said, trying to get his attention. "I'm Molly. Have you been to Lockdrest before? I just want to know if there is—"

He gave her a look of such annoyance that it made her stop talking. "This is my first year. I plan to only learn what I need to so I can get back. I have no answers for you."

Molly's voice was smaller this time, echoing her confidence. "It's . . . my first time too."

"Cool," he said, turning his head away from her.

He refused to look at her again.

Namu

Chapter Four

Namu's hard, beating pulse sent a wave of panic through him, forcing his eyes to open and a gasp to escape his trembling body. He was on the floor. One of his legs was pressed against the cold metal leg of a desk, and his free hand was trapped under his back. He tried to sit up.

Mr. Vero was there helping him. Namu clasped his hand tightly, needing something to hold on to so that he wouldn't slip back to where he had come from.

What happened? Had the tree . . . ?

Namu ignored Mr. Vero's face and looked over his shoulder. The tree was dead. Its leaves had fallen and were brown and crusted around the twisted and now rotting stump, proving that it was one of the many things that needed a spirit in it to be kept alive.

"Namu! Are you okay?"

Namu tore his hand away.

Mr. Vero seemed taken aback by his reaction. "Do you want to check?"

He did not. He knew he wasn't healed. He knew the holes were still there, like before. He could feel them. Big, gaping, empty, hollow, and hopeless.

"No. This was stupid to try." Namu scrambled to his feet.

"We'll figure it out."

"How can you say that!? You haven't had to go through this! You don't even know if it's possible! You don't know if I'll ever heal!"

"I may not have chosen to heal myself, but I do understand how it may feel at a level—"

Namu cut him off. "How? You have only a couple of holes inside you! How could you possibly know how . . . ?" He made himself stop, focusing instead on trying not to grab one of the marble slabs and throw it at Mr. Vero's face.

The symbol on the marble was mocking him.

If only he had been smarter, like his teacher had been when he had gone through the door. No, not smarter—if only he had known magick for years like Mr. Vero had, maybe he would be okay. Mr. Vero had grown up in the magickal world. One time, he'd explained to Namu how he would drink the same transformation drink to turn into a weasel and play tricks on his friends for years. Because he had devoted himself to only that one drink and his soul had become accustomed to it, he could use transformation magick on himself and turn into a weasel at will. That was what Mr. Vero had done as soon as his body had been turned into a metal husk beyond the door. Before the husk had glued itself to his skin, he had turned into a weasel and stayed inside the metal statue of himself for days, far enough away from the walls that it kept those other creatures from obtaining access to every bit of his soul.

Unlike Namu.

Lockdrest

When the world had released Mr. Vero by melting the metal casting away from the weasel inside it, Mr. Vero had fallen to the ground and turned back to a human, too exhausted to keep himself a small animal any longer. He then expelled his entire spirit, just as Namu had done, by separating his entire soul from his body, even though it might have killed him to do that. But he had done it just in time. His body had been turned to metal again a second later.

Mr. Vero had then made his way out the door as a spirit and astral projected to get into a teacher's dream. It was then that the teacher had gone in to get Mr. Vero's body out.

If their souls stayed outside their body for too long, their souls became too easy to destroy. If the creatures had eaten a majority of their souls, they would have died. That was probably what had happened to the other students who had gone in through the door.

After Mr. Vero had been the one to save Namu, Mr. Vero had been surprised at Namu's ability to expel his soul from his body while he was in the husk. He had said he had been unable to do that while in animal form and that he couldn't turn back into a human because he was too scared to be trapped in a much smaller space. But it didn't matter what Mr. Vero was impressed with because it didn't matter what Namu had done for himself. Whatever it was that he had done, it had been too late. Mr. Vero's actions had worked. Mr. Vero had survived without losing too much of himself.

They both turned when they heard rustling behind them. Someone was at the door.

Lily.

"Something wrong?" Lily's already tall stature looked even taller with their shoulders pressed back and their arms crossed, leaning against the door frame. Lily was studying Mr. Vero intensely and then examining Namu with their big brown eyes of calculating judgment.

Namu shook his head and put up his hand up to wave goodbye to his mentor without giving him another glance. He was over the day and over hoping. Hope just ate him away from the inside.

"What's wrong?" Lily asked as he walked right by them.

Although Lily was Namu's best friend and had been since non-magickal elementary school, he had not told them about the door. Mr. Vero had begged him not to in case someone else got hurt. Namu knew that if he told Lily, Lily would want to check it out, and Namu couldn't let that happen. He couldn't put them in danger. What if they got killed?

But it was hard, since they used to tell each other everything. They used to be the most comfortable around each other and only with each other. Especially since Namu never judged Lily when many changes had happened. Those changes weren't when Lily had realized they were gender-fluid. They had found that out at a very young age, and Namu respected that. Lily leaned more toward girl but sometimes was a boy, so they decided to go by they/them. No, the real changes had occurred when Lily's family became rich and known for the Pathon Airlines.

Lily's dad had been the one to mix techno magick and science to create the magick needed to make airplanes that could go through a cloud and appear wherever they needed to go in an instant. This worked by accessing memory magick within water vapors in the clouds. That meant it only worked if the airplane had been where it needed to go before, but it was still really impressive. Although right now, that type of magick was only used for the magickal schools and certain rich and magickal people. The magickal division of the government called the Magickal Society still wasn't ready to mass release it. They wanted to use it slowly to phase out the everyday modes of transportation over the years, to avoid sudden unemployment and panic. Lily had hinted at their dad working on many other secret projects but had never elaborated.

After Lily's family had gotten rich, they moved away from the apartments where they had grown up together into a mansion instead. But even after Lily's move, Lily and Namu had remained good friends. Their parents were also friends, which was why Namu was at Lockdrest. Lily's parents did not want them to go to Lockdrest, one of the magickal schools that their dad had gone to, alone. Namu had agreed to go with them.

And he ended up here with holes eaten out of his soul and a secret about a door that made it impossible to connect with Lily like he used to.

"Namu." Lily's hand was on his shoulder, stopping him from heading up the grand staircase from the basement. He knew they were heading to lunch together before they broke away. He then would head to Symbols One, while Lily went to Runes Two. "What. Is. Wrong."

"Nothing. Just got in an argument," Namu answered, avoiding Lily's eyes.

But Lily got in his face and made eye contact. He could feel their small, pointed nose almost inches from his since they were the same height. "An argument? With your mentor? When no one else gets that privilege?"

He could almost breathe in their jealousy as Lily stepped back and crossed their arms. They looked menacing, their long glossy brown hair hanging dead straight over their wide shoulders, paired with their piercing brown eyes.

"Yes. It happens. I didn't like how he was teaching me."

"With a dead tree?" Lily paused. "How did it die?"

Namu sighed. "That . . . that was my issue. I didn't want to kill anything. He had me draw the spirit out."

"But for what reason?" Lily didn't sound shocked. They sounded calculating.

Namu could not come up with an answer fast enough, so he started heading up the stairs to the cafeteria to give himself an extra second to think. "To see how different it is compared to unalive spirit essences."

"But we already know that from books. Trees don't need to die for us to learn that hands on. Seems unreasonable, especially for a Spirit Magick Four teacher."

Namu shrugged, trying not to show his annoyance. He tried to calm the festering buzz under his skin and in his veins that made him want to lash out. "I don't know what to tell you, Lily. I just do what he says."

Molly

Chapter Five

While Kren had his eyes closed and his head back against the gray headrest, snoring during the flight, Molly tried to look up as much as she could about Lockdrest on her phone using the plane's WiFi. Surprisingly, she had found a lot of information. So much that it was hard to sift through and know what was true or false. She had found that some students who went to Lockdrest had large social media accounts and many followers, but those students posted pictures and told stories about what went on inside the school that seemed too far-fetched to be believable. One student had said that her teacher had turned another student into a pink spider to punish them and had posted a picture of a creepy pink spider on a wall and then the same one trapped in a jar. The comments posted below these stories were often calling those students out, claiming they were attention seeking. Some said that Lockdrest would never let anything like that happen to a student.

She sure hoped so. She was already scared about going to another school, let alone one full of magick, when she knew so little about magick. She just hoped that she could make friends quickly and they could teach her the right or wrong thing to do so she didn't mess up or make a fool of herself. She also didn't want people to find out that she was an empty vessel. Molly knew there was a chance that the term "empty vessel" would be understood or accepted in this school, especially compared to her old friends, who would have found a way to make fun of her for being "empty." But Kren had said it was rare, and she was still self-conscious about it. She was not ready to let anyone know—not without knowing how this world felt about it first.

Turning off her phone and sliding it back into the same shorts she wore yesterday, Molly sighed, overwhelmed. She reached for her bag on the floor by her feet, which Kren had carried onto the plane with him. She couldn't wait to unpack and change into new clothes for tomorrow. For some reason, Kren had not wanted her to waste a set of new clothes today and told her that, when she needed to wash her clothes, there was a laundry area in each of the bathrooms in the hall where her room would be.

She had never stayed at a school where she would be there day and night.

A voice came over the loudspeaker, announcing that they would be landing soon.

It was then that Kren partially opened his brown eyes with disinterest.

"How far is the school from the airport?" Molly asked as Kren yawned and stretched up his short arms. Today, he wore a dark-brown suit that went well with his green hair, although it pulled a little tightly at the seams.

"Airport at school."

Oh.

Molly couldn't look out to see because the closest window was covered. Anyway, it was near the boy who wouldn't tell her his name or look her way. She hated how the boy's aloofness made her quiver inside and want to cry. She hated being rejected, which was why she hadn't tried talking to anyone else on the plane. She didn't want to meet another person so cold right away again. If she did, she was sure she would want to turn around and head back home.

The plane landed, and they were told they could disembark. Kren led her off the plane. She kept her head down until they took the steps onto the sun-warmed pavement of what looked like a massive parking lot. That was when she looked up and saw the long runway behind them facing the airplane's tail and another aircraft that hooked her attention immediately. It was an old run-down plane at the edge of the lot that looked well past broken, as though it were a memorial piece. It had moss, grass, and weeds growing all over it, cracks along the worn gray sides, and no letters to name it. If a troll or giant came and picked it up, it looked as though it would break in half immediately.

"Adults don't like to send kids in it alone," Kren mentioned as some of the other students walked past them as they got off the plane, although a few stopped and stared at it with her.

"I don't blame them," Molly whispered. "How does it even run? Magick?"

Kren snorted, which made Molly turn to look at him. He was actually smiling at her, with yellow but straight teeth. "Does not fly. Techno magick. Finicky but okay. Need a little device. Few teachers have. Can take anywhere if used if enter inside."

"Like a portal?" Molly covered her mouth, embarrassed at her surprised outburst. Her embarrassment grew when she saw the boy from the plane staring at her, his lanky figure tilting with most of his weight on one leg and his arms crossed. "But if you guys can . . . If that can . . . Why do we have cars, planes—why do we have anything?"

Kren laughed again while waving her off before he began to walk away from her toward a mighty building of bricks many stories high that had to be the school. "Too young. Dumb. Would collapse economy."

Oh. Molly was about to follow him but stopped. He was right. If everyone used something like that, too many people would lose their jobs. And he did say that it was finicky. So, did that mean it didn't always work? And he said only certain teachers could use it? What for and why? Were there other things like this that she didn't know about?

Molly shook her head to realign her thoughts, then took a few quick strides to catch up with Kren and the others.

The sidewalk from the airport curved around to the right so they could see the side of the school, which was beautiful. The side they were facing had no windows, only tan bricks and an ominous presence.

"Where students and teachers sleep," Kren said, pointing to it as it towered over them. Its shadow stretched to cover them, blocking out the sun.

"How old are students when they come here?"

"Seven if smart. If adult and need learn, have classes elsewhere. In cities. Kids leave at eighteen."

Molly swallowed hard. The building looked menacing. As they made their way around it, they encountered many windows, all lined up together in uniform rows, staring at them like hostile eyes. She also wondered if she would have classes with kids half her age.

Large windows that Molly could not see into lined the bottom floor as they continued to walk around the building. It had to be more than thirty school buses long. She counted eight rows of windows with over fifty windows on each floor and a couple of gaps containing more oversized windows in between.

"Easy location for students to get to with least property tax. Used to be useless land. Built by Reeneme Yurr and Jarcob Wills with chaos magick. Let chaos stir in walls. Do what need to for children. Know what needs to provide."

The few other students who were with them turned and looked at Kren. The girls smiled at what he was saying.

"The school would know what it needed to provide? For the kids?" Molly felt guilty whenever she had trouble understanding him.

He nodded. "Help from goddess of beginnings. Help from gods of fate. Lockdrest was first one made."

Now he sounded like he was just making up rhymes.

The sidewalk grew broader as it curved and then plunged into a corridor-like hall outside the building.

Molly was shocked at how the bricked walls lined this pathway. They were approaching a set of giant wooden doors that must have led to the inside of the school. It was a cool design, but Molly didn't see the benefit of it being shaped like it was. It felt like a waste of space, having a chunk cut out of the school to make an outdoor hallway, unless it was to slow traffic. Molly scratched at her arms and saw a couple of the other students do the same. It felt like something was crawling all over them, leaving little threads.

"When did school start?" Molly asked. She figured it couldn't be the first day, since there were only four students arriving, including herself.

"Days before. But it is fine," Kren answered.

One of the students looked even more nervous at his words. Molly wondered why the few others were arriving late.

The door seemed perfectly normal at first until it glossed over green the moment Kren knocked on it twice with his knuckle.

Then the door creaked open, allowing only enough room for one to enter at a time. Kren allowed all the other students to go in first before he beckoned Molly inside.

"When first come," Kren said, "didn't think me real. Or Trennly. Mini-trolls not exist. Did tests. Checked age. Decided we were okay."

Molly first noticed the dark, lustrous hardwood flooring when they entered. Then, as the door closed behind them after Kren tapped the side of the door with an easy touch, she saw a wall of names directly in front of them. There were hundreds of them in flawless white cursive letters on the smooth black marble wall. Then there was a sizeable TV that was shut off over the top of it, tilted down at an angle so everyone could see the screen.

"New," Kren said, studying the TV with his head cocked to the side. Then he looked down to the names, which he seemed more familiar with. "Names of witches honored." He gave a nod of respect before he walked past it to the right, where there was a giant staircase leading downward that could fit twenty kids across. A pristine-looking maroon-colored carpet traveled down the middle of the dark wood.

Molly followed Kren, although she was desperate to look around the main floor. Right before they descended, she noticed that, if they had continued right, there was what looked like a cafeteria farther off after a set of restrooms and offices.

As they went down the stairs, she noticed the school was very clean and, at this time, very empty. There were no students around except the ones she had arrived with, who were ahead of them now. She wondered if the other students were all in their classes.

Although the ceilings were not as high as they had been on the main floor, the basement was massive, with a harsh concrete ground. There was also no chunk cut out of the basement structure like in the building above. The basement seemed to run along the whole building, with many light wooden doors that were closed. From where Molly stood, she could see to the right three sets of restrooms, what looked like a small office, and a large library. To the left was a small pool of water shaped like a half-moon buried into the concrete, trickling in through an underground river with stone set all around it.

Molly and Kren walked in that direction. The water was a beautiful emerald blue.

"Given by Closedrest. Nice gift. No one knows what for," Kren said as he strolled with his hands behind his back to where the other students had already made it. The two girls were in front of an office that looked like a ticket booth. There was counter made of flecked brown marble with a window set in between and a college-aged smiling man behind it. The man was wearing a green beret and had a birthmark the size of a quarter on his right cheek.

He handed one of the girls a large old silver key. She took it and hugged it to her chest before running off with one of the other students from the plane who must have gotten there first because she was already holding a key and a piece of paper.

The boy from the plane, who had ignored Molly the whole time, was next in line. She looked back at the two girls running up the stairs together. It made her desperate to know someone here. She suddenly missed her friends.

"Name?" the young man asked, smiling down from his window.

As Molly approached, she saw his name tag: "Mr. Bell (Key Giver)."

"Derrin Nimper," the boy from the plane said.

Mr. Bell nodded and picked up a metal box that was a little larger than his hand from the desk on his side of the window. He pushed it across the marble to Derrin.

Derrin looked at him, confused.

"You put your hand in. Don't worry; it won't bite you," Mr. Bell said, laughing.

Without hesitation, Derrin put his whole hand inside. There was a wide enough gap around Derrin's hand so Molly could see deep purple-and-violet streams of floating liquid. It didn't seem to hurt; he didn't flinch. He only held his chin high. He looked to Mr. Bell to tell him when to take his hand out.

Mr. Bell turned away from the window to examine a wall behind him filled with hundreds of miniature golden drawers. Molly had to stand on her tiptoes to get a closer look. After a few moments, one of the golden drawers opened.

"We got one. You can pull your hand out now!" Mr. Bell announced cheerfully.

Mr. Bell pulled out an old bronze key with an angled R fixed on its head. It was ancient in design, yet had a beautiful luster at the top. Over the symbol was the number 96 made of the same bronze material. He handed it to Derrin.

"Raido Hall, Room 96," Mr. Bell said, heading to a filing cabinet and pulling out a paper. He handed it to Derrin with a wink. Derrin stood blankly.

"Oh, yes. Those two girls had parents here before. I'm guessing you don't know where to go," Mr. Bell said and then pressed something behind the counter. "Someone will be coming to show you around. Don't you worry."

Derrin only gave a stiff nod, then took three steps away before he found a new place to stand with no emotion on his face.

Mr. Bell looked to Molly next, studied her for a second, and then pressed whatever he had pressed for Derrin again. "And who do we have here?"

"Molly," Kren said. "Paperwork just under Molly."

Mr. Bell had to lean over his window to figure out who was talking to him. When he did, he looked at Kren questioningly.

"It's Molly Reese," Molly said nervously.

"I am guessing you signed her up?" Mr. Bell asked Kren, eyeing him.

"Yes. Under Molly. Just Molly."

"Okay." Mr. Bell returned to the filing cabinet and riffled through it. Apparently not finding anything, he then went to a printer and pulled out a sheet of paper. "Found it! You are right. It's under just Molly."

She wondered how often kidnappers knew their kidnappees' last names and if that was why Kren hadn't used her full one. She swallowed a nervous laugh.

"Hand in the box, Molly Reese," Mr. Bell said, sliding it toward her.

She did as he said, while holding her bag with her left hand. She didn't know exactly what she was expecting but was surprised to find warmth. It felt as though she had immersed her hand in a stream of dry sand as the purple swirled around her. What felt like the cool end of a pen traced every line on her palm.

Mr. Bell was watching her and Kren carefully. When he heard a pop from one of the tiny drawers unlocking, he smiled at her.

Molly took her hand out of the box and gave it a shake, trying to bring it back to a normal sensation as Mr. Bell pulled a golden key from her drawer. It had two lines forming a sideways vee and the number 260 below it.

"Kenaz Hall, Room 260, Molly Reese," Mr. Bell said, handing her the key and the thin sheet of white paper when she set down her bag.

The key was warm in her hand, the sheet cold and light.

Kren said, "You get books from classes. Will catch up. Couple of days late. Leave when think can protect self. But ask first. You start tomorrow."

She glanced down at the list of classes she had to take or that he had signed her up for. She had breakfast at 7:30 am, then her first class was at 8:15 am: Divinations One. After that was Symbols One, then a break, then Transformation Drinks and Remedies One, a break, Spirit Magick One, Technology, a break, then History and Transformation of the Magickal World, online classes before dinner and then more online classes. She didn't know what the online classes meant.

"Why do I have to take all of these if I'm just trying to learn to protect myself?" Molly asked, a little taken aback. The schedule was worse than non-magickal school.

"Can't only take a few."

"He's right." She hadn't realized that Mr. Bell had been listening. "This is a school leading you to magickal job opportunities in a magickal division of society if you need them. It isn't like college, where you can take a couple of classes. Even if you do not want to take that route, Lockdrest believes in knowledge for all bases." He paused with a lopsided grin and a pinch of his hat. "Also, it's free. Free board and free food. So, you take a full schedule in exchange."

"What are these online classes?"

"Your non-magickal schooling so you don't fall behind. Everyone here does that," Mr. Bell answered, then turned away.

All of this was free? She supposed public education was also free, but who was providing money to the school for this? Maybe there was a tax she didn't know about.

Molly hadn't noticed anyone approach them, but there were two older students standing next to each other, staring at her and Kren.

Well, the boy with the pasty skin was staring at her. The girl with the big blue eyes and messy brown hair that looked like it was supposed to be straight was staring at Kren.

Derrin had walked off with another older student.

"You go," Kren said, waving her off. "I get key for guest room." He turned away from her and gave his attention to Mr. Bell, leaving Molly awkwardly alone with the two other students. She didn't know what to do or say.

"Regretfully, our tech teacher was in the room today and kicked us out to help," the boy said to her. He narrowed his brown eyes. "I'm Koz."

"That's a troll—but mini!" the girl said. "How big are—"

The girl took a step toward Kren, but before she took another, she glanced over her shoulder back at Koz, who gave her a grin but shook his head.

The girl straightened and took a step back to her original spot.

"This is Rem," Koz said. "We are, apparently, supposed to show you around the school."

"We have things to do, so it needs to be quick," Rem blurted out.

Molly could feel her cheeks burning red.

Koz didn't correct the girl; he only laughed and then started walking away.

Molly followed.

Namu

Chapter Six

Namu knew he should have gone into his next class. But as Lily had gone into their Runes Two class, he had walked up to Symbols One's door, then turned around and went upstairs instead.

He was done for the day. He was unsettled after he had destroyed that tree.

After he had sucked it dry.

He had to do something to calm himself. Something to get his mind off things.

He headed outside. The warmth of the end of summer surrounded him, but, somehow, it wasn't enough. He missed the blazing and blaring construction sites. To hear anything like that now would be nice to drown out his fear.

The terror he had for his future was becoming too clamorous.

It pounded against his skull every second of every day in the form of anger. He wanted to understand how a school could let what had happened to him happen to a student. He wanted to figure out how to destroy that door.

Namu took out his phone and lay down in the smooth, vibrant green grass. It was perfect because no one else was outside.

He had a text from his little brother, Minis. He had sent a picture of him with their dad at a site.

Namu was too empty to reply.

Instead, he opened his gallery and found videos that he sometimes tuned into at night. The nights when his breathing and the beating of his heart were too deafening, just like they had been when he was in that metal cocoon.

He played one of the videos and closed his eyes.

The sounds of a demolition resonated with his soul. A building being torn down. Machines carving into what once was a stronghold to build something new.

Molly

Chapter Seven

olly followed Koz and Rem around the school, staying a couple of steps behind. Rem kept looking back at her, but she didn't seem annoyed that Molly preferred to stay away.

Molly found the pair intimidating in a way. They were two people who needed to only check her off their list of things to get done. She could tell they couldn't care less about getting to know her.

But they were full of information.

The first place they showed her was where her classes would take place in the basement. The class names were written on golden plates by the sides of the doors to make it easy for her to find. The other important locations downstairs that they passed, with only a wave and a small explanation, were the restrooms and the library, which was bigger than the one she had in her school back at home and was not closed in but instead a portion of the basement. They then took her upstairs.

On the main floor, they showed her the nurse's office, the computer lab, which was where she would be taking Technology and looked like any other computer lab she had been in, and then the stairwell that led to all the halls, where her room would be.

"We will show you the halls and to your room after we grab something to eat," Koz said.

Rem nodded more than a few times and skipped ahead to a three-level cafeteria.

It was a large room in three tiers with two open balconies of clear glass staggered on top of each other. The steps leading up to the two floors were glass, too, with a pudgy blue gripper on each one. On the floor they were on, there were glass tables with metal chairs placed around them, looking out at a giant window that reached the uppermost ceiling so all the floors could see the grounds. The main level held the kitchens. There was a counter for students to walk along to grab food and people working in crisp white uniforms in the back.

The people in the uniforms were pouring liquid from long, clear bottles onto hot pans. Molly was mesmerized as they flipped and tossed the cooking meat to give it a dose of air to calm the smoke. The meat had looked like chicken in two of the pans, but one of the slabs of chicken had turned a golden crisp with what looked like glitter on the top. When the cook pressed a spatula onto a section of the sparkling crust, it was as if the glitter itself oozed a thick cheese onto the pan before it was tossed onto a plate. The other chicken had turned dark brown from whatever liquid they had poured on it, and when the spatula pressed onto that one, the brown crust produced a clear glaze.

Her mind was blown. She had never seen anything cooked like that before. She turned to ask Koz what she had just witnessed but then clamped her mouth shut when she saw he was staring at her.

Her cheeks flared again.

"You are from the non-magickal world, huh?" Koz asked.

Molly didn't know what to say. She didn't want to single herself out. She imagined that it wasn't common for someone to come straight from the non-magickal world into here.

She didn't say anything.

Rem danced over to the counter and grabbed the two plates with the chicken that Molly had watched them make. She then went over to a table close by and sat down. Around them, more kids were getting into lines to get food. Classes must have been let out.

A few younger kids had found each other and started laughing.

"Lockdrest accepts younger kids, but it's rare they come here so young," Koz said in reply to her watching them. "There are maybe ten, if that."

"Eleven," Rem corrected. She took a bite of the cheesy chicken, and, somehow, more cheese leaked out.

Koz sat down next to her and pointed at the seat across from them. Molly sat just as he pushed the dark-brown chicken across the table to her. She put her bag on the metal seat next to her.

Rem handed her a fork.

Molly took it and sliced into the chicken with ease. She waited until Koz and Rem weren't looking before she took a bite.

It was sweet. Almost as sweet as a donut but more hearty, full.

Koz pointed above them. "The seating arrangements look the same on the other two levels, only smaller the higher you go up."

Molly nodded.

"You don't talk much, do you?" Koz asked.

She tried to slow her heart. She thought by being quiet that she was being safe and that she wouldn't drive them away like she had the boy on the plane. But now, she wasn't sure if Koz thought she was too dismissive.

"Um . . . it's nice." She looked up to the levels above them and to the students starting to climb the steps. "Organized. Neat."

Koz laughed. Rem continued eating. Molly wondered why Koz wasn't eating anything.

"The last thing I would comment about this school is that it is organized and neat," Koz said. His long pink lips stretched into a knowing smile. "More like unsupportive. Ambivalent. But what else can you expect from a magickal school, I guess."

"Chaotic," Rem said.

"Yes. Chaotic is the best term for obvious reasons."

Molly didn't know what the obvious reasons were.

She waited until he looked away before she took another bite of her chicken. To her dismay, he looked at her again while she was chewing. Thankfully, he glanced to Rem instead the moment she froze.

Amusement played in his brown eyes.

"I don't want to take up your time, as much as I'm sure you don't want to take up ours. As soon as you finish your food, we will take you upstairs. But while we are here, I am curious—how new are you to this side of things?"

Molly swallowed. "Side of things?"

"What are your views on the magickal world?"

"Compared to the non-magickal," Rem said with her mouth full.

Molly took a deep breath in and looked down at her plate. Her chicken was only half eaten, but she was full. Uncertainty had filled her stomach in the form of butterflies.

"I don't really have any views or opinions," she lied. "I just . . . I appreciate magick. I'm happy it's here." And she hoped it would help her. The problem was that she had never let herself form her own opinion on the topic. She had always gone off what her friends thought of it. She had always followed the trends. She hated parts of magick, like the fact that ghosts could take over her body and, apparently, corporeal beings too. But she had never hated it as much as her parents did.

"Lockdrest is far away from non-magickal areas," Rem randomly said. Maybe to fill the silence. "On an island, like a video game drop-off where kids are placed on an island and have to find a way off. We even have game ghosts!"

Koz smirked before he sighed. "This is true. Even if we compare our magickal school to the smaller establishments in the city closest to this island, there is a significant difference."

Rem nodded. Her chicken was now gone. "It's like a video game world, where the creators believed in different gods and creatures and *bam*, shoved them together."

Molly was caught on something Rem said before. Something that had made her heart stop. "Game ghosts?"

Koz crossed his arms. "The game ghosts in her hypothetical scenario are only projection spirits from techno magick blending with memory magick. Not real ghosts."

Molly held in a sigh of relief. "Are there any ghosts?"

"Here? So far, no," Koz said, looking around. "We are on an island, so it's pretty hard for ghosts to get to the school, and there haven't been many traumatic deaths here, where the spirit has lived on outside the body. The school would know how to clean up the situation if there were and, hopefully, pass the spirits on in some way so they could either enter into their reincarnation cycle process or stay with the god or goddess they decided to bond themselves to."

Molly had to take a moment to let that process. It sounded like a traumatic death was how a spirit was made, which was news to her. She had never cared where they came from. She had always been more focused on how to stay away from them or get rid of them. "So, no ghosts?"

"There are game ghosts," Rem mentioned again.

"Besides game ghosts, no ghosts. Are you scared of ghosts?" Koz asked.

Molly could not help but to let her shoulders fall. The breath of relief she let out was so loud she covered her mouth. It sounded like here was the best possible place she could be to learn to protect herself if there were no ghosts.

"No . . . Not—Kind of," Molly answered Koz's question.

Koz stood, took Rem's plate and then Molly's. "Well, there is nothing to worry about. And the video game analogy is the best way to describe our world. It is also best—if you are new— to think of it in a similar dissociative way."

Molly got up and followed after him. She needed to know what that meant or it would torment her. "What—what do you mean?"

"What I mean is that, if you pay too close attention to what you *assume* may be the meaning of certain things instead of looking only to the facts, this world could drive you crazy and make you go mad."

Rem brushed right past her a little too close, which made Molly jump. Rem then stood next to Koz as he put the two plates on a conveyor belt that moved to an opening so they could be cleaned. Then she followed closely beside him as he led them to the stairs.

Molly made sure to stay a little behind once again, now more unsettled than ever. She decided to focus on the beauty of the hardwood in stone that made up the stairs as they climbed up until they reached the first hall, which entranced her with its beauty.

It was blinding. It was all gold, even the carpet and each door.

"This is Fehu Hall," Koz said. "Each hall is based on a rune from Freya's Aett." He nodded to a symbol embedded in the golden wall: a single straight line with two lines coming out of it at an angle.

"Why Freya?" Molly asked, still mesmerized by all the gold. She remembered that goddess from Norse mythology.

"Because, although the school encompasses all gods and pantheons, like Rem said, this school was made by Freya's chaos magick. Fitting, since it is believed that Norse religion is more intimate with the human condition—with how it touches the darker aspects of life," Koz explained.

She wanted to walk down the golden hall. She wanted to touch it and let her mind take in how each door and every part of every wall was gilded.

"*Fehu* is assumed to mean 'for the rich.' For those with wealth and strength. I'm telling you this so you don't waste your time trying to look it up only to fall down a hole of incomplete information," Koz said, continuing up the stairwell without her.

The next hall was darker. Koz said its rune represented *Uruz*, for resentment of power and creative force. Molly swore she saw spider webs growing and disappearing along the dark walls, which had no speck of gold. But she didn't think that could be right. Why would there be a hall that would do that?

Next came Thurisaz, which Koz said was meant for extra protection for those who needed it most. It catered to them and made life easier. It made life more accessible. There was something Molly's size strolling down the hall that made her heart stop for a moment. It was a creature with giant insect-like legs and a furry torso. She couldn't quite make out the head as it reached a door to turn the key and slip inside.

Rem nudged her. "Not polite to stare."

"What was . . ."

"Another student who happens to be an intelligent creature," Koz said with a shrug and then continued up.

Ansuz was the hall on the fourth floor. She swore there was dust falling from the ceiling in random places. Koz said it was for those who need to be more aware.

Next was Raido, where Derrin's room was. Apparently, it was for journeys.

Finally, they reached Molly's hall, Kenaz, on the sixth floor. She saw the same rune that was on her key embedded in black marble on the wall by the stairs.

Koz stopped.

"What does this one mean?" she asked nervously. She couldn't believe she would be living and sleeping here.

He paused. For a moment, she was worried that he wouldn't tell her, but then he sighed. "Discovery. Destroying for something new."

Her eyes shot wide. "What does that mean?" She wondered what that meant about *her* and how that box or the school thought this hall would fit her needs.

"For everyone . . . the meanings mean different things. Remember what I told you? Don't read into things without facts so you don't drive yourself insane." Koz pulled out his phone and looked at the time.

Molly turned away from the both of them to her hall and then sneezed, which made Rem laugh.

Molly's muscles tensed. She smelled something burning.

"Take a deep breath," she heard Koz say.

What? She glanced at him, but he was looking down her hall with his arms crossed.

They had said they had things to do.

She quickly did as she was told, not wanting to be a bother. When she took a deep inhale, there was an odd smell, something like burning hair but not quite. She couldn't place it.

"Burning feathers," Koz said. "Now, touch the wall."

She took a few steps into the hall and put her hand on the wall near the imprinted rune. She snatched it back, sucking air sharply through her teeth. "It's hot!"

Rem nodded with an impatient glance at Koz.

Molly looked down the hall again, walked a few paces, and then tried to touch another wall. This time, it was only warm. It was calming at first, until she could picture the skin on her hand starting to melt, and she swore she could see it steam. She pulled it away, checked her palm, and saw that it was unharmed.

Why had she been placed here?

She pulled out her key and looked at the number. Room 260.

She began walking down the hall, carpeted in the same deep maroon as the stairwell that led to the basement, but then realized Koz and Rem weren't following her.

"Are you coming?" she asked.

Rem shook her head, but it was Koz who answered.

"No. We have things to do." He pointed up the stairwell. "The next hall is Gebo. It has tree branches that have grown with no tree. When a branch is touched, it lights up different colors and happiness flows through someone. Teachers and guests reside there. The one after that is Wunjo. Those with a key on that floor hear peaceful music. That is also a hall where teachers and guests live and stay."

Molly glanced over her shoulder at all the doors in her hall once again. She wasn't ready for Koz and Rem to leave her. She didn't know what to do.

Rem pointed down her hall this time. "Every hall is different. Doors count by three, some five, some two."

Koz nodded. "Yes. Your room numbers count off by fives."

"Why?" Molly asked.

"Chaos." Rem grinned. "There is always chaos in numbers."

But that had to mean something.

"One last thing," Koz said, already turning his body to head back down the stairs. Rem started down ahead of him. "There are two gender-neutral bathrooms, along with one girl bathroom and one boy bathroom, with everything you need. There is a creature in the bathroom. Don't worry about it. It's called a vigilplunk and will only attack if someone is bullying someone else. They are there for that reason."

"Oh . . . Okay . . ."

He shook his head with a lazy grin and then left her all alone.

Alone to find her room . . .

As she made her way down the hall, her brain swam from the burning fumes. She saw right away that Koz had been right: the rooms were counted off by fives. She was now at 100, which meant she would reach her room soon.

But then she saw something that made her shriek and drop her key and bag to the floor.

Floating out of the carpet ahead of her were two creatures that could have been fairies. They were blue, with slender bodies that grew translucent from the light fixtures above them as they floated to one of the doors before her. They had no wings and long fingers, with small feet with normal-sized toes.

One of them started to mess with the keyhole on a door. It looked like they were trying to get in and that they couldn't just move through the door like they had the floor.

Molly then heard students coming up the stairs. She wanted to check to see what time it was and where everyone was at with their schedules, but those fairy things were breaking into someone's room. She couldn't pull her attention away. What would the students think if they came up the stairs and saw her doing nothing to stop them?

But before Molly could shoo them away, they had succeeded in opening the door by using their long fingers in the keyhole, sitting on the knob, and then pulling at it together.

"Not again!" a girl yelled, running to the door and slamming it shut. The two creatures scurried away in shock, but another one rose from the ground and floated right in front of the girl's face, looking annoyed.

A few older kids walked by and snickered.

"How do you keep on opening on your own!" the girl yelled at the door, completely looking through the thing in front of her.

Couldn't she see it? Or was it like a spirit? Was it something only Molly and others who worked with spirit magick long enough could see?

Molly instantly felt panicked that there were spirit creatures here. She grabbed her stuff and walked right past the girl and the thing floating in front of her, ignoring them both as the older kids had done. But then something pinched her, making her shout and slap her hand to her lips. She turned around to see what it was. That thing had followed her. It was looking directly at her now as the girl stared after her, probably because she had shouted. Molly watched in horror as it reached out to touch her and stood paralyzed as its finger went right through her, convulsing her muscles in pain. She didn't yell out this time, though. She just let tears well in her eyes as she turned and tried not to run away from it, tried not to look too panicked, too out of place, too weird.

It was her first day at this school. She did not want anyone to think she was odd or that something was wrong with her. She did not want to give anyone a reason to make fun of her or hate on her right away.

She saw her door was four doors away and ran toward it. The number 260 was in gold in the middle near the top. She fumbled with her key, then shoved it in the hole right when she touched her door. When the door opened, she ran into the room and closed it behind her, holding the handle so the spirit creature could not try to work its way in. It rummaged with the door handle on the other side for a while until it seemed to give up and finally let go.

Molly sank to the floor and cried.

Namu

Chapter Eight

Namu was exhausted. Spirit Magick Three and Runes Two that morning had taken a toll on his brain, even though both classes covered basics. It was going to be a challenging year. It didn't help that he was still drained from his time with Mr. Vero the day before, which hadn't fixed his problem.

Now he had an hour break before meeting Mr. Vero again for another round of what he was sure would be the same as what had happened the day before.

Shoulders pounded into him as too many students tried to go up the stairs from the basement, heading outside, to the cafeteria, or wherever else for their breaks. Namu didn't understand why they didn't stagger schedules. It wasn't as if the school was too full of students, but it was still annoying when the halls were brimming with them, which was why he was excited to get to his room to relax for a moment.

The giant TV placed over the top of the wall scribbled in white cursive flickered as Namu arrived at the top of the stairs with a number of other students. The scribbles were the names of deceased witches meant to honor them. He hadn't known any of them personally, but he knew Lily's dad's name would be there one day.

The TV had been recently placed there, another effort to blend technology into the old school, which wasn't working out for the best. The screen flickered a few more times as he walked by it, which meant something was going to happen that he didn't want to deal with. A display of how blending old and new sometimes didn't work.

Namu couldn't cut across the room in time.

From the corner of his eye, he saw one of the white names light up as if a flashlight were behind it. The TV flickered again, covered in static, before a ghost emerged and floated to the floor, the ghost of the person whose name had been lit up with projection spirit magick. This magick was mainly used during balls, speeches, or even some history classes to illustrate some aspect of the deceased person. But adding projection magick to technology obviously came with some glitches: sometimes making it turn on itself and choose a random name carved on the wall—names that had been put there with memory magick.

The projection magick and memory magick combined with techno magick to create projection spirits who sometimes had minds of their own, especially a particular few. They would eventually flicker in and out, but how long they lasted always varied.

Namu wasn't a fan.

One of these spirits was now roaming among the students and harassing them.

Mister Quivver—"Mister" spelled out on the wall with each distinct letter, thanks to his constant badgering after his death—

was a spirit the same height as most of the younger students with a glare that could burn a soul. He kept trying to jab at the foreheads and shoulders of the students who passed him as he shouted about how techno magick would be the end of them all, although he was thankful that it had allowed him to come alive again and spout his nonsense.

A few students laughed.

Namu scurried away to the stairwell that led to his hall. He didn't entirely disagree with the spirit projection. He hated how people were so distracted and worried about pixel magick and apps when there were bigger things to be worried about, like the door in his room. Because of that distraction and because, apparently, according to Lily, people were idiotic enough to give up bits of their soul to use magickal apps in the non-magickal and magickal community, he was sure something bad would happen. It annoyed him how often he heard students talk about all the different kinds of apps, including some created by a student named Koz. Namu was sure this Koz guy could find a better use of his time, but at least Koz's apps didn't ask for the absurd price of pixels from a soul for payment. Why would anyone use those apps when they didn't know how much a pixel of a soul really was?

But maybe he was being too harsh, once again irritated by his own difficulties and taking it out on everyone else. Would he be like them if he weren't already missing pieces of his soul?

Something made him stop. It wasn't the fact that he was alone on the stairs. He was expecting that. It wasn't common for students to go to their rooms during breaks, since they spent most of their time at night in their rooms doing their online non-magickal classes. It was that something smelled weird. Something smelled too nice. Too alluring.

When he turned the corner to Raido Hall, he saw an odd, familiar mist that he recognized as an astral mist. A transformation type of magick that one could only perform using a drink that turned your body into a soul-like mist. It scooted right past him, then he heard a clang from behind.

A small black cauldron, small enough to fit in his hand, had fallen from somewhere. Someone must have made a concoction to turn themselves into an astral mist. Maybe a student was practicing what they learned from their Transformation Drinks and Remedies class?

He shook his head. Another thing that wasn't his concern. He just needed to get to his room so he could relax and clear his mind before he had to join the swarm of students again.

He left the cauldron and headed to his room, number 114. It wasn't that far because the doors on his hall counted off by threes, making his room precisely in the middle.

He pulled out his golden key to unlock it. The click of the lock and the turn of the knob sent a calm wave through him. That feeling grew when he saw how clean and neat the room was. He had most of his things glued down with glue magick so the spirit sprites wouldn't steal or mess anything up.

He plopped down on his bed, arms spread wide, and stared at the ceiling, wishing it was the sunny sky. He could almost hear the construction workers and machinery in his mind, dissolving his thoughts. He was tempted to take out his phone and listen to the videos he had of past summers working with his dad again.

Then beeping from across the room called for his attention.

He threw his head back, extending his neck farther to exhale all the air from his lungs. He knew who it was—his brother, who knew when his breaks were and loved to call him up to bother him.

Namu kicked his legs up and strutted across the room to grab his tablet off his desk. When it wouldn't budge, he cursed, undid the glue spell, and hit the talk button.

Lockdrest

The face of his eight-year-old brother, Minis, popped up on the screen. His skin was darker than Namu's, his eyes a mischievous dark green, and his smile beaming.

"What do you want?"

"Just wanted to see you! And *Lily*. H-How is Lily?" His brother was trying to look over his shoulder through the screen for their friend. Minis always teased Namu about Lily and called them hot all the time, which they were. But Namu had expressed more than a hundred times that they were only friends.

"Lily is Lily. They're fine. What's up?"

Now his brother looked bored. "Nothing. Just wanted to bother you."

Namu went back over to the bed and fell onto his back. "Of course. Wouldn't have expected anything else. How's Dad?"

Molly

Chapter Nine

The first thing Molly did when she had gotten herself to calm down was unpack. There was a large wooden dresser in the room to put her clothes in and an empty bookshelf. A desk with a black laptop was sat in the middle of the room, against a wall. The one window in the room looked out to flat grass plains for about a mile before the land dropped off the island to the sea. Molly pulled out the fragile wooden chair, sat down, and opened the laptop. The screen came to life and burned her eyes for a moment, displaying a background that showed the front of the school. In the left-hand corner was an icon that said "Online Non-magickal Documents." She did not want to worry about non-magickal classes right now.

She moved her mouse around aimlessly, thinking about clicking on the other small icon on the far bottom right of the screen, which was a search engine for the internet. But there was nothing she wanted to look up.

Biting her lip, she closed the laptop and took off her shoes. The parts of her room with hardwood flooring were cold on her feet. She placed her shoes by the dresser and opened a drawer that she designated the spot for her dirty clothes, since she did not have that many clothes yet and had no hamper. A rug in a calming blue gave her ease when she stepped onto it. It was set under her bed and extended in a giant square two feet on each side.

She was disappointed that there was no bathroom in her room until she realized it was because she was scared to go back out into the hall, which was stupid and made her feel ashamed. She couldn't be afraid to leave her room forever.

It felt like being little all over again, finding out that only she could see spirits and then being too frightened to leave her safe space of home. It had taken her years to begin going anywhere without making up excuses that she couldn't.

She took her phone out of her days-old shorts and realized that, more than anything, she wanted to shower and change into her pajamas to try to rest. She didn't want to wait until tomorrow morning, not when her day had started so early, not when she was never that good at getting sleep.

She wondered if the app she used on spirits before would work on the spirit creatures she saw in the hallway. But she didn't want to use an app yet when she didn't know if anyone used anything like them at the school. She knew they used old magick, so they might look down on cell magick. But if she knew for sure no one was looking, maybe she could try. No, with her luck, someone would catch her. What if they thought she was lame and a cheat when it came to magick?

She went to her dresser and grabbed one of the tank tops and pajama shorts that Kren had bought her. She could try to go a couple of days without using one of the magickal apps. The blue spirit creature had hurt her, but it didn't seem to be trying to take her over. When it touched her, it didn't send her back to that place with the purple ice.

She put her phone in the bottom drawer of her dresser so she wouldn't lose it and wouldn't be tempted to use an app. Then she went to the door. She patted her pocket first to ensure she had her key and wouldn't get locked out before opening it. She didn't know where she would put it when she was showering, but there had to be a place.

Stepping out into the hallway, she was greeted by the smell of burning feathers again. It assaulted her nostrils, making her sneeze. The hallway felt warmer than it had moments before; even the carpet under her bare feet felt hot.

She headed back the way she had come before. Not far away from where she had seen the spirit creatures come out of the floor were two pairs of doors on opposite walls, with a gentle glowing hue coming from inside them. On the left side, a boy symbol was engraved in a black marble square on the wall and on the other, a gender-neutral symbol. On the right side of the hall was a girl symbol and another gender-neutral symbol. So, she had three choices. She decided to go with the girls today.

The warm glow welcomed her as the flooring transitioned from maroon carpeting to gentle stone. The walls were a soft-brown brick that was so spotless she wanted to run her hand across it.

She turned into a large room with mirrors set over sinks of black marble, large bowls sitting on a long white marble counter. Stalls, seaweed-green in color, were lustrous in the now-white light that differed from the illumination of the hall. There were four standing showers at the end made of stone, with sea-green curtains decorated with white petals. And there was—

Molly let out a scream, dropped her clothes, and jumped back.

There was a thing lying over one of the green stalls. A monstrous thing that looked like a lopsided ball. It was the size of a large stuffed animal with hair. Pink hair. So much pink hair that it poked out every which way. The blob was staring at her with blue eyes as it stretched its mouth wide into a yawn and showed her its sharp teeth.

It finally shut its mouth, but Molly could barely stop shaking. The thing kept watching her lazily, then blinked.

Molly gathered up her clothes and ran out of the restroom to try the gender-neutral bathroom next door. But there was another creature there, this one a little smaller, with brown eyes and hair a darker shade of pink.

Molly wanted to cry but decided to shower there. What choice did she have if they were in every bathroom?

When she walked past the creature, she remembered that Koz had warned her about not being scared of a creature in the bathroom. Did he call it a vigilplunk? How could she not be scared of the thing that was following her with its gaze wherever she went?

It still gazed at her as she walked to the showers, pushed the curtain away, and noticed a small clear safe box with the design of a key etched into its glass.

There was a little square indent on the side of the key impression with an etching of a thumbprint. This must be where she put her key.

She grabbed the tiny handle and pulled the glass container open to set her key right-side-up inside of it into the stand to hold it in place. Then she closed the door, put her thumb where the thumbprint was, and watched the box glow yellow before it faded to clear again.

The water spouted in the shower that instant, and a shelf extended from the wall below the box holding a white towel, a washcloth, soap, a comb, brush, and anything else she might need to clean herself, along with a place to set her clothes. Her house was nice but nothing like this. She'd never seen a shower so modern or advanced.

She looked over her shoulder at the vigilplunk, then started undressing. It averted its eyes. At least it wasn't rude. And the longer she looked at it, she began to think it was kind of cute.

Molly patted her hair with the white towel, then headed to her room. It felt nice being in her clean pajamas. She couldn't wait to throw the old ones in the designated dirty drawer. Too many things had happened while she had been in them the last two days.

Stutter-stepping momentarily, she realized that the maroon carpet was turning a light blue beneath her wet feet. Behind her, where the carpet was drying, her footprints were starting to disappear.

She sighed in relief to be back near her room and put her key into the lock.

She was happy that she hadn't run into anyone else. Although she was desperate to make friends and fill the emptiness inside her, she was not ready. Not tonight. Not after those blue spirit creatures. She was not ready to make a fool out of herself again. Not before tomorrow, when she would be around so many people.

She put her dirty clothes in the drawer, pulled out her phone, and fell onto her bed, exhausted. She laid the phone on her stomach as she looked at the twisted silver light fixture above her. It was dark in her room, but she did not want to turn the light on. What she should have done, though, was get out the charger in her bag to plug in her phone for the night if she happened to pass out, but her body was telling her it was too late.

She lay there, listening to her heartbeat in the empty and quiet room.

She already missed home. She had that sinking, sick feeling in her gut that she had gotten at summer camp when she had only wanted to go home. It made her want to run to the bathroom and get sick. It probably didn't help that she had only eaten a few nuts on the plane.

She rolled over onto her side, letting the phone fall off her onto the bed. If she figured this out and learned quickly, she could go back home and live normally for once. Or at least as normally as she could pretend to be. Then she wouldn't have to worry so much about losing her friends and everyone again. She also wouldn't have to worry about completely losing herself . . .

That was her biggest fear.

Losing herself in that large body of water. Drowning and never being able to breathe again.

She heard a rummaging and a click.

Molly grabbed her phone and shot up straight to see two of the blue spirit creatures, with their thin blue bodies floating into her room. They began to roam around.

She wanted to hide and scream, but she had nowhere to go. She also knew if she screamed, she might draw attention, which she didn't want.

So, she held it in.

The spirit creatures looked as though they were trying to find something. They looked at her empty bookcase, pulled open her drawers, shifted around her clothes, then grabbed her bag. They pulled out her charger by its prongs, lifting it to the ceiling. Then they let it fall. She cringed when it clattered, then cowered when they turned to her. She scrambled under the bed's covers to hide as she whimpered.

"Please leave me alone. Just go! I don't have anything for you!"

But then that stabbing pain returned, going into her back. They could reach their fingers through the sheets.

She couldn't do this. She couldn't. Another one jabbed her legs, and warmth entered her calf before it withdrew, making her cold and tight. She turned on her phone and went to that screen she had used to get rid of spirits before throwing off her covers to direct it at them.

The lines that she was supposed to navigate were there, but the square in the corner that told her which lines to move was blank. It was black and empty, shredding all her hope.

She threw the phone at the creatures instead. It hit the rug as she scrambled for her bag. She grabbed it by one of the straps and swung it. It went through one of the spirit things floating close to her face.

Although the bag had passed right through it, the blue creature still looked disturbed.

The other one tried coming toward her, and she swung the bag once more.

That one shook its head after the material of the bag, and its body didn't mesh or collide.

After a few more swings, Molly found herself sitting on her bed. She swung all night until the blue-spirited beasts finally gave up and went away. By then, Molly couldn't check the time on her phone, plug it in, or wipe away the angry tears from her cheeks. She dropped the bag to the floor and passed out.

Namu

Chapter Ten

Namu stared at the door. He wanted to leave it alone. He needed to ignore it.

But he couldn't.

There was a hole in his wall that had fallen away to sand with magick moments ago. Namu stared into it, sitting where his small dresser had been before he moved it. He peered through into the small room, which contained a petrified wooden door that was much like the trees in the world behind it. Its handle kept shifting and changing the type of metal it was made of every few seconds. Sometimes, it was black, sometimes, gold.

He hated it. Even though the door and that world had made *their* world a better place.

Once technology revealed that magick was real, witches knew that people resistant to the idea of magick would react. Hiding in plain sight would no longer be possible.

Witches from all over the world found a way to contact each other through the internet. They put aside their own strife and their own wars, for one thing. To work together to eliminate the objects that had killed many of their kind in the past. The items that were impossible to fight against.

Magickal people were the minority then; they still were today, even though more people than ever in the last twenty years had taken advantage of learning magick. Before magick became a world topic, most would allow themselves to be hunted or killed in order to protect the secret that magick existed so it wouldn't turn the world on its head.

But now, with the secret out, they decided to make a spell that only their combined knowledge and talents from all parts of the world could create. A spell that still lingered today and would most likely last forever.

That spell got rid of all the weapons in the world. The spell disintegrated any weapon held with any intention of violence.

But all those disintegrated weapons had to go somewhere.

With their skills, the magickal people of the world had created a door to a different dimension. One where the cycle of death and rebirth roamed in the form of petrified things and black matter that they didn't understand. One where creatures fed off any kind of soul.

It was a place of nightmares.

All the chaos of future death had been sent there and still was there, in the form of disintegrated metal, warped and black, creating something new. And they locked that place away and closed that door, in a child's room in a children's school.

Namu had been told that the school would decide by way of keys who would be sent to the room and who would find it. He was told that, since he didn't die when he had found it, he was meant to watch over it next.

He was meant to give up his life to watch over a door that had taken bits of himself.

Lockdrest

He was expected to toss out all his dreams and stay at the school. To be like Mr. Vero was and stay near the door for the rest of his life. And for what? Did they have a plan for it? Was it just supposed to sit here?

He sighed. He had every reason to hate that door. It did not belong here. It was a terror, a danger, not to mention all the kids in the past who had gone inside it and perished.

And the stupid school had not done a thing. They had never even warned them.

Namu looked down to see a glimmer of its chaotic metal now crawling up his arm. A thin, silver snake slithering through his veins, fed by anger. One of the fights between him and Mr. Vero spun through his head as the door continued to linger in front of him.

"Why can't the school just get rid of the key!?" Namu had yelled in Mr. Vero's face.

"From what I was told, that's not the way of the school. The school will start to break. Cracks will form. Don't suggest things when you don't understand. Tell me, what would happen if everything behind that door were released back to the world? Chaos. It would be worse than it would have ever been before. The non-magickal people who are already furious, you want to give them back what could destroy so many so easily? This is unmanaged magick we're dealing with. I don't know what would happen if that door were opened and it began to leak to the outside. We need to watch the door and keep it closed. If you can't do that, just ignore it and move on when you're done with your schooling. I'm sure the school will find someone else."

Someone else to be tortured the way Namu had been?

"Why can't you just stay in the room?" he'd asked Mr. Vero.

"It would be too obvious that something is there. Don't you think students are already suspicious as to why I live in the hall above, where there are no other teachers? Thankfully, my room is a normal room. If any students were curious and decided to break in, they wouldn't find anything. And, at some point, the job of protecting the door needs to be passed on anyway. This is a sacrifice to make this world a better place. Stop asking—"

A knock at his bedroom door tore Namu away from the memory.

He knew it was Lily coming to get him for breakfast before their classes. He couldn't allow them to see—

"Hold on!" Namu yelled, crawling to the dresser to drag it back into place.

All it had taken was his eyes darting away from the spot for the wall to re-form itself.

The dresser screeched across the ground as Namu pushed.

"What are you doing!? Come on!" Lily knocked harder.

"Hold on!" Namu repeated, pushing the dresser against the wall. He looked down and realized he wasn't dressed in day clothes yet. In a panic, he looked to the door and then to the bigger dresser that had come with the room and back to the door again. There was another violent knock.

He didn't have time.

He opened the door, and Lily barged in.

"What took you so long? What are you—" Lily went from looking around the room to staring at him. Perplexity had their brows drawn in. "You aren't even dressed yet."

Lily smelled like cheese puffs. Even though they had tried to hide it under perfume, they still had some residue on their fingers. They must have been watching sci-fi movies that morning or last night. That was the only time they ate those.

"And you smell of junk food and junk movies."

Lily waved him off, going to his dresser. "Sci-fi is not junk movies. If anything, especially with our world, I would say fantasy movies are junk movies." They turned and eyed him.

"Too bad I'm not the biggest fan of the fantasy genre anymore," he whispered. He hadn't been since he had entered the magickal world.

Lily opened one drawer, threw him a pair of underwear, then pulled open another and tossed him a tight pink shirt and cargo shorts. He hated tight shirts—Lily knew that, but Lily had bought him some this year anyway, along with the shorts.

"Are you going to tell me what you were doing? I heard noises. Like you were moving something around." They eyed the room again and turned away from him so he could get changed.

He was used to this and stripped behind them, then tugged on the tight shirt. "I was just rearranging things."

Lily waited for a few more breaths before they turned around. "Everything looks the same."

"Lily . . . it's none of your business . . . What if I were doing something you wouldn't want to know about anyway?"

They gave a short laugh at that. "You're quieter when it comes to that."

He rolled his eyes, knowing they wouldn't even know.

"Does it have anything to do with how you've gotten so good at spirit magick?" Lily asked.

He turned away to put his dirty clothes in his hamper. "No."

"Because it's strange to me that you had no background whatsoever in magick and then, ever since the middle of last year, you've had your own tutor for no reason at all. You never told me why they gave you one."

He clenched his jaw, annoyed. "They just decided to."

"But why?"

"It isn't your business, Lily."

They looked taken aback. Lily's eyebrows shot up, and they pushed their lips to the side. "Why have you been panicking?"

What was he supposed to tell them? He couldn't tell them about the door. They would try to go into it, study it, or even tell their dad. But if he didn't say anything, Lily would never back off.

He went for an easy lie. One that he could maybe convince Mr. Vero to go along with later too. "I'm practicing for a special exam for an apprenticeship . . ."

This time, Lily's eyebrows drew inward. "What kind of apprenticeship? I didn't know there were special exams. I didn't even know you were interested in any magickal divisions."

"I don't want to talk about it." He tried to feign defeat as if he were scared of the prospect of failing. "If I make it, then I'll tell you. Hell, if I fail, I will tell you. But not before. Not yet."

Lily only stared at him.

And stared.

Finally, they opened their mouth. "Okay . . . When is your exam?"

"I don't know. Mr. Vero will tell me when it's closer."

"Can I ask you questions on what it is about?"

"I would rather you didn't."

"Does it deal with spirit magick?"

"I would say that's obvious."

More silence.

Namu sighed. "Are you ready to go to breakfast?"

Hopefully, the kitchen witches would be there today so the food would actually be good. Sometimes, as a perk of their job, the kitchen witches traveled to learn from elders worldwide. When that happened, the students were left with sandwiches they had to make themselves and popcorn or chips. It was interesting to Namu that the kitchen witches had no concern about rushing to leave together on what he would call a vacation and didn't find some kind of rotation schedule. But he assumed they didn't want to give up an opportunity to have a distraction or break from their jobs.

Lockdrest

Just like Namu could use a distraction. Really any distraction at all.

Molly

Chapter Eleven

M olly woke up on the floor, leaning against her bed with the sun shining through her window. Her back hurt. She ached all over. Her eyes were strained, and her arm was heavy from swinging her bag all night long. She wanted nothing more than to crawl into bed, pull the sheets over her, and pass out again to regain the night of sleep she had lost. But instead, she got herself up on twinging legs and made her way over to her phone on the ground.

She bent over to pick it up and nearly toppled over from exhaustion. It had lost half its charge, and it was already 7:20 am. She had no time to plug it in. She had to get dressed and get down to breakfast now. She knew that Kren would be waiting for her to say goodbye, if he weren't waiting for her already.

She quickly opened a text message to him and typed that she would be there soon, then threw her phone on the bed, scurried to her dresser, and tore open a drawer. She tugged on a pair of purple jean shorts and a white-blossomed blouse before putting on her socks and shoes. She would have to find a way to make money while she was here and get herself sandals or something easier to slip on.

Snatching up her phone, she saw that only five minutes had passed, so she grabbed her key and foraged in her bag for her folded-up schedule. When she found it, she made a mental reminder to put it on her desk. She then headed out the door.

Her first stop was the restroom. She ran into the gender-neutral one, ignoring the vigilplunk in one of the stalls, but all the showers were in use. She'd hoped to use her key and obtain a brush from the extendable drawer since she didn't have her own.

Knowing she'd likely find the showers equally occupied in the other bathrooms, she ran to the mirror in front of the long white marble vanity and ran her hands through her messy brown curls. She tried to ignore the dark circles under her eyes and her wide, grimacing mouth.

Then she went back out of the bathroom and down the hall.

Her phone vibrated. She pulled it out.

Kren: waiting . . .

Molly realized that she hadn't peed . . . Her bladder was practically sloshing, needing a release, but she decided to hold it.

Why was everything going wrong on the first day?

Afraid to meet anyone's eyes, she ignored everyone in her hall and headed forward and down the stairwell. Many other students were coming out of their rooms to head down the stairs, too, clogging it.

Molly: almost there

When she finally reached the bottom step, she immediately noticed Kren with a paper cup in his hand. His eyes widened when he saw her, and he brought the cup to his mouth for a sip.

"What took you?" Kren asked, pulling out his phone to check the time. It was 7:33.

Lockdrest

When Molly didn't answer because she was still trying to catch her breath, he seemed to notice her exhausted face and grabbed her unsteady hand as if to check her pulse. "What happened?"

She drew her hand away and let it rest on her chest, trying to calm her beating heart. "Those blue—things snuck in my room and bothered me all night."

His eyebrows raised. "Spirit sprites?"

He knew about them? Of course he did. He had gone to this school.

"I don't know. They kept trying to put their fingers into my skin."

"Into soul," Kren corrected. He put his phone into his brown pants pocket and then his sizeable finger to his chin. "Didn't think . . . Normally not bother students. Only steal. But with empty vessel . . . Maybe see toy."

"They see me as a toy!?" Molly was angry now. "They steal? Why don't the teachers do anything about them? I saw that some students can't even see them!"

"They're nuisance. Teach things not always seen, which will learn from spirit teacher. You need to learn glue spell and banishing. I don't have time to teach you."

Molly wanted to cry. A part of her had been hoping that Kren would at least have some way to help her. "But I need—"

She was interrupted by a teacher approaching them.

"Mr. Kren, is this who you were telling me about? The student who brought you all the way back to Lockdrest for a day?"

Molly couldn't tell if the teacher was male or female. Their head was twice as large as any human's. The creature had big green eyes and stringy flint-gray hair that lay in clumps around their head.

"Murs. Eddl, yes. Molly," Kren said with a smile and a slight bow. "Molly, Divinations One teacher. Made sure first class."

"Excellent!" Murs. Eddl said, clapping their hands. "I wonder if you will be as fun as Kren. We used to go to school together. Just don't go randomly giving people concoctions like he did. Still good at transformation drinks in a whole new way, though, as I noticed last night. Best sleep I've had in years." They winked at Kren.

Kren smiled awkwardly and slurped from his paper cup.

"I'll be seeing you soon, then! Safe travels back, Kren. Hope the tethers of our lives meet again." Murs. Eddl gave a small wave and smiled in Molly's direction with their perfect teeth before heading downstairs.

"What is . . . ?"

"Rude to ask," Kren stopped her. "No matter. Goes by Murs. When child, came here from far away."

A sudden pain stabbed Molly's lower stomach. She thought it was a spirit sprite again for a moment but then realized her bladder was still full. "I need to go to the bathroom. I didn't—I—there was no time."

Kren nodded and pointed to the restrooms by the stairs before the cafeteria. She rushed to them, trying not to make a scene.

But then she ran into someone hard.

The boy stopped, grabbed her shoulders before she could fall over, and stared into her with hate-filled brown eyes.

She stepped away, expecting him to yell at her, while her stomach cramped again.

"Namu! Apologize and let's move on. It is already your fault we're late," his companion behind him yelled.

The boy named Namu, who looked older than Molly, did not apologize but gave her a sneer, then turned and walked away.

Why were there such rude people here? First, the boy on the plane, and now him?

She didn't watch him and his friend walk away. She instead barged her way into the girls' restroom and one of the stalls. Then she sat down, looked up, and screamed. She had picked a stall with a vigilplunk resting on top of it.

It did not turn to face her as her pee turned to soft trickles and still didn't look at her as she lifted herself off the seat and slowly pulled up her pants. It wasn't until she exited the stall that she turned and saw it was now staring at her with its lopsided mouth hanging lazily, as if it were about to fall asleep.

Breathing heavily, she went to the sink to begin washing her hands.

She heard a toilet flush and then a shriek as a stall banged open, and a girl jumped out with her hands up.

It was the stall farthest away from the vigilplunk. But the vigilplunk was tense now and baring its teeth until it saw the girl breathing heavier than Molly had been just moments before. The girl tried to relax her hands at her sides but could not and darted backward from the stall into a sink.

It took Molly a moment to realize it was Rem.

"Hey, Rem. Are you okay?" Molly asked, still running her hands under the warm water.

Rem turned and looked at her with wide blue eyes. Her face dropped in fear, but she did not speak. Molly found herself wanting to see her thin lips smile, like she had the day before. Her skin was pale, as if she had seen a ghost. Molly waited, but Rem did not respond to her question.

"Man, you scared me!" another girl said after a flush that made Rem, who was beginning to wash her hands, flinch again.

This girl walked out of the stall with her blue romper pants flowing at her sides. She had light-brown hair in tight braids that matched her golden-brown skin. Her thin pink lips turned up in a smile. She fixed her hazel eyes on Molly, which made Molly realize that she had been staring while someone had been coming out of a bathroom stall for the second time in a row . . .

Molly turned away from this other girl, mortified, trying not to grimace at herself as she turned the water off and went to dry her hands. Her first day could not be going any worse.

Before she knew it, the girl she had been staring at for too long was drying her hands right alongside her. Had Molly been drying her hands for too long? Had this girl noticed?

"You look new." The girl smiled. "What's your name? I'm Ova."

Molly gulped and hoped the girl hadn't heard it. Rem was still washing her hands. She was either cleaning every inch of her skin or waiting for Molly and this other girl to leave. "I'm Molly. Yes. I'm new." She didn't want to be rude and exclude Rem, especially if she was having as hard of a time as Molly was, so she called out to her.

But before Molly could say anything else to Rem, two other girls came into the room, talking loudly. They were arguing.

"No. No. No. Don't blame it all on her. You saw her doing it. Why wouldn't you—"

"I thought she was joking," the other girl interrupted with a shake of her head.

"Even if she was joking, I would have never let someone put any kind of concoction they made near your hair!"

Molly saw that one of the girls had a strand of hair in her black locks that was different than the rest. It was green and seemed greasy, like she had dunked it into a bowl of melted butter.

"I worked on it all morning and all night. I can't fix it!"

"Ask a teacher," the girl with her hair nicely done up and no dark circles under her eyes said.

"No! You ask a teacher what to do!" The girl with the green strand had her hands clenched into fists. Her face was turning red.

"Why would I do that? It's not my hair."

The girl was close to tears now and took a step toward the other girl and grabbed the straps of her tank top to yell in her face, "Because it's your f—"

The vigilplunk growled, fell off the top of the bathroom stall, and started hopping its body toward the girls with its sharp teeth chomping.

Molly gasped, body shaking, and took a step to run out, but Ova grabbed her arm, stopping her.

The two girls screamed and scrambled out of the bathroom. For some reason, Rem seemed more at ease now than she had moments before, even though she was pressed against a wall. She had a small smile on her face.

The vigilplunk's body stopped hopping for a moment. Its eyes darted around as it munched on nothing a few times before it hopped around and made its way back to the bottom of the stall.

Ova went over, picked it up, its pink hair completely covering both of her hands. It seemed to melt a little in her grasp. She lifted it and set it back in place on the top of the stall.

It opened its mouth into a big yawn once it was settled and closed its eyes.

"Want to be friends?" Ova said, turning around and looking directly at Molly. She took something out of her pants pocket and started rubbing it between her hands. Ova stopped what she was doing and held it out to show her, also revealing an axe tattoo on her right forearm. Molly wondered what it meant but saw Ova was holding out an amber rock. "It calms me. Same with this." Ova grabbed at the gold band that adorned her left bicep.

"That's nice," Molly said, forcing a smile. "The most I have is a . . ." She stopped herself. She wanted to say an app, but then she knew she would have to explain the magickal one she used all the time with the sounds. She still didn't know if that was acceptable or not here. "My . . . phone."

"Oh! Would you like to exchange numbers? Why don't you give me your phone and I'll put my number in it? You can text me later when you have time. What classes do you have?"

Molly handed her phone over as they walked out of the bathroom. Rem dodged around them to get ahead of them and met someone who seemed to be waiting for her. It was Koz.

"You okay?" he asked Rem before holding something out for her. It looked like it was his phone. She smiled at him as she nodded twice before grabbing the phone from him. He took a second phone out of his pocket before they both walked away.

He hadn't seen Molly wave.

"Here you go."

Molly had to shake her head again to bring herself back to attention. She felt her cheeks burning red. Here was someone willing to talk to her, someone actually nice, and she was ignoring her and worried about getting the attention of someone else.

"What classes do you have again?" Ova asked after Molly finally took her phone back.

Molly took the paper out of her pocket to name them off.

"We have our first class together! Divinations One and then later Spirit Magick One at one thirty!" Ova exclaimed. "We'll have to meet up later, since it's 8 o'clock now. You'll have to tell me all about yourself. Do you want to head . . ."

Molly wondered why Ova was trailing off but then saw Kren approaching them, looking quite stern.

"Yes. That sounds great," Molly sputtered as Ova stood there frozen and confused. When Ova realized that Kren seemed to know Molly, Ova gave her a nervous smile and left.

"Made friend?"

"I . . . Maybe," Molly said, her voice trembling with nerves. She had probably ruined it. She had been thrown off by everything this morning and with not knowing what to do. This was a whole new setting for her. This was a whole new place. She didn't know how she was supposed to act. How she was supposed to react. What she was supposed to say. She was overtired and frightened by how terrifying and rude some people were here. She couldn't believe she had gone into the stall with the vigilplunk. She hated that there were spiritual creatures here that thought she was a toy and were apparently supposed to teach students a lesson.

She was falling into insanity. She missed her friends. She missed normality. She missed knowing the right or wrong thing to do—or what at least was close to acceptable.

"You need food," Kren insisted. "Then class."

His hand wrapped around her arm to pull her through the students, most of whom were heading to the stairs that led to their classes, then into the cafeteria where he nodded in the direction of the food lines.

She went to the long, smooth counter the color of sand and reached for a plain bagel on display in a heap of them. She shoved it into her mouth, then turned to see that Kren had gone. Panic filled her once more, making the bagel sour in her mouth, until she saw him. He was getting a second drink.

When she went over to him, he handed the drink to her. "Calm nerves," he said.

She took a sip of it. It quenched her dry mouth. Then the little sparks of anxiety on the outer layer of her skin went out, even though the world was spinning inside her. It wasn't as effective as the one Kren had made in his home.

"After classes. When have time, you need to see Koz." He pointed to the pocket where she kept her phone. "He will explain."

"Explain what?" Molly asked, taking another bite of her bagel. She didn't think that he had noticed who had shown Molly around yesterday. But maybe he had. Or maybe he knew him. "Do you know him?"

"Personally, no. But know from teachers he is knowledgeable. With trends," Kren spat. Then he sighed. "You will find Koz. This is where we say goodbye. You will be okay."

"Where are you going to go?" Molly asked. She didn't know how she felt about him leaving her here. Apparently, based on Ova's reaction, mini-trolls might make it harder for her to make friends. She wasn't really helping herself as far as that went, but for some reason, he was a comfort. She didn't feel judged by him. She knew he only wanted to help her. He had taught her that she could do old magick, something she had never thought was possible. He knew what she was, recognized it, and cared, when her parents hadn't. She had never felt that from anyone before. And not only that, but he was a bridge to her old world. Her old life. With him gone, she would have only this. She would have only herself, which made her uncomfortable.

"To look for Trennly," Kren said. "You will be okay."

Namu

Chapter Twelve

"No, *you* move out of my way."

Namu shook his head as he picked up his Runes Two book. Lily was outside the classroom door, probably actively blocking it, waiting for him to come out. That was how Lily normally talked to the people they saw as beneath them. It wasn't because their dad was famous; they had been like that their whole life.

"Namu! Come on! You're wasting our break." Lily stomped their foot, then groaned when they noticed him carrying his book with him.

"It isn't my fault you left your class so fast." Lily had just come from Divinations Two, which was a few rooms down from his. "I can't hang out with you anyway. I've got to put this book in my room. I have homework tonight."

"I'm not fast. You're just slow. And can't you drag it around with us?" Lily said as they headed to the stairs that led to the main floor.

"To where? Where do you want to go?"

"Outside."

The thought made the book grow heavier in his hands. "I can eat outside with you later, but I'm not dragging this book out there with me. Plus, I have my time with Mr. Vero next."

Agitation flitted across Lily's face as they threw up a hand. "And let me guess. You want to rest. Fine, I get it. I'll catch you later."

Then they took off, taking two stairs at a time. Namu watched as their long, glossy brown hair swayed alongside their hips as they moved through the people.

He rolled his eyes and took the turn for the stairwell when he got to the main floor.

When he reached his hall, he paused when he smelled that odd, alluring scent again. Then he saw something strange. Well, it wasn't too strange: just, that morning, he had seen something similar downstairs at breakfast, after that student who had looked scared to death ran into him.

He couldn't believe there were two here.

It was a mini-troll. Standing in his hall. But this was not the one he had seen downstairs. This one had a bright violet mohawk, unlike the green matted mess the other one had. This one was also dressed nicely, with shiny black shoes and a purple suit.

Was he interviewing someone?

He had heard of mini-trolls before briefly and was told that they had been made by magickal means. Apparently, a couple had been students here years ago, maybe around the time when Mr. Vero attended. But he had never seen one before today. Neither of them looked much like the giant trolls he had seen pictures of. These smaller ones had faces that were a little more squished in. Also, everything was a little smaller and compacted, a little off, but they looked quite nice. Quite professional.

Lockdrest

It was almost as if someone had combined two kinds of magick—or even more—to make them like that. Possibly visionary magick and transformation magick. But how had that someone gotten it to stick if a spell had done it at all? Lily's dad had mixed science and magick together. Was it like that? There was no way that Lily's dad was the only one who had tried to mix various types of magick together to create something new, like he had done with techno magick and memory magick.

The mini-troll was talking to another student outside their room. He must be a first year, since it was a boy Namu had not seen in the hall last year. The boy, whose skin was a deep tan, a little darker than Namu's, looked skeptical of the mini-troll but nodded and let the troll in.

Namu didn't know what to think of it, but he kept walking. Maybe he would get started on his Runes Two homework for the night before he went down to Mr. Vero's.

But then an idea came to his mind regarding combining magicks. What if he combined a healing-plant soul or essence and something with another kind of soul or essence that might help it stick better inside him? Like glue? No, that was stupid. But maybe the plant's healing properties would transfer in soul form to his own soul. Maybe, if combined with something else that Mr. Vero might know of, it might actually stay.

He would have to bring that up later to Mr. Vero.

Molly

Chapter Thirteen

Divinations One was horrible. Molly had been so lost, and she could not find any reason to care. The tarot decks were interesting, but since she had already missed a couple days, the class was already through learning the beginning of the standard cards and their meanings. They each got a worn deck to work with that had faded emerald backs. Each card looked like it had been eaten by moths on the sides.

Symbols One wasn't so bad. All she had missed was some history of the first set of symbols they were studying. Apparently, Lockdrest would tackle a wide variety of symbols from different areas of the world throughout the years.

It was like normal school, just more stressful. Molly couldn't have been happier to see Ova waiting for her outside of Symbols One class.

"How were your classes?" Ova asked. She was not carrying any books with her, even though Molly was.

"Overwhelming," Molly answered, clutching the heavy textbooks to her chest. She didn't understand why no one had bookbags around here.

Ova nodded and smiled apologetically. "I take it that you're not from a magickal community, then?"

Molly's heart stopped. Was it that obvious? "Why do you say that?"

"I mean, obviously, it's different for everyone, but it's the start of school. The beginning of first-year classes only go over basics. So . . ."

"So, this is all supposed to be easy, or I'm already supposed to know it . . ." Molly's shoulders slumped.

"But it's okay." Ova smiled brighter this time. "If you're new to the community, what made you come to magickal school?"

Molly didn't know what to say. She couldn't tell Ova that she was an empty vessel. She wanted to keep that to herself until she understood what it meant. "Just . . . I wanted to check it out."

Ova nodded uncertainly, as if she didn't trust Molly. Because of course she didn't. Molly's answer had been suspicious. Why would she have shown up a few days late if she had just wanted to check the school out? Also, if she had never done magick before, that probably meant her parents were reluctant, which they were. So why would they have chosen to let her come?

"I'm sorry, I . . ." Molly grabbed onto the wooden banister of the stairs that led up to the main floor and stopped. "I just . . ."

Ova held up her hand. "You're okay. Trust me."

Molly noticed that two coin-sized red bumps had risen on Ova's arm. Ova saw Molly looking at them and tucked her arm away. "I just want to be your friend and help guide you. Do you want to take those to your room, or do you want to bring them to the courtyard with us?"

Molly's heart pitter-pattered in her chest. She was happy that someone wanted to help her, but it still made her nervous that someone knew she needed that kind of assistance. She focused on the two books in her hands, one with a periwinkle binding and a lavender cover and the other a sticky red, and decided to take them to the courtyard. She didn't want to waste time taking them to her room when this was her time to bond. She also wanted to use them if something awkward happened, to say she needed to put them away or use them to hide behind.

"I'll take them with us. I would love to see the courtyard."

Ova pulled the purple book from Molly's arm with a *s-l-o-w* sticking lug as it rubbed across the red one. "Then, I will take half your load, as a friend would," Ova said. She started back up the stairs, and Molly followed her. "What hall are you in?"

Biting her lip, Molly remembered how Kren had said that the name of her hall meant "destroy for something new." Would that make Ova think badly of her? It wasn't like she could escape that, though. She was stuck in that hall and in the room they gave her. She was sure she couldn't change it. If they were going to be friends, Ova would find out sometime. "Kenaz. Room 206. Yours?"

"Uruz. 150," Ova stated. "Which . . . I don't know why. It isn't like I resent power. I love the power of the gods and goddesses."

"Yeah. I don't understand mine either." Molly was relieved that she wasn't the only one worried about the room the school had allocated her.

Ova laughed. "There's a deeper meaning for sure. Freya wouldn't have it otherwise. My parents said it takes a couple of years for the meaning to come clear. It's like divinations. It's a look into ourselves that we refuse to glance at until we are brave enough. This school was built on Freya's chaos magick, meaning her essence. So, in a way, the school has an all-knowing soul of its own. You were placed there for a reason."

Adora Michaels

Ova guided Molly past the cafeteria, where a few students sat and chatted during their break. There was a giant fountain in the middle of the open floor that Molly hadn't noticed yet because there had been so much going on. Water fell down in countless streams from its top to various piers of smoothed gray rock until it emptied into a large open sky-blue and cloud-gray basin.

Molly followed Ova past the fountain to a door near the largest three-set restrooms she had seen in the school. The silver-handled glass door led outside; Ova opened it and let Molly through.

At once, fresh air filled her lungs, and Molly could hear birds chirping over the students chatting. There were students sprawled out over the beautifully rich, freshly cut green lawn. The shining sun warmed her skin, welcoming her outside. The distant horizon collided with a mountainous drop, and the broad expanse let her imagination run, dreaming of adventures and wonders in many worlds. It felt as though they were on their own planet, their own island, high up near the heavenly sky.

"Spectacular, isn't it? Freya truly blessed us." Ova headed to the sidewalk that ran the length of the front of the school. It was the same path Molly had taken yesterday when she arrived from the plane. But now, Ova was taking her to the grounds on the opposite side of the school from the airport.

As they walked, Molly could see a forest reaching out behind where the grass plains stopped, where students from all years sat, laughing. As she and Ova turned the bend, they came to what felt like a circular courtyard, except there were no buildings surrounding it. It was just a giant circle of tanned brick with stone benches cemented to the ground all around its curves, and a giant statue of a man watching over it.

Molly stopped to stare at it. The statue had to be four times the size of any human. Black as a moonless night, the warrior-

144

like man stood, with one foot raised on a platform of onyx stone, extending a long, thin horn into the sky. The man was depicted in armor, with a beard that fell to a cloak that draped over his broad shoulders, and stone fur sprouting out near his wrists and soft-detailed boots. The thing that entranced her the most was his very own horns that curved around from the top of his helmet to the back of his head.

"Heimdallr," Ova said. "Born of nine sea monsters. A gift from Opendrest." Maybe because Molly had stopped, Ova decided to sit down there in the grass. She stretched out her legs, her blue romper blanketing around her thin frame.

"A gift from Opendrest?" Like how the pool in the basement was a gift from Closedrest.

"Yes. Opendrest is another one of the three main magickal schools over on this side of the country. Each with their own island. Each school gave the other schools a gift," Ova said.

Molly sat, too, and set her book down. Some of the students nearby seemed to be waiting for something. A few were sitting on the stone benches, staring at the statue or the middle of the brick circle, wringing their hands together nervously and pulling at their fingers. They were sitting in twos or threes, whispering and talking.

"I'm excited to hear what your favorite class is later, after you've taken them all," Ova said with a yawn, which prompted Molly to yawn too. "Are there any you're most excited about?"

"Spirit Magick One," Molly answered without thinking. She continued to watch as a few teachers came into the courtyard. One wearing a red shirt was holding out a black container to the waiting students. Molly watched as each student pulled something out of the container, something long and white that left dust on their hands. Was it chalk?

"Oh, really? That's a hard subject. Why that one?"

Molly didn't want to explain too much about herself by answering that question, so she deflected it by feigning to look around. "Who is the principal of this place?" she asked.

"Principal? Oh!" Ova gave a quick laugh and then covered her nose before putting her hand down into the grass and plucking a single blade. "You most likely won't see the heads of the school. They are elsewhere, probably living in their mansions or all together. I hear they are pretty eccentric."

Interesting.

The teacher had finished handing out what looked like chalk and tucked the small black box under her right armpit as she headed to the statue. Looking annoyed, the teacher dropped the black bag she had on her shoulder to her forearm and pulled out a small horn. The horn didn't exactly match the one on the statue. It was shorter and not as beautifully made. She faced the statue, placed the chalk box on the ground, and blew a light note.

The students around the courtyard stepped back as a rumbling started deep in the earth, and the bricks began flipping and changing. They were transforming into a mirrored black pavement that might have been onyx.

Once it was done, the teacher picked up the chalk box and walked away with a huff.

"What just happened?" Molly asked, still mesmerized, as the students walked onto the glassy black slate and started writing on the ground.

They were writing symbols. Molly could already identify some of them as runes.

"Oh. Depending on the note played, the statue can change the terrain of the courtyard to nine different landscapes. Mrs. Heard is apparently the only one who knows how to play all of them. That wasn't her, though. That was the Projection and Memory teacher, Mrs. Refra."

Lockdrest

Molly turned to Ova, watching the red-shirted teacher as she disappeared into the school with an annoyed sigh. "Most teachers don't like doing it," Ova added. "But Lockdrest's main focus is symbols and runes, so the students need time to practice, and some like the sport."

"Sport?"

Something suddenly drew her attention back to the courtyard. One of the symbols, made by a girl with braids, had risen from the ground and had tilted itself right-side-up. The symbol had a few twists and turns, making it look like numerous number 8s flung together haphazardly. Molly heard Ova tsk.

The boy the girl was facing, who had long hair and determined eyes, stood up next as his symbol began to rise. His was perfectly connected Os, maybe even 8s, forming their own circle.

The symbols flew toward each other and connected with a small flash before the girl's disintegrated and before the boy's twisted itself into a perfect full circle and then shone a light up to the sky as bright as the sun for one second before disappearing.

Molly didn't know what to think. She didn't even know what the symbols meant.

"She should have taken her time," Ova said, shaking her head. "It's called chalk-rising. If you pair up, you need to decide what symbols to use against each other. You can test to see if you are faster or which ones are stronger. Some symbols are naturally supposed to be stronger but may fail if not drawn correctly or if the incorrect amount of incentive is given into the chalk while you transfer it to the ground. Hers was supposed to be stronger. If you team up, you can also practice mixing symbols with others to create something new. This is the place to practice the power of runes and symbols. It has safeguards to let the earth ground them and not hurt anyone. It also streamlines the magick. Some things you can do here you can't do anywhere else. A lot goes into it. It's a hard sport."

"Sounds boring," Molly said, falling back a little to relax. She imagined Rexa and Val would have thought that too. "It's like studying."

Ova's mouth dropped open an inch. "I would not say boring. This school is all about the academics of runes and symbols. They form the very foundation of many things. Like the halls . . . It only makes sense that the school's sport would be . . ." Ova stopped herself.

Molly hadn't meant to offend her, so she tried to change tack. "What's your favorite subject?"

Ova sat up straighter, scratching at a small red welt on her arm right below the golden band that hugged it. "Runes. I also like symbols, but I've been doing runes my whole life."

"Your whole life?"

"Yes." Ova leaned over, pulled her pink phone out of her right romper pocket, then leaned the other way and pulled out a small velvet navy bag. "With my family's profession, it's important."

"What is your family's profession?" Molly asked.

"My family runs the temple of Freya."

Sliding open her screen with her finger, Ova hit a few buttons and then showed Molly an app. The logo had a bag much like the one lying on the ground next to Ova. But on the app, the bag was spilling out wooden sticks with runes on them.

"This app shows what each rune means. There are even rune games on it. There is another one for symbols too. It might help you. Koz made them both, so you would have to go and ask him for them."

Koz had made them?

"How many pixels?" Molly asked.

"Pixels?" Ova asked.

"Yeah, pixels. Of your soul?"

Ova blanched, which made the blood drain from Molly's cheeks.

"Pixels of your soul? What?" Ova asked.

"Um . . . in . . . well . . . where—my old friends. The apps . . . They cost pixels of your soul to use."

Ova's shoulders dropped. "You're kidding."

Molly shook her head as Ova put her phone away.

"It costs no pixels of your soul. How does that even work? Why and how would the gods allow that?"

Molly thought she could explain. "Before you use one of them, it asks if you want to give a pixel of your soul. You hit yes, and you feel something small get sucked out of you, and then you can use the magick of the app." Molly was talking fast. "It's only a little bit. That's all."

"And where do those apps come from?"

"I . . . I don't know."

"You've done this?"

Molly wanted to shake her head no, but she could not move her head at all. She only watched Ova's hazel eyes widen.

"Oh, Freya, Metis, and Dagda, you need guidance. Who do you follow?"

"What?"

"What pantheon or gods do you work with? All are accepted here."

Molly didn't follow or work with any.

Ova covered her mouth for a moment and then took a big breath. "I work with Freya because she is our family goddess, which is why I was sent to this school of first foundations and runes. We have worshiped Freya for a long time. These runes, they help consult her. I mainly use these runes that I keep with me at all times, like all my family does, to consult Freya."

Ova took the bag and emptied the contents onto the grass, her hands shaking. What came out of the bag were small wooden blocks with runes on them that were shaped just like the symbols for the halls.

"I also follow Metis for guidance, cunning, and wisdom. I have a tarot to consult her. Then I follow Dagda because she has power over life and death and is associated with Druidry, which I—well, that doesn't matter. The last two were my choices. My gods. Not my family's. You can worship anyone. Anyone. And then garner their protection or guidance. Please—please don't tell me that you follow no one . . ."

A shadow passed over them both just as Molly was about to pull some random god or goddess out of her head. She was willing to go along with whatever god or goddess she chose for the rest of her life, as long as it got Ova to settle down.

But the shadow over them spoke first.

"Leave her alone about it," the person said with so much disdain and authority that Molly felt obligated to give them her full attention. They had their arms crossed against their chest, their straight brown hair flowing in the wind over their shoulders. Their shrewd brown eyes stared at them both. "Not everyone needs to follow someone, a pantheon, god, or goddess."

Ova started scooping up her runes and then clenched the bag in a fist as she stood to face this person. "Not everyone needs to, no, but it's in their best interest."

"Why?"

Molly went to stand up, too, but took a step away from the two of them because their new visitor looked ready to take a step forward and stand pointed-nose-to-pointed-nose with Ova.

"Protection. Guidance. For when you have a question on what to do."

The person gave one sharp laugh. "Sounds like knowledge would fit that need."

Ova shook her head. "Who are you?"

"I'm Lily Pathon. Please use they/them when referring to me in your minds or elsewhere. Thank you," they said with a tilt of their head, eyeing Ova up and down. "I had come over to apologize for my friend Namu earlier, who ran into her"—they looked to Molly—"but then I heard you terrorizing her."

"I was not terrorizing her! I was helping!"

Molly took in too much air when she realized that Lily's last name was the same as the airline's. She started coughing.

"How is it helping to overwhelm someone about religion and act like it's the most important thing there is?" Lily asked, leaving their mouth slightly open to showcase that they were biting their tongue on one side with the back of their teeth.

"It is the most important thing!"

Lily tsked. "Let me guess. Your family owns a temple?" They shook their head. "For some, it may bring comfort. For some, it doesn't." They shrugged. "For me, money is my comfort. I like to have it so I can use it to help people. Other things can help people, not just religion."

When Ova opened her mouth to interrupt, Lily put their finger up. "And I don't care about anyone else's opinions. I know what is best for ME, and I am offering variety for everyone else."

Ova closed her mouth, then opened it again. "So, you follow no one?"

Tilting their head to the side, Lily answered, "I didn't say that. My family follows Aine of Knockaine, as do I. A goddess who has brought hope to many women. I also follow Cernunnos."

"For wealth . . ." Ova hissed, clenching her runes tighter.

Lily turned and gave her a wink. "For wealth," they confirmed, then walked away.

Ova's eyes followed Lily as they went to the courtyard to watch the students perform chalk-rising. Once Ova saw that

Lily would not turn their attention back to the two of them, she peered down at the grass, and a tear fell from her eye.

Shoving her bag of runes back into her pants, Ova started walking away. "I've . . . I've got to . . . go to the nurse. Or Mrs. Heard. Someone. I'll talk to you later, Molly."

Ova left Molly in the grass with her two books on the ground, not knowing what to do or what had happened.

It seemed like Ova had been questioned about her religious beliefs—or had she? Honestly, it just seemed like Lily had been the one who was pushing their beliefs.

Whatever it was, at least now Molly knew it was a topic to stay away from—or at least to be cautious about around Ova. Molly would have to try to understand Ova's position a little more. Obviously, religion was very important to her, and Molly wanted to know why, if it ran that deep. She was also curious about what Ova's parents did.

Molly pulled out her phone and saw she still had about half an hour until her next class. She could return to her room, but the thought of the smell and possibly encountering the spirit sprites bothered her.

She looked at the impression that Ova had left on the ground and the spot where her bag of runes had been. She could try to find Koz right now, as Kren had wanted her to do. If she did that now, instead of later, it would be done, and then she could use whatever app Ova had to start practicing and catch up on her classes tonight. Maybe then she would not feel so overwhelmed and behind.

But where would Koz be? If he made apps, would he be in the computer labs?

It was as good a place to check as any.

Lockdrest

She should have taken the sidewalk around the school back to the front entrance so she could enjoy the outside more, and maybe it would have saved some time. When she finally reached the labs on the other side of the school by the stairwell, almost ten minutes had passed.

There was a sign on the outside hanging from the glass enclosure that said the lab was open at all times, so she went in without knocking.

The room was dark, quiet, and the air buzzed with electricity, although no computer made a sound as each flat dark screen stared at her, and each soft upholstered chair offered her a seat.

A faint glow came from a corner on the far side of the room, many rows of computers away, with the sound of typing click-clacking from that direction. She cautiously went over, afraid to touch anything.

There were Koz and Rem. They were so engrossed in their computers that they didn't notice her at all. It looked like they were playing a game on their screens with weaponry and monsters from a far-off world.

She didn't want to interrupt them and was turning to leave when she bumped into a chair, making it squeak.

Koz paused the screen and swiveled in his chair to face her. He looked at her, confused. "You again? May I help you?"

The girl stopped what she was doing too. "Come on! I want to play!"

"Hold on, Rem. Is it about your phone?" Koz smiled at Molly.

When Molly nodded, he held out his hand.

"Phone," he demanded.

She dug it out of her shorts and handed it over.

"Who directed you here?" he asked, opening up the screen. He slid it along the side of his own computer screen without touching it and then drew some kind of symbol on it that allowed him to bypass her setup.

"Kren, the mini-troll. And Ova, my friend."

"I know Ova," he said.

"In the game I play that Koz developed, my troll has four-inch-wide back teeth! I need to know how big a mini-troll's teeth are compared to that! Do you know?" Rem asked.

"Oh . . . okay," Molly stuttered. "Next time I see Kren . . . I'll try to ask him."

Koz nodded. He was deep into her phone now, his feet tucked under his chair, leaning back. "That would be great. Then Rem here can correlate, and I can make sure my data is correct." He slammed his feet down. "Now, I see that you have some apps here."

Molly froze.

"Oh, don't worry, I didn't touch them. But I suggest you delete them. It's stupid to sell pixels of your soul for these apps when you don't even know who makes them." He eyed her for a second before looking back at her phone. He used one leg to kick out the chair next to him. "Have a seat."

Reluctantly, she did.

"Um . . . How long have you guys been going here?" Molly asked, wanting to fill the silence and wash away the judgments. It was something she hadn't asked them when they had shown her around. She knew they were at least a year older, so it wasn't important to ask, except maybe it would remind Koz that she was new so he wouldn't form a harsh opinion of the apps she used. She had no idea until recently that they were bad to use.

Rem spoke up as Koz swiveled some more, biting on his bottom lip. He pushed a few more things on her phone.

"My adoptive parents let me go to magick school because I wanted to," Rem said.

"Oh. You're adopted?"

"Yes. Because my parents loved me."

It was a statement that didn't allow for any slack.

"This is my second year," Koz said, lazily raising his hand without looking at her and then putting it back down to type more things into her phone. "We started together."

It took Molly a second to realize that he was returning her phone. "I gave you some good studying apps on there from my own database," he said. "Obviously, I didn't allow you access to my database, but with how clueless you seem about techno magick, I'm guessing you won't be able to backtrack to access it on your own. So, I don't need to erase my imprint. Next time you come to me, though, it will be faster and easier to add apps from it."

"I wouldn't . . ."

"Are you sure?"

"Yeah . . ." Was she? Why was he making her second-guess herself?

"Now, about those apps. They're stupid because, one"— he held up a finger—"why not just make your own apps and sell your soul to yourself if you're going to do that? Once you learn technology, it's not that hard. The apps are just taking and reusing spirit magick." He held up a second finger. "Two, you don't know how much of your soul they are really taking. No one knows how to measure a pixel in souls. And how can you measure it yourself? There are no regulations about it yet because it's so new, so it's very dangerous."

"But . . . I know lots of people who . . ."

"I'm sure you do. Whoever made the apps can't take too much of a soul because it would be too noticeable, and they would get tracked and taken down. Do you know anything about spirit magick?"

Molly shook her head. "I haven't taken—"

"Then, you don't understand how it works at all! It takes some of you and transfers it. Depending on the app and who's behind it, who knows how much it is taking. It can take too much of your essence too fast. Your essence, you can grow back slowly, but once too much is taken, it is impossible. It's complicated and disgusting, frankly, how people are taking advantage of the young and dumb when it comes to these things."

"But . . . I . . ."

"Yeah. Yeah. I've heard it all before. *But you use them all the time. But these certain ones*," he whined. "Just use apps made by someone you trust. I know you don't know me, and I know it's insane for me to ask you to trust me. But I promise you, I don't want any ounce of your soul."

Namu

Chapter Fourteen

Namu slammed his laptop shut. His conversation with Mr. Vero kept spinning in his head, stirring anger inside him, and he could not focus on his online non-magickal schooling.

He had suggested combining plant magick with something else, but Mr. Vero had disagreed. He had said that the healing plants might be worth a try, but other things with less organic matter, which didn't have much relatability to Namu, may not work. Which, in turn, meant that a healing plant might not connect with him because Namu wasn't very healing in nature when it came to helping others. It all came down to "like calls to like" and, in this case, "like sticks to like" too. Also, if they did combine two things, those two things would need to connect on a spiritual level, which might be hard to do.

He didn't even know what "not being naturally healing in nature" meant! Did it mean he tormented people when he was around them?

His hope had slipped from his grasp in that conversation, as it had done repeatedly this past year. Whenever he had hope, his logic started building around it, but then it came crashing down, burying him in the rubble until he couldn't breathe.

He threw his head back in his chair and took a deep breath. Looking up to the ceiling, he stared in the direction of Mr. Vero's room, which was directly above his room in Kenaz Hall. It was the only hall with both students and staff, although Namu swore that Mr. Vero was the only staff member there.

Namu slid his key off his desk and shoved it into his pocket as he stood up. He would go to Mr. Vero's room and talk with him. If he went now, they wouldn't waste the allotted hour they had tomorrow. Namu couldn't focus on anything else anyway.

He knew it was late, at least after 8 p.m., but he didn't want to check the time. He didn't want anything else irritating him, and he knew that seeing how late it was and how much he had not accomplished tonight would do just that.

Something thick, stiff, and long came out through one of the cracks in the hall, making Namu jump. He nearly banged his back into another student's door. It was a tongue about the size of Namu's middle finger in length, swiveling around, looking for something to taste before it retreated back into the wall.

Namu shivered. His own tongue now felt heavy in his mouth. It was a relief that whatever measures the school had in place ensured that no creatures could harm anyone in this hall. If those creatures had any powers, magick, or poisons, it dulled them. But the thought of some random tongue coming out of the wall and almost licking him revolted him.

"Aha! You got it!" Namu heard from a few doors down.

Then he heard a croak from what he swore was a toad from the same room as he passed it.

Namu realized it was the same door the mini-troll had been let into earlier today. That seemed strange, but he could be wrong.

When the door banged open behind him, he saw he was not wrong. He caught a glimpse of the troll as the boy fell out of the room onto his bottom. His eyes were larger than normal, with black diamond pupils that darted around in fear. His mouth was flat, with no lips, and opened for a long frog's tongue to jump out.

The mini-troll stepped out of his room and grabbed the boy's hand, pulling him up.

"You can't be terrified each time we do this," he said, pushing the boy back into the room. "Now, to get rid of it, you do this." The mini-troll closed the door behind them.

It was uncommon for a tutor to be teaching extra lessons not in a classroom, but that was not his concern. Namu understood the need to practice late into the night, and he was heading to Mr. Vero's room right then, when, maybe, he shouldn't be.

He just didn't understand why anyone would want to practice transformation magick like that. It creeped him out. He couldn't believe that was something that Mr. Vero had also done at an even younger age.

Namu missed non-magickal school.

Namu reached the stairwell that led to the other halls and headed up to Mr. Vero's hall. He had to keep his hand off the banister to avoid touching a few dust eaters that had come out of the school's nooks and crannies to clean. The dust eaters were about the size of his thumb, although varying in thickness, and were furry and black with big eyes that reminded him a little of the vigilplunks in the bathrooms, except the dust eaters looked softer. He was also sure that the dust eaters didn't have teeth.

They cleaned during the day, too, if there were large random messes, but it was rare. If anyone wanted to see them, they had to roam the halls at night, like Namu was doing now. The dust eaters were not that entertaining and not that cute to look at, being only little furballs that roamed around and ate up messes, but the logistics of it had always interested Namu, especially how they could fit so much in their tiny bodies.

He remembered the first time he had seen them. He had stared at the countless little ones spaced inches apart up the banister, eating away all the germs from the handprints that day. He had been fascinated and had stayed there, staring at them for an hour, trying to figure them out. Many non-magickal houses would benefit from such things, which made him wonder how to obtain them and if magickal places typically used them. He knew Lily had some, but he didn't know if it was only because their family was rich.

When he reached Kenaz Hall, the smell almost knocked him back; it was like rotten eggs or an overheated sewer. He squeezed his nostrils shut. He had never asked Mr. Vero what exactly it was and why he continued to live on this floor. Namu might have left the school right away if he had been forced to stay in this hall.

Mr. Vero's hall counted off by fives, unlike Namu's, which counted off by three, so Mr. Vero's room, 190, was exactly halfway down the corridor, just like Namu's below. The smell was still reaching his nose. At least he knew that it would stop once he was in Mr. Vero's room, like it had before.

The number 190 stared down at him as he knocked.

Mr. Vero groaned as he opened the door, a quesadilla in his hand.

He stepped aside and let Namu into the room before closing the door and heading to a desk, much like Namu's, to grab up a trendy drink that he must have had one of the staff members make for him. He took a sip after swallowing the bite he had been chewing.

Lockdrest

"A little late to be eating, isn't it?" Namu asked Mr. Vero. His dark black hair was a little shorter than earlier today. He must have had it cut.

"A little late to be coming into my room to start a fight," Mr. Vero stated, putting the rest of his quesadilla in his mouth while staring at Namu, his blue eyes unblinking.

"I couldn't work."

"And what if I was working?"

"You don't have homework or online work. I figured you had time."

Mr. Vero nodded, swallowing a big gulp before chewing his food all the way. "True. Although I study and do research for you and your case. You are lucky, though, that you caught me when you did."

He went over to a red leather seat adorned with golden buttons and pulled it out for Namu to sit on. He pulled out a second one from behind a dresser. "I had just come in."

"From bothering the staff to make you a late supper?"

Smiling, Mr. Vero took the lid off his drink and tilted it back. "What else am I supposed to do when I've been stuck here for so many years, longer than any child would be?"

Namu looked around the room. It was small, just like his, with an old dresser and a bookcase, although organized differently. Mr. Vero also had a few nicer things to accent it, like a red-and-purple Persian rug under the bed, a standing lamp in the corner, and an extra desk tucked between the other side of the bed and the window, giving no room to walk. The desk was stacked high with books and various measurement tools.

"You have your classroom," Namu commented.

Mr. Vero sneered while wiping his mouth with the back of his hand and set down his cup. "What do you want, Namu?"

"I want to talk about that door. I want to talk about how to fix me. I want to talk about why the school isn't doing anything!"

161

Holding up a finger between the two of them, Mr. Vero sighed. "I told you, Namu, just ignore it. If you do not want anything to do with it, if you do not want to stay and protect it or protect children from it, then ignore it. At some point, someone else will come along that the school will pair with the room."

"I don't want to ignore it!" Namu spat. "How am I supposed to ignore it when that thing is in my room with me? I still don't understand why they would place it around children. I still don't understand why no one warned me! I can't stop thinking about it! How!? How do you expect me to ignore the thing that took so much from me?"

Tears, tears were wetting Namu's hands now. Hot, warm tears that he had held inside himself for so long. Tears he honestly didn't know he still had. He wondered if the hot metal inside him, the terrible metal from that chaotic place, was contained in each drop. Maybe he was tainting the world, poisoning it.

He looked down at his arm and saw the metal slithering through his veins. He needed to calm down.

"I know . . . It's hard . . . Trust me, I know. I tried, too, came back, but . . ."

"No! I'm not myself anymore because of it and because of you! It took me and tore me apart! I almost DIED! Why don't you understand that? Even after—after being away all summer—" Namu swallowed. "I—I couldn't stop thinking of it. I couldn't stop feeling empty. I cannot, I want to, I need—I need to heal. Don't you understand?"

Desperation seeped from him. He wanted to be given answers to the questions plaguing him. He wanted to be understood. But Mr. Vero's face only held uncomfortable hollowness as a deafening silence fell between them. Namu held back a sob that was choking his throat.

Mr. Vero looked away. "I was told the door is here in the school because teachers care for children. They are not looking for power or much else. Children aren't as deadly as adults, but they are more curious." His hand went around his throat. "Curiosity can kill. I do believe that. That's why I . . . why *we*— don't say anything."

"Because children are curious? That's your excuse for letting them die?"

Mr. Vero's hard, dead eyes breached through to Namu's soul. "No. Listen to me. After I found out, after it was made in MY room, I decided to go inside it. From curiosity, much like yourself. Even though I knew. *I KNEW* that it was a place that fed off chaos. That it was *THE* place that got rid of weapons from people's hands. I knew that. The headmasters told me. They told me I was supposed to only watch it, but I went in. How is a teenage boy supposed to listen when he is told to leave a one-of-a-kind thing alone? I was lucky I was saved. And after I was saved, I left. I left this school because I hated it. I hated it because of that damned door and the staff who let it be here. The staff who trusted me not to go inside. But when I left . . . other students knew about it too. I had vented. I had told them."

Namu's breathing grew heavy.

"When I was gone, when I was not there, apparently, those other students went into it and died. The reason I came back was the nightmares. That was when I found out about my fellow classmates. That was how I learned that kids will find a way in if they know. And that was when I decided I needed to protect people from it. That I needed to study it. That I needed to be here until someone else took charge."

Namu shook his head. Deep down, he knew that was why he couldn't tell Lily about the door, or they would go inside. But to protect people from it? The thought exhausted him.

"I don't want to protect anyone from it. I want to find a way to get rid of it."

Mr. Vero half rolled his eyes to stare at the ceiling. "You can't."

"You haven't tried."

"Yes. Because I know better. What has been stored in there is too dangerous to mess with."

"Letting that door be there for children to wander through and die is too dangerous!"

"I know that, Namu! That's why we don't say anything! That's why I didn't tell you about it during your first year. I had hoped that—"

"That I wouldn't just stumble upon a secret door hidden behind a wall in my room?"

Mr. Vero was silent.

Namu got up to leave, pushing the chair away from him as he stood.

"Namu," Mr. Vero tried again, "I didn't want you to be like me. I didn't want you to know about it until you were a little older. Until you maybe knew a little better and understood. I thought then you wouldn't have . . ."

Namu's shoulders tightened as he walked to the door. "I'm pretty sure I would have understood the same way I do now. That the school, that the staff, and the headmasters do not care about the students. They care more about a stupid door, since no one seems to be trying to find a way to get rid of it." He opened Mr. Vero's door and slammed it on his way out.

The big question was *why*.

Heading down the hall, he forgot to plug his nose and let the scent burn his insides until a sickly sweet, welcoming aroma teased past him. He turned his head to look for the source. Far away, near the end of the hall, he swore he saw something, but he couldn't make it out.

Lockdrest

He thought it might be a spirit sprite—another perfect example of the school not caring that much about the students, since it just let the mischievous little creatures torment the first years until they figured out how to protect their things from being stolen.

All the way down the stairs back to his own hall, Namu considered what he was going to do. He understood the predicament of not being able to tell the students. He understood the danger in that. But he was going to destroy that door. He would never let anyone else fall to the torment that was inside.

Molly

Chapter Fifteen

M olly had decided not to delete all of her apps. She just deleted a few, the ones she knew she didn't need and that weren't important to her. The few that she kept, she would delete down the road. She wasn't ready to throw them away when she had already been taken away from home. She couldn't give up all the things that gave her comfort. That wouldn't be fair.

She stared at the sound app, the one that made noises come to life, trying to convince herself not to use it to put herself to sleep. She was fighting with the choice of either giving away another pixel of her soul to fall asleep quickly—something that she had done over and over again that obviously hadn't hurt her soul too badly because she was still here—or trying to fall asleep the harder and more natural way.

She had tried to go up to the Spirit Magick One teacher during class earlier that day to ask about the spirit sprites and how to protect herself, but she couldn't bring herself to do it.

No one else had approached the teacher; no one was talking about anything that had happened to them the night before, so maybe no one else was affected. She didn't want to go alone and seem weird. She also didn't want to stay after everyone had left and make people think she had a problem—or worse, be late to her next class on her first day. Not when there was a chance that the spirit sprites might leave her alone tonight. She always had tomorrow to try again if they came back. She could ask then. But not on her first day.

Blood swelled to her pumping heart at the thought of the little creatures coming in anytime soon. That prompted her to start the app that always brought her sweet dreams and let the magickal rain pitter-patter all over her skin.

Frigid prickles of pain danced under Molly's feet. She was on ice. Purple ice, threatening to break, calling for her to fall into its depths. She was cold, shivering, too frightened to move, until the ice shattered, water coming up around her as she was dragged through it. The shards cut her face. The freezing water hugged her close as she tried to scream. She was paralyzed. She couldn't breathe. The only thing she felt in the freezing, numbing liquid was warm tears in her eyes.

Something was holding her under. Something was holding her still.

She was drowning.

Her lungs burned. Her eyelids closed as the purple world began to turn black . . .

But then her lungs burst open, and she gasped.

She was back in her room. A spirit sprite was there, looking at her.

But something else was there too. She couldn't see it before it grabbed her again, gripping around both her arms.

She was shoved back under again.

Straight back into the icy water that was trying to kill her.

Something was trying to take her over. Something in the outside world. Something was dragging her here.

But she could kick through the water this time.

Whatever had her before had less of a hold. She tried to swim up before everything went black, but she was met by a solid sheet of ice forming over her.

She pounded her hand against it, her body screaming. She ran out of air just as her hand broke through. The plate of ice was thinning, weakening, along with the grasp of the thing holding her.

She grabbed on to the edges of the ice as it slipped away from her, slicing into her skin.

And then she woke up.

A spirit sprite was driving its fingers into her arms. There was shuffling on the floor beside her bed and then a token of some kind in that spot: a bronze coin with a twisted, knot in its middle.

The spirit sprite dug its fingers in deeper. Molly screamed, grabbed the creature's spindly arms, and yanked its fingers out. She shoved the creature away from her.

The token was gone, and her door slammed shut.

She had no idea what had happened. She didn't know if another spirit sprite had been in there with her and had somehow tried to take her over. But that night, she had not slept again.

Another thought crept into her mind the moment she picked up her phone as her room began to brighten.

Did that happen because she sold another pixel of her soul?

She wanted to text Kren and ask him, but after she had used another app that night when she was told not to, she knew she couldn't. She wanted to see if it happened again when she didn't use the app to make sure she wasn't getting herself in trouble for nothing. But none of it made sense. The only times she had ever gone to the place of ice was when a spirit had almost taken over her body, which started happening before she ever had a phone.

She didn't want to risk going to that place again, but the only thing she could think to do was wait another night to see if it happened again. She didn't want to look like an idiot and didn't want anyone to know she had used an app for a minor thing, like falling asleep. She also didn't want to make Kren angry or make him think he couldn't trust her.

But she would ask for help with the spirit sprites today like she had promised herself she would. The ache in her arm and wrists still throbbed, reminding her that she needed to do something about this.

She decided to skip breakfast to see if her Spirit Magick One teacher, Mrs. Sleck, was in her classroom.

A small wave of relief washed over her when she saw that the classroom door was open and that Mrs. Sleck was sitting at her desk eating a glazed donut.

Molly invited herself inside.

Some of the classrooms Molly had been in the day before had been interesting, but Molly had found Mrs. Sleck's classroom the most curious. It had spiritual magick posters all over the walls, symbols carved from metals and different types of wood hanging off-center in various spots, and the non-magickal schools' alphabet that Molly was familiar with, along with others in different languages, lined on wallpaper cradling the ceiling.

"Can't you see I'm eating? It's not class time," Mrs. Sleck snapped, turning her head away from Molly. The blue dye at the ends of her curls bounced, while the gray dye in the middle stayed flat. She was maybe in her thirties, and was built in a way that had made Molly think she had children. But someone in class yesterday had asked her if she did, and she said no. There were also no pictures of children on her desk, only of a man that Molly assumed to be her husband smiling out at the world, next to a man-shaped candle. This was presumably a representation of the god she worshiped, although based on her first introduction to the kooky teacher, the thought of it being her husband had crossed Molly's mind.

"I'm in your one-thirty class," Molly said. "I'm sorry I'm bothering you during your break time. I just had a question about the spirit sprites."

Mrs. Sleck's green eyes rotated slowly to stare at her as one widened and the other grew smaller. She knew that Rexa and Val would not have liked her, but Molly felt fondly of her, even if she was slightly unfriendly now.

"You see them? Already? If you're in my one-thirty, you have to be a first year." Mrs. Sleck stood up, abandoning her donut to come around her desk. She wore a blue tulle dress with many ruffles falling in layers. "You don't look like you grew up around magick. Oh! Did an older year tell you?"

"No . . . I see them. They've been hurting me."

"*Hurting* you?" Mrs. Sleck let out a laugh. "They only steal and pry. They don't cause any harm."

Molly stood still as Mrs. Sleck grabbed her by both shoulders and moved her to a more open space before she let go and walked around her in a circle. "I remember you. You had an extra hard time in class yesterday. You could barely do a slight expulsion to look at yourself. However, that was a hard lesson. I admit that."

Molly felt her face turning red.

Mrs. Sleck stopped behind her. "Are you going to tell me why?" she asked.

The question made Molly jump. She didn't know if Mrs. Sleck was referring to why she could see the spirit sprites or why expelling a part of her soul hadn't worked, although the answer was the same for both. Did she really have any choice but to tell her? Would she tell anyone else? Would Mrs. Sleck be willing to help her if she knew?

"I . . . I am a . . . an . . . empty vessel," she stammered out.

Mrs. Sleck grabbed her arms with warm, sweaty hands. Her green eyes bore into Molly's. "You're an empty vessel? How do you know?"

"I . . . I was told . . ."

"Oh. Wow. What bad luck, child!" Mrs. Sleck bit her lip. "I'm so sorry. That was insensitive of me. That makes sense— why they are hurting you, then. I can teach you a glue spell and how to ban them from touching you for brief periods of time."

Mrs. Sleck went to the other side of the room where there was a big table.

"Come here. Come here before breakfast is over." Her teacher beckoned her with a wave of her hand.

Molly rushed over and stared at the Spirit Magick One book on the desk.

"Glue spells are very quick and easy. They will stop the spirit sprites from stealing your things, but you can only unglue your own glue spells—unless you're a teacher and more of an expert. Complications." Mrs. Sleck waved her hand, dismissing what she was saying before she put her hand over the gray textbook. She looked at Molly. "You can't do a glue spell on the doors either. No spells can be done on them for safety reasons. The spirit sprites will always be able to get into the rooms, but since you are more prone to being practically bitten by them"—she wheezed a laugh at her joke that made Molly squirm— "well, certain ones live mainly on certain floors. They are territorial. I can teach you to ban the ones on your floor. So, if they come into your room, they will leave you alone and you can sleep." She seemed to be eyeing the dark circles under Molly's eyes.

Molly nodded, biting the inside of her cheek.

"Glue magick combines spirit magick and symbol magick. You want to make the soul stick. To do that, you need to give it a reason to. You draw this symbol."

Molly watched as Mrs. Sleck traced a squiggly line down the middle of the book with her right hand, which was adorned with a gaudy plastic purple ring. "It's that easy, although I didn't do the other basic step. You need to call to its soul and mesh your want for it to make a permanent bond to something, while drawing the line. It will take some time, but, soon, you'll find it as quick as signing a name." Mrs. Sleck drew the squiggly line straight down the middle of the book, then turned to Molly, motioning for her to try to pick the book up.

Molly grabbed at the edges of the book to lift it from the desk, but even the pages wouldn't release from themselves.

"To unglue it, you do it the opposite way." Mrs. Sleck did so, then waved her hand for Molly to try again. Molly was surprised to find that she could lift the book. It didn't feel like it was set in stone.

"Now, you try."

Taking a deep breath, Molly concentrated on wanting the book to stay in its place as she drew a squiggly line down the book's center. Mrs. Sleck poked at the book, and it budged.

"Again."

"But what did I—"

"You need to *feel* the want. You need to have the right incentive."

Molly breathed again. When she drew the line this time, she felt her want seep into the book like melted glue, trying to keep it shut. But it moved again when Mrs. Sleck touched it.

Mrs. Sleck had her try again and again until, finally, Molly felt the warming of her soul inside her hand as if it were melting the soul of the book and convincing it to stay in place. When Mrs. Sleck tried to move it, it wouldn't budge.

"Good. Now want it to lift. Take it away. And if you get any pages stuck, you will take this book with you, work on it the rest of the day, and bring it back once all the pages are unstuck."

Molly tried to do it. She drew the line backward, sliding her finger up the soft plastic casing of the book until it got to the top, wanting it all to unstick, for the soul to form back together and be tightly bound again, not be loose and re-form separately through the pages.

Mrs. Sleck prodded at the book and smiled with one side of her mouth when she saw that the book had moved, but then she scrunched her nose when she picked it up and tried flipping through the pages to see that some of them would not turn.

She pushed the book into Molly's chest, then walked to a desk.

"Come on, come on, barely any time now."

Molly followed after her.

"Banning something as simple as a spirit sprite is easy too. They are meant to cause mischief, so your own incentive will be strong to keep them away. Because they are hurting you, you will have a strong incentive that I'm sure you will feel deep within your soul. They also don't have the magick or wits to fight against the ban. When a spirit sprite approaches you, you think in your mind how much you want it to be gone, then you call to your god, goddess, or whoever"—she eyed Molly again—"and if there is no one, that's fine too. You then draw this symbol with your spiritual essence."

She drew the symbol in the air. Molly thought the invisible lines she traced looked like a lock. "We will be talking about spiritual essences in class later today and how to draw your spiritual essence out at least a little to work some magick, so you should be able to make the banning work after today."

Molly was confident that she would be able to since she had drawn her spirit out before at Kren's house. It was just that asking her spirit to come out all the way was hard for her. Some students had expelled an entire arm or leg in spirit form from themselves. Some had expelled their whole body as they had sat slumped in a chair.

Mrs. Sleck made Molly draw the symbol a few times to ensure she got it right.

"All set. Off you go," Mrs. Sleck smiled, pushing Molly to the door.

"But I have another question."

Annoyed, Mrs. Sleck crossed her arms but then smiled. She was a conundrum.

"I need you to help me learn how to protect myself. Since I'm an empty vessel, sometimes, spirits try to take me over, and I . . . and I almost lose myself."

She didn't want to tell Mrs. Sleck what had happened last night.

Mrs. Sleck's face fell, but she did not uncross her arms. "I'm sorry, girl, but I can't do that. Not yet. I can when you're ready, though."

"Ready?"

"I can't teach you how to protect yourself because you have no foundation for your learning yet. Protecting yourself in the way you are thinking will only get you hurt. Spirits are not like spirit sprites, where you can just ban them. They are more complicated. You're not yet ready to tackle that. You've only been in school for one day. You could get hurt and then that would be on me! The school is the safest place you can be, though. You'll be fine here until you learn some basics. Then we'll figure out a time slot in your next schedule if you really need me to help you learn."

Before Molly knew it, she was being pushed out the door, which was then shut behind her. When she checked her phone, it was 7:55. She still had twenty minutes until her first class. The thought of getting breakfast skimmed through her mind until the book in her hand reminded her that she had left the two books for her other classes back upstairs. That was perfect, since she could then drop off the Spirit Magick One book while picking up the other two.

Ugh. She was so annoyed. She had started online classes last night before she went to bed, and the work wasn't too hard, but it was time-consuming. If she had to do that again tonight, she wouldn't have much time to get the pages in the book she was holding unglued, especially if she had any homework from her History and Transformation of the Magickal World class like last night.

There was not enough time in the day.

On top of that, Mrs. Sleck, the teacher she hoped would help her, refused until she knew more. When would she know enough? And how could she possibly gauge that?

Molly headed up to her room to put her book away. She decided to visit the library later, when she had time, to find her own ways to protect herself. Then she would rush through her online schooling tonight, unglue her book completely, and practice banning the spirit sprites when she got the chance. She just hoped that her History and Transformation of the Magickal World class at the end of the day didn't give her as much homework as it had the day before. Although that could have been because she was behind and had to catch up.

She had tried to get Derrin, who had been in that class with her, to meet up and do their work together, since they had arrived at the school the same day and he had a mountain of work too. But he had still refused to talk to her.

It had been an interesting class, at least. They had discussed names in technology who had transformed the world, many of whom Molly hadn't known because they were on the magickal side, except for Lily's last name. Molly had caught that. Apparently, in the class, they were to start discussions closer to the present and then work back in time. A major thing she had learned was that the magickal community called the period when technology showed the world that magick was real, the All-Seeing Time. That era was already bringing up topics that Molly felt uncomfortable with, like the protests when humans thought their rights were being taken away, religious communities that rose up, and many jobs and systems in the magickal and non-magickal world that were lost.

It was interesting hearing from the magickal perspective about how the world had changed and how the non-magickal and magickal communities were working to find ways to live together.

Molly's phone vibrated.

Ova: Where are you?

Molly: Heading to the library during break. Sorry!

Ova: Don't be. Hope you like it!

Molly was heading against the tide of students going in the direction of their rooms or the outside. It was after Symbols One. She had to lean against the wall so the mass of students could get past her. She was near a door that had been left ajar and was surprised to hear squealing coming out of the room.

The boy she had run into yesterday, Namu, was inside it with a teacher who had long black hair. There was a creature squirming and screaming in a medium-sized cage sitting on a desk. It looked like a chinchilla but had a yellow duck bill and duck feet. The most alarming thing about the scene was that the sounds coming out of the creature were not ones a duck would ever make.

"Focus harder," the teacher, who had his back to her, demanded.

The boy was focused. His eyes were closed. It looked as though he were drawing the spirit out of the creature with his hands raised above it. No, not a spirit; it was two spirits. He was drawing two spirits out: one of a duck, which Molly could clearly see outlined in a translucent green soul and one of a chinchilla, outlined in pink.

"That's it. Good," the teacher encouraged. Then the teacher slapped a slab of marble onto the table that the cage was sitting on.

In a flash, the single creature became two sleeping animals in one cage. The boy held the two spirits separate from each other as the teacher ran to the other side of the room to grab another cage. He then scooped the duck out of the first cage and placed it inside the second.

"Okay," the teacher breathed.

The boy let the spirits go, and Molly watched as they sprang back down into their rightful bodies. The creatures stayed asleep, their breathing deeper than before.

Molly tore herself away from the scene, not wanting them to know she had been watching, and then ran to the library. She had no idea what she had seen. Was it separating two combined souls? But how?

And that creature . . . that poor creature before they had helped it . . .

Was that something that could happen to her or someone else if she tried to do magick beyond her means of control and understanding? She wanted to find the spirit magick section and educate herself. Then maybe she could get someone to teach her how to protect herself. Maybe if Mrs. Sleck wouldn't help her, the teacher she had just seen would—or that boy. If not, she would have to text Kren and beg him to come back and teach her something or persuade him to ask someone else to.

The library was a big open room that she could not see the end of, placed after the hall of classes and the restrooms. It contained hundreds of freestanding bookshelves lined up in rows. It was overwhelming, and she did not know where to start, so she walked outside the library to the library office she had noticed to ask for help.

Before she reached the enclosed glass library office, which looked much like the technology room upstairs, she found empty desks filling the library, some with computers and some without. A tall woman with many dark braids was bent over, helping a student at a desk. She wore a vibrant navy-and-light-blue striped romper that clung to her thin shoulders, with a little yellow sunflower pinned to her right shoulder.

Molly drifted over to ask for her help just as the student, who had a book opened on the desk, read a sentence out loud with broken words as he scanned the page with his finger. Molly could not hold back a gasp when she saw a spout of water rise from the page over the student's finger to nuzzle it for a moment before returning to the page.

The student, with big bright eyes, turned to the woman, who was smiling.

"See," the woman whispered. "Isn't that scary at all. I don't know why Mr. Young insisted on making such a chaotic show in the classroom with a live display much bigger than that, but tell him to warn you next time before he does and send you to me. If he doesn't listen, I'll have a talk with him."

The young boy, who had to have been about ten, nodded, closed the book, and ran off. The woman nearly stumbled and grabbed hold of the chair, then saw Molly and straightened herself.

"Yes, dear?" she asked, her kind light-brown eyes turning to Molly.

"Are . . . are you the librarian?"

"Well, yes, dear, I am. My name is Mrs. Yitter. Anything I can help you with?"

"I'm looking for the section on spirit magick, but . . . it's my first time here. I don't want to waste any time."

Mrs. Yitter smiled. "I completely understand. It can be overwhelming. All you need to do is tap three times at the start of each connected row and think about which section you need. That section will glow brightly for a moment only for you." She pointed to the side of her head. "If you have any problems, just come back and get me."

"Thank you," Molly whispered, then whisked herself away, not wanting to disturb the tired librarian any longer.

She went to the first row after the desks and tapped three times, thinking about the section she needed. When nothing lit up, she went to the next row of dark wooden shelves and tapped again. Then again, and again, until finally, something in the back ate away the shadows indicating that it was the row she needed.

The books surrounding her varied in size, age, mustiness, griminess, and color. Some looked ancient, while others looked brand-new. The names of the sections appeared along the bottom of the wooden shelves. She walked past some labeled with locations, some with eras of time, and then one labeled *fiction and nonfiction, non-magickal.* She wondered if there was any organization to the shelves at all.

Lockdrest

Finally, at the end, she found the spirit magick section, taking up about twelve shelves.

She scanned the bindings, some with words and some without, and put her fingers against an old one with faded black letters that read Spiritual Guidance in a Helping Hand. Then she heard a familiar voice behind her.

"Hey! Molly."

Molly's arm jerked. Her finger missed pulling out the book as she turned to see Ova smiling, with an adult standing beside her.

"Fancy seeing you here," Ova continued until her happiness flipped to a look of worry. "I promise I didn't follow you. I just came to see Mrs. Heard since you were busy during break. She literally works right over there sometimes." Ova pointed around the corner, and Molly stepped back to peek out. There was a half-circle of bookshelves around a big round purple rug on the floor, forming some kind of special selection.

Mrs. Heard reached out her hand and shook Molly's a little too vigorously, with a wide smile. "Please call me Celta. I am the religious coordinator."

Oh. That would explain why Ova was with her.

Celta wore a bright yellow top that complimented her dark skin. The outfit reminded Molly of a sunflower.

"She's married to the librarian, Mrs. Yitter!" Ova squealed, then shut her mouth with her two hands before giggling. "Sorry, Celta excites me in general. She also went to Opendrest! She liked it there way better."

Opendrest? One of the other schools?

Celta laughed. "Well, yes. Who wouldn't? That school is filled with music and art. Something this place needs." Her hazel-brown eyes twinkled.

"But if you and Mrs. Yitter are married"—the sunflower on Mrs. Yitter's romper came to mind— "why do you have different last names?"

Slapping her leg, Celta laughed again and pointed directly at Molly. "Trust me. I tried to get her to change it. I said I would go either way. But she didn't want anyone getting confused." She rolled her eyes.

"Because they work together," Ova chimed in. "If you ever have any questions on religion, she is the one to ask. She's here to help students with research, finding objects connected to certain gods to pray with, or researching whom you may want to follow if you are lost. She follows Guan Yin and Oshun."

Molly then noticed the two necklaces hanging from Celta's neck. One, on a golden chain, was a circular golden portrait of what looked like a goddess and the other of a green jade figure encased in gold.

"Yes! Please do! When I was in school long ago, I HATED how everyone fought about different religions. After growing up in a bustling city where everyone followed one religion, I had expected things to be different when I went to magickal school. But of course not! I'm here to make that change."

Ova nodded proudly. "Also, you can ask her about the other schools too."

"Opendrest is one of the three, right?" Molly asked.

"One of the three, yes," Celta said. "What is your name?"

"Oh! Molly," Ova stammered, obviously embarrassed that she hadn't introduced her friend correctly.

"Listen here, Molly. This school and all the others are about acceptance. Everyone, and I mean EVERYONE, deserves peace in religion. Peace in general. One day, our world will make it there. Non-magickal and magickal religions are all good. We are just trying to teach that we don't want anyone falling into the bad side of things that could hurt them," Celta said, winking at her.

It was comforting to know how keen some of the staff were on acceptance. It made Molly feel safe and like she might be accepted one day.

She looked back to the spirit magick section and felt a pit open in her stomach. She still did not feel safe enough, though, to tell Ova about being an empty vessel. Also, what if there was a bad choice regarding religion and this school? Ova had seemed less than accepting earlier regarding Lily and their beliefs. So, where would that land her?

When she looked back, Molly saw that Celta had gone, but Ova was still standing there studying her. "Do you want me to leave you alone? Or do you want me to show you some of the religious books?"

Molly could see the slight hint of a smile playing at Ova's lips.

"I'll follow you," Molly answered.

Namu

Chapter Sixteen

I t had been a week since a couple of students had accidentally combined two creatures into one with spirit magick and Namu had had to help Mr. Vero separate them. Mr. Vero usually didn't need Namu's help with things like that, but that incident had been such a mess that he needed some assistance.

The image was still burned into Namu's brain. It was something Mr. Vero had apparently seen on various occasions, but it had been a first for Namu and one he never wanted to see again.

After they had separated the two souls, Namu and Mr. Vero dove into research on combining two living things, at Namu's request. That research had consumed him, more than his school work and the door. It was taking everything to hold himself together, especially when he felt he was close to possibly being whole again. If only he could wrap his head around being combined with an animal spirit.

They had found in their research that the animal had to be on the brink of death but would still want to stay alive. The animal needed to have will power and be willing to bestow their soul on someone who hadn't been responsible for setting it on the path to death.

Namu wasn't manipulative or conniving. He couldn't kill an animal for his own gain, even if it resulted in him becoming whole again.

And the chances of them running into some animal like that, on the edge of death, especially in the school, was slim. And he didn't have time to scour the woods constantly and have all the materials he needed ready, along with Mr. Vero, to do the spell.

Not only that, but what if it was some magickal creature that they ran into that did not mesh with his soul or that the animal had a conflicting reaction to him? Or what if their spirit was too big to fit? Mr. Vero had said that he knew symbols and runes used together that could condense a spirit's form and make it smaller . . .

Still . . . the chances. All of it was just chances. And no hope.

Ugh! He was so frustrated.

"Man, I feel the anger steaming off you," Lily said, taking a bite of their cucumber sandwich. "Why aren't you eating?"

Namu pushed away his tray, where his hamburger sat with a single angry bite taken out of it. "I'm not hungry."

"Worried about the exam again?" Lily fished.

"Of course."

Dropping their sandwich, Lily put their hands up. "Hey. Just asking. I'm worried about you, and I just don't get it. This last week, you have been more than distracted. You are barely even talking to me anymore."

"I'm just busy, Lily . . ."

"With an exam . . . an exam for an apprenticeship in a magickal division? When you didn't even want to come to a magickal school? You wanted to be a construction worker like your dad, Namu! Maybe even own your own company one day. Do something like that, and I'll fund you."

Lily would fund him? They would give him money to get him to stop trying to heal himself? No. That wasn't fair. They didn't know. They didn't understand what he was doing. But couldn't they just back off?

"Lily, I appreciate it. I do. But just let me do what's best for me. Please. I know what I need."

"You know what's best for you? Are you serious? You're falling apart!"

"I'm working on putting myself back together."

"If you were doing that, you would be following your dream."

"If you wanted me to follow my dream so bad, why did you let me come here?"

It took a moment for his hazy vision to clear and for him to see that Lily was breathing heavily in the silence.

Finally, Lily answered, "Honestly, I didn't want to be alone, and I didn't want to lose our friendship. But seriously, I thought maybe it could give you a one-up in the construction world if you learned something on this side. If you pushed yourself a little more. Got a little uncomfortable." They shrugged, then got up, pushing their chair back with their thighs. "Prove yourself, and I'll give you the money you need to help your dreams come true, Namu. By then, hopefully, I'll have proven myself too."

"I am not a charity case!" Namu yelled as Lily walked away.

He was sick of feeling like he was wasting everyone's time, including his own. He was sick of not knowing what the right thing to do was.

With a big sigh, he got up and threw the rest of his food away before putting his tray on the belt. The last person he wanted to see again was Mr. Vero, but he didn't know where else to go.

He walked himself to Mr. Vero's classroom to see if he was there. He opened the door without knocking.

It was unlocked.

Mr. Vero jumped and then narrowed his eyes at Namu with a shake of his head. "You wouldn't think so, but I do enjoy my privacy, Namu."

Namu shut the door. Mr. Vero was standing at a long black desk with a cauldron that had the symbol for heat written on it with chalk. There was a liquid bubbling inside. Namu couldn't see the color because of the cauldron's dark walls.

"Did you have any close friends?" Namu asked Mr. Vero, who rubbed the symbol off the cauldron with his long dark sleeve.

"After the incident? Of course not."

Mr. Vero went to a cabinet. The clinking of small glass vials pierced through the silence. He brought them to the desk.

"If you are going to interrupt me, why don't you help?" Mr. Vero walked to the other side of the room and pulled out a small white-speckled ladle made of granite. A nonporous rock, so it wouldn't absorb what was transferred from the cauldron to the glass vials. He handed it to Namu.

Namu picked up one of the flat-bottomed vials and dipped the ladle into the warm mixture. He poured it carefully into the vial, which he learned to do in Transformation Drinks and Remedies. The liquid was a thin purple.

It was an astral-transformation spell.

Mr. Vero was gathering the supplies he had used to make it and putting them away in the same cabinet he had taken the vials from. Namu caught a glimpse of Alteress powder, an ultra-fine golden powder that teachers treated like gold.

Namu poured another spoonful into a vial. "Why are you making these?"

Lockdrest

"I want to introduce my students to the theory of spirit altering with a focus on transfiguration at the beginning of this year. I know they will learn how to make an astral-transformation spell in Transformation Drinks and Remedies Three. But I want them to feel how it displaces the soul and how long it may take a soul to mold itself back into its original form, if it can do so at all. I figured doing an astral-transformation spell is easier and quicker than the students turning into animals. Also, a little less annoying."

Namu didn't know about that. If he was a teacher, he would be annoyed if there were a bunch of mists floating around the room. But he would probably be annoyed with anything. It was smart, though, to have the students test that within themselves so they knew what they were comfortable with and how much their soul could handle. Namu had done an astral-transformation spell before with Mr. Vero. It was the least invasive, although maybe the most disorientating. The soul felt a little out of place afterwards, but it wasn't that bad. It reminded Namu of when he had been on a boat all day and still felt the movement of the water beneath him even when he was on land. It took a while, but that feeling always faded.

It was his belief that, after transforming into something else, a soul could completely fix itself back into its original form, but it all depended on the person. If the soul or person was strong enough.

And if the transformation tore a soul apart.

Molly

Chapter Seventeen

Molly thought History and Transformation of the Magickal World would help keep her awake, but she was wrong. Maybe putting students to sleep was just what history classes were meant to do.

It had been a week now since she had banned the spirit sprites in her hall from touching her. Although it took her a few tries the first time to get the banning right because she had to fully concentrate and catch the spirit sprites off guard, it was easy for her to do now. She just had to be careful. If they touched her before she banished them, sticking their little fingers into her nerves, her concentration was lost, and she became too frazzled to do the spell.

Now, thanks to the banning, she could sleep most nights. Also, even after using the app that helped her fall asleep, she had not returned to the place of ice.

Her hand slipped off her face as Miss Weelt discussed the fear many had when magick had first become known to the larger world. But why? Molly never understood why so many feared it when it was accessible to anyone who was willing to learn. She wondered if, once the fear was quelled completely and the kids her age grew older, most, if not all, of society would use magick, it would take over the majority one day.

From what she had learned throughout this last week about the magickal side of society, they faced many of the same issues that the non-magickal society did. Throughout history, the magickal community had worked hard to keep their children from falling into the bad ways of magick, much like the non-magickal community did regarding drugs and crime. Before the All-Seeing Time, and still now, they had systems and jobs in place to manage the once-hidden society. Only a few of those jobs in the magickal divisions had become redundant after the All-Seeing Time. The trolls and even the griffon Molly had seen multiple times no longer needed to be hidden, so the divisions that had worked to hide magickal creatures disbanded. Another division was now required to protect and manage magickal creatures.

What they were learning in class right now was how the magickal community had gotten rid of all the guns and weaponry in the entire world.

The magickal community had called those weapons unnecessary and deadly and expressed that they were watching nations fall for no reason to machines that required no power, strength, or talent to wield. They wanted to show the world that magick did exist but that it was not to be hunted or messed with; it was to be left alone, and it was here to help create a better life.

All the witches and magickal beings who had been brought together because of technology had put aside all the strife they had with each other to find a way to get that point across, and they had. Molly admired them for that.

Lockdrest

Derrin, who was a few seats away from her in class, was continuously rotating a vial of blue-green bubbling liquid, which he'd been doing since the beginning of class. She was surprised that the teacher hadn't said anything to him but wondered if Miss Weelt had even noticed, since her glasses were fogged up on her thin face.

It seemed like Derrin was also trying to stay awake. His head drooped, then he snapped back up to look at the teacher with wide eyes, and a few drops from the vial spilled out onto his fingers.

Derrin cursed.

Molly wondered why it was open in the first place. Maybe to allow in oxygen?

Suddenly, feathers began sprouting from his finger where the liquid had soaked into it. Gray-white feathers emerged. First, just a few, but then they covered his whole hand until he had what looked like a small wing attached to his arm.

Miss Weelt was standing over him, her glasses nearly falling off her nose. "What are you doing besides interrupting my class?"

"None of your business," Derrin shot back, trying to hide his hand under his desk.

But the teacher grabbed it before he could.

Molly watched as the teacher quickly drew out what looked like a blue-green soul's essence from the feathers with her own, then closed her hand into a fist. The feathers disappeared, turning to dust on Derrin's desk before vanishing.

"I will tell you this, if you wanted to keep that, you are bad at holding onto magick."

Molly couldn't help smiling as Miss Weelt returned to the front of the classroom.

After class, Molly didn't look in Derrin's direction, wanting to avoid his wrath. Instead, she headed straight to dinner, hoping to catch Ova there.

A line of students hung around near the cafeteria, waiting for friends coming from their classes. Ova was there waiting for her while playing with the bronze buttons on her red blouse.

"How was class?" Molly asked, coming up to her.

Ova shrugged. She had several red bumps on her arms and a few on her neck. Molly hadn't yet had the courage to ask her what they were. She felt it might be rude, especially since Ova often seemed to overshare and hadn't yet brought it up herself.

"Yours?" she returned.

"Somewhat entertaining. A boy in our class basically turned his hand into a wing," Molly said, then walked with Ova to the line on the first floor of the cafeteria to get their food. They had eaten on the top floor a few times last week, but it was more crowded than they liked.

"Really? In History and Transformation? How?"

"He had a vial of liquid."

"Weird. What's his name? Maybe he's in one of my classes." Ova grabbed up a freshly made peanut-butter-and-jelly sandwich, while Molly went for the fish, tempted by the lemony steam curling to the lights above it.

"Derrin. I don't remember his last name." Molly scooped some steamed carrots sprinkled with nutmeg onto her plate before filling a cup with clear water.

Ova pondered for a moment. "No. I'm pretty sure he isn't in any of my classes."

They sat down at one of the only empty tables they could find, which was close by the fountain.

"Do you mind if, after I eat, I run to Mrs. Heard? I need to ask her something." Ova took a bite of her sandwich. Ova still refused to call Mrs. Heard "Celta" out of respect, although Molly couldn't help to let the name Celta slip past her tongue.

"Of course. Are you okay?"

"Yeah . . . Just . . . I know I shouldn't have, but the tarot app that Koz made—I used it. Sometimes I compare it to my own decks, and it . . . well . . . it said something different. A little more sinister. And I can't decide whether it's because Metis is upset at me that I second-guessed her guidance, or if I'm overthinking everything. I'm sure it's fine. I'm sure that she isn't upset. I'm sure I'm fine. I'm fine." Ova laughed, then itched at her neck. "Unless maybe Metis wants me to go to Mrs. Heard today because she's cunning. Metis is, not Mrs. Heard. This could be her plan all along."

"You don't think the app just messed up?" Molly knew little about tarot decks and had never really cared to learn. When Ova had first mentioned it, it had seemed like it would be handy to see what was approaching one's life until she saw how Ova was acting now, freaking out about it. Molly did not want to be like that. She wasn't sure if it was worth it.

Ova started scratching at her arm, hard enough that Molly thought it might bleed. "What usually goes wrong is the interpretation of it OR if my thoughts went a different direction when asking the question. But this was different. Look." Ova shuffled through her small bag and took out three thick cards. "I brought these to show Mrs. Heard." She laid two of them down on the table in front of Molly. One had an interesting compass in the middle of it, and the other had a woman holding up a thick, short stick that was glistening and silver. "Two cards came up the same as my physical deck, the Wheel of Fortune card turned upright—which could mean that a change is coming—and the Magician reversed, which could mean trickery, illusion, or being out of touch." She laid down the last card she had pulled out. This one had a giant, haunting building in the center. "But the last one from my physical deck was the Tower upright, which means that a sudden upheaval is coming. I don't know what that means! Then when I turned to the app, the last card was the Ten of Swords instead, which means failure or collapse or defeat!"

"Why do you do it if it upsets you?" Molly asked her friend, who had gathered the cards and was clutching them at her chest.

"It opens awareness to the world and connects you to the universe and energies. It helps the practice of watching out for something. I'm sorry. I'm not meaning to . . . I . . . Usually, people don't freak out as much as I am . . . I just—" Ova was trying to catch her breath.

Molly extended her hand across the table and tried to grab for Ova's, but Ova withdrew hers with tears in her eyes.

"Ova. It's okay." Molly understood the fear that came with not knowing what would happen. "I'm here for you, just like I know you are here for me." Molly laid her hand out over the table again, waiting until Ova took it. When she did, Molly squeezed it tight. A few tears fell from Ova's eyes as she took in a deep breath. "If something happens," Molly said, "we will figure it out. What else is the magickal side of this world for, if not finding solutions?"

Maybe she was depending on the magickal side a little too much and giving it too much credit. But it was where the only hope she had lay too.

"Thank you, Molly. I think I'm going to find Mrs. Heard right now." Then Ova got up and one tear dropped onto the table before she left. Her tray of food had barely been touched.

Molly got up to throw it and hers away, having lost her appetite. She wanted to find Koz. She was sure he was in the technology room again. She wanted to ask him if maybe the app was wrong so that she could calm Ova down.

But before she made it to the conveyor belts, she saw that boy again—the one who had been separating the creature spirits over a week ago.

He was standing by the fountain, talking to Lily.

Molly set the trays down at an empty table, then went over to the boy. She wanted to ask him what exactly he had been doing. She wanted to see if maybe he knew more about spirit magick than what she had seen. If perhaps he could give her a little guidance on the right way to set her own foundation so she could learn as much as she could. This last week, Molly had only been able to make it to the library alone twice with how busy she was, and she did not find anything that helped her. Everything was confusing, and there was no order to things, as if the teachers wanted resources there for the children but did not want them to get too ahead of themselves.

Then, when she tried looking up empty vessels—which didn't seem to exist—or protecting herself against spirits on the internet, she got so much conflicting information, spells, and options that she didn't know which ones to try without hurting herself.

The closer she got to Lily and that boy, she swore she smelled the welcoming aroma she had smelled before on Trennly . . . as if either Lily or the boy used the same shampoo.

Lily noticed her staring first and nudged the boy, who was the same height as them. Molly stopped, waiting for his attention.

"Namu," Lily growled, nudging him again.

He turned and lowered his questioning brown eyes, filled with hate and anger, to Molly. Molly felt small under his gaze.

He didn't introduce himself. He didn't say a thing. He seemed to be waiting for her to state what she wanted.

"I—I saw you the other day. Last week. In that room. Separating the two spirits . . ."

Lily stiffened and looked at him.

Molly noticed. Namu seemed to stiffen too. "You don't know what you saw," Namu declared.

"That's why I . . . I just want to know what it was you were doing. I want to know how you knew how to do that. Why you have one teacher in that period," Molly rambled.

"Yeah, Namu. Why?" Lily sneered.

Namu shook his head, and his eyes turned to daggers. "It's none of your business."

Molly had to avert her eyes and ended up looking at his hand as he gripped the lip of the fountain. Clear water sprinkled his skin as it splashed up from the dancing falls, but something else was there. A small pink vial was floating near his hand, tipping into the water.

"You came over to talk to me. Why aren't you looking at me?" Namu's shout forced Molly to return her gaze with a grimace.

"She's just curious. I would be too. It's your fault for showcasing what it is you do," Lily snipped at him, dipping their hand into the now bubbling water and splashing it at Namu's face.

He winced, but neither of them had noticed the water was bubbling.

"Mr. Vero must have accidentally left the door open when he brought in the cages. It was a rush of a—never mind. It's none of your business either."

"Yeah, seems like nothing is anymore!"

The fountain exploded behind them. Not the fountain but the water. It continued to bubble over, now a hot pink. The first explosion shook the ground and had people screaming, then the bubbles continued popping like balloons, as if gas had been building inside them and then releasing.

Molly covered her ears.

"What the hell!?" Namu yelled, staggering away.

Lily and Molly fell back, too, as the bubbles continued to grow and pop.

Teachers stormed into the cafeteria. Some dove to the ground and began drawing symbols on the hardwood floor with crystal-looking wands. Some had containers and were trying to collect bubbles in them before running off again.

Miss Weelt, Mrs. Sleck, and Molly's Transformation Drinks and Remedies One teacher, Mr. Ferrer, were there too.

"Out now! This needs to be contained! Leave! Scatter!" Mr. Ferrer bellowed.

Some kids were recording the scene on their phones, but another teacher took out her phone and hit something that made all their screens turn black.

This made the students moan as they left.

It looked like Namu had already gone, but when Molly walked away, Lily followed after her.

"That was strange, wasn't it?" Lily asked once they were out of the room. The teachers then put up an invisible shield to keep the bubbles and themselves inside. The pink mess continued to grow, eating the teachers up. One teacher passed earplugs to the others inside the encasement.

"I don't understand what happened! I saw this vial," Molly tried to explain but realized that Lily was not listening; they were watching the teachers try to control the chaos.

But what if the vial hadn't been there? Would Molly have sounded stupid if Lily had heard her say that?

Not wanting to further embarrass herself, Molly turned to leave, but then Lily grabbed her arm. "I'm sorry Namu wouldn't answer you. He has not been answering me either lately. I'm worried about him, actually. Him snapping like that is not like him. He never used to be like that before we started this school together last year."

"I'm sorry I bothered him. I was just looking for—" Molly stopped herself. She didn't want to explain to Lily why she was so desperate to learn more than the other kids in her year about spirit magick.

Lily waited for her to continue, but when they saw Molly wasn't going to, they did instead. "It confuses me. We grew up together, side by side. He was never interested in anything magickal but came to this school for me. Then, all of a sudden . . . Well . . . this is his second year, and he skipped a Spirit Magick class. He's in Spirit Magick Three now and has a tutor on the side. He also says he's preparing for some kind of internship exam. But obviously, it's changing him and eating him up. Plus, personally, I know he has other dreams he wants to pursue."

Lily was staring over Molly's shoulder now as if trying to collect their thoughts.

Molly didn't know what to say, but then Lily shook their head and smiled down at her. "I'm so sorry. I'm just at a loss. I'm worried about him. And confused. It isn't your problem, of course." They let Molly's arm go, turned away momentarily, and then turned back around. "Here." They held out something. It was a solid gold bracelet.

"I . . . can't," Molly said, stepping back with her hands up. It was beautiful, but she couldn't take such a thing, and she didn't understand why Lily was offering it to her.

"My family is rich. It's not a big deal. It's an apology for Namu, and I'd like to be friends. You're interesting, anyway. I saw how you came to the school with a mini-troll. I would actually love to discuss that more one day." They tried handing Molly the bracelet again.

Molly stretched out her hand reluctantly to take it, and Lily slid it onto her arm. "It should bring you comfort. Even if it's just in the fact that it's pure gold." Lily winked. "I'll see you around."

They turned, flipping their hair over their shoulder.

Molly stared down at the bracelet in wonder. It was the first thing she had received from a friend here, and it was better than any of the gifts that Rexa or Val had ever given her. It was heavy and solid, and it did feel like it grounded her in a way. It also made her feel important and accepted. Someone in high standing in Magickal Society—the child of the owner of the magickal airlines, no less—had noticed her and given her a token. She had befriended someone who knew so much about this world and might help her navigate it. Someone who could guide her if she asked. Someone she could lean on.

That reminded Molly about Ova and how she had wanted to check on Koz's app. Molly still had thirty minutes of dinner left, which should be enough time.

Molly entered the dimly lit technology room and saw Rem and Koz playing another game together, but this time on a tablet. They were sitting with their chairs touching but their heads far apart as they took turns touching the screen, creating symbols in the illusion of mud. Items sprang out from the mud and then points built up in golden coins on each side of the screen.

Molly wondered if it was another studying app.

"Umm . . ." she said hesitantly.

They both jumped.

"Oh, come on!" Rem complained, spinning in her chair with her head thrown back and the tablet in her lap continuing its rush of music.

Koz shifted, dug into his black cargo pants to pull out a green crinkled straw, and handed it to Rem. She took the straw from his hand and put the tablet on the computer desk in front of her before pulling at it. The straw extended to an unbelievable length and then shortened without making any noise. Molly could almost feel the crinkling beneath her own fingers as if it were imbued with magick.

Rem continued to play with it as she looked at Molly.

"What can I help you with?" Koz asked.

"I just wanted to ask about this app you made for Ova. The tarot one."

Koz shook his head. "I don't understand why everyone is so interested in knowing the future, especially when the future comes close to death, something people don't look at long enough to examine anyway. Let me guess, she got a bad reading, and it scared her?"

"She got a reading that's different from the physical reading she did," Molly explained.

"And you're asking me if my app is wrong?" Koz asked with a sly smile.

"Well . . . yes."

Rem intervened. "Koz is really good at making apps."

Koz nodded as if that were all the acknowledgment he needed. "My app is not wrong," he insisted.

"But how do you know?"

"Because it grasps onto the same wavelengths of energy as when Ova asks the cards. There could be many factors as to why the reading was different, but if she used a physical deck, then the chances of the app being wrong are even fewer. The energy from the physical deck would still be lingering. My app would have grabbed onto that energy if she had asked the same question."

"But what factors could have made it different?"

"Well, she could have been asking a slightly different question, wanting to dive deeper into the answer she just got. There is also the factor of whether or not technology was involved in either the answer or the question. If technology was involved, then my app's reading would have been stronger. Sadly, not much is known about techno magick yet. It's like a whole other world and magick system. Its own timeline, even. It has its own presence and awareness that *knows* whether it itself is involved in the future because of the links it creates and establishes. It can make some things in the physical world a little duller—like a tarot card reading."

Molly was confused and regretted asking. It sounded like nothing Koz had said would help Ova feel better.

"Do you want it on your phone? I have downloaded it for several people in the school. Even some teachers." Koz rolled his eyes but then smiled.

"I have it too," Rem said, holding up her straw.

"It also helps in divination classes," Koz added.

Molly didn't really want it, but if so many others already had it, and if it would help her with her classes, why not? It didn't mean she had to open it and use it to scare herself like Ova had.

She nodded and took out her phone to hand it over, then felt her face grow hot. Koz looked down at her phone with a look of disgust, then glanced back up at her with a shake of his head.

It was probably because of the other apps.

Not wanting to hear about it or be judged, when her heart already felt as though it might beat out of her chest, she decided to distract Koz. "So, since you're really good at computer and technology stuff, what do you want to be when you get older?"

Koz didn't look up as he answered. "I want to work for a legit big techno magick company—mainly on computers—or build my own company once the fear of technology and magick calms down. Not anything huge. Although I admire high-tech magick wizards like Yimmet Simmo, I don't want to be that busy. A few conventions and a few big jobs every year would be great. As long as I still have time to play games."

He handed back her phone without a smile, then turned his chair away from her to pick up the tablet and resume the game he'd been playing with Rem. Molly took that as her cue to leave.

Namu

Chapter Eighteen

Namu had no idea how the water in the fountain had bubbled and exploded. The teachers had fixed it later in the evening, but it was obvious that they suspected a student was responsible because a teacher was stationed nearby, keeping a watchful eye on it for the rest of the day. It unnerved Namu for some reason. It had never happened before, and it had been just after that girl had asked him what he had been doing.

Or maybe Namu was unnerved because some student he had never met had approached him and asked about his personal life. He didn't like the idea of someone spying on what he and Mr. Vero were doing.

He hoped that the fountain incident had scared the girl off and she would stay away from him now. He couldn't deal with anyone else, on top of Lily, trying to figure out what was happening with him.

He barely knew himself.

He needed to fix himself, and he needed to find a way to destroy the door. Then he would have time for questions. And he could take Lily up on their offer to help him follow his own dreams.

Namu rolled over in his bed. It had been over an hour, and he was still unable to sleep. Too many questions were nagging at him. Too many questions he wanted answers to, but the only way to figure them out was to wait.

Unless . . .

He suddenly felt as though the bag of runes from his class last year, which sat at the bottom of his dresser drawer, was somehow pulsing, begging to be used.

He groaned. He was growing delusional.

He threw off his covers.

Normally, he wouldn't do this. Normally, he detested divination. But he couldn't let every single question he had weighing on him sit in his head and slow his mind. He would get nothing done that way. What was wrong with throwing at least one question out to the world and leaving it to the gods?

He tore open his drawer and pulled out the black bag. While some students had many runes, he only had the ones of Freya he'd gotten for completing the class last year.

He had only used the runes a handful of times with Lily, mostly in class, and had forgotten most of the spreads, but the fastest and easiest one was impossible to forget. He just hoped it would give him a decent answer, one that would calm his mind enough for him to sleep.

He spilled the runes out onto the floor and closed his eyes. Then, with his right hand, he felt for the wooden chips and selected four before separating one from the three in a line. He knew he could have picked three out of the bag, one at a time, but he knew himself too well: he was too impatient and would give up on the reading after just one bad tile.

He opened his eyes.

He moaned. All the tiles were reversed, their blank sides staring up at him.

He flipped over the one he had separated from the others to show him the nature of his question. It was *Fehu*, as in Lily's floor. When in reverse, it meant suffering and having lost something of value.

So, that was the road he and the tiles were going down . . .

He flipped over the first of the other three.

Raido, as in his floor, meaning disruptions and things that might go wrong.

Oh, great . . . This was backfiring. And to think he had hoped this reading might bring him an ounce of peace.

The next one. *Thurisaz*. Secrets, enemies, luck running out.

And lastly, *Wunjo*. Period of unhappiness. Personal decisions postponed.

He swept the runes away, scattering them across the floor.

Well, screw the runes. He was not about to put his personal decisions aside. He would make them happen. He would heal himself. He would destroy that door.

He would find himself again, whether the world was against him or not.

Molly

Chapter Nineteen

Molly decided to wear the bracelet Lily had given her to bed. She didn't want to do a glue spell on it just yet and knew the spirit sprites would try to steal it if she left it out. Even when she did a banning spell to keep them from touching her, they still entered her room.

The gold glared at her in the dark, the sturdy metal lending a sense of security as she pressed her fingertips against it. She couldn't keep her mind from spinning with all the things she might be able to do for Lily in return for such a gift as she turned it around on her arm. She could try to carry Lily's books to class if they ever needed her to, even do some of their reports, even though Lily was a year ahead of her. Maybe she could let Lily practice some magick on her outside in the courtyard.

She shook her head, the pillow, and her hair, ruffling chaos to her ears for a moment.

She had to think of a way to repay Lily for their friendship, but letting Lily practice magick on her might seem too desperate.

She let other ideas swarm her head and had not realized she had fallen asleep until she woke up on the biting, cold purple ice. She would never grow accustomed to it. She was stuck to the ice this time, and it threatened to peel her goose bumps away from her skin.

She heard the cracking before she saw it.

In a panic, she searched around for land, shelter, anything to crawl to or hold on to.

She had no idea why she did, though.

There never was anything.

Her foot burned the moment it broke through the ice.

She bit back a scream for only a moment before the water made its way into the pores of her bare foot and then froze.

She tried to pull her foot out of the water, but it wouldn't budge.

Her right hand went in next.

The fingers of her other hand sank into the water as the ice around them splintered, giving way before her whole hand fell through.

Then her arm.

The arm her bracelet was on.

Somehow, all she could think about was Lily. What would Lily say if she lost the bracelet? What would that mean for their friendship? Wouldn't that show how careless Molly was? Who would want to be friends with her then? How was she supposed to explain that she had lost it in a random world of violet ice?

The water was slowly pulling it away, sliding it off her arm with its frozen touch.

She tried to grab the bracelet, but her other hand was going numb in the water, turning purple, then blue.

Her eyes shot open. She was in her room, and something hit the floor loudly. Her hand that had been trapped in the ice shot up to her bracelet, where long blue fingers were pulling at it. It was another spirit sprite. One she had banned from her before. The spell must have worn off. It was trying to pull at the bracelet as if it were too enchanting to let go. Its eyes conveyed greed.

Molly yanked her arm up over her head away from its grasp, slid the bracelet off her arm, then shoved it under the blankets to sit on it before giving the sprite a face that made it look at her in shock, then fly away since it could not touch her skin.

Molly plugged her nose to block out the smell of burning feathers, then saw that the door was slightly open, even after the spirit sprite had flown through. Had it been open this whole time?

But something had hit the floor. When she looked over the edge, still squeezing her nostrils closed, she saw a mist there that raced after the spirit sprite and then vanished.

Molly jumped up, grabbed her bracelet, and ran to shut the door, hoping the smell would leave her room soon. She did not know if she could go back to sleep.

At lunch, Molly learned that the kitchen witches had left, which was humorous. A handful of students walked around with slumped shoulders and complaints building on their lips. Ova told her that it was common now for the kitchen witches to leave, since they learned more from elders when they traveled to far-off places. They took trips together as often as they liked and still got paid. But the students were left making their own sandwiches and eating leftovers.

Molly was building her own sandwich, which consisted of lunch meat and lettuce, then grabbed some popcorn before she was stopped by Lily, who put their hand on Molly's tray.

"I need you to do something for me," Lily said.

The golden bracelet on Molly's arm winked at her, letting her know that this was her chance to pay Lily back. "Of course. What is it?"

"It will have to be quick. Here. Give me your phone."

Molly didn't hesitate to hand it over, not even when Ova came over to them, anger etched on every line of her face. She looked down at Molly's tray and then at Lily.

"What's going on?"

"Exchanging numbers, Miss Templest. How about you? We're good friends now. Hasn't Molly told you?"

Ova looked at her, alarmed.

Molly could only smile back at Ova.

"Unless you want to listen to me bash religion and talk about money all lunch period, I would suggest you sit by yourself. I have some business with Molly to attend to . . . quickly." Lily looked over their shoulder at the busy cafeteria before handing Molly back her phone.

Ova stared at Lily and then looked to Molly, a few red bumps rising on her fingers as they twitched. "I think I'll go eat outside . . ."

Then she took her tray and walked off.

For some reason, Molly didn't want to go after her. She found herself not caring at all. The only thing she cared about was Lily's mischievous smile.

"I need you to sneak into Namu's room."

Molly's heart skipped a beat but did not stop. Instead, it rushed on with a desire to fulfill Lily's request.

Molly couldn't believe she was going to sneak into the room of a boy she barely knew during lunch when it was almost over, but she knew Namu was hiding something. Not just because Lily told her he was—and she wasn't just doing this because Lily had convinced her to—but because Namu was a level three in Spirit Magick who had a special tutor on the side.

She needed to sneak into his room. She had no choice. Besides the fact that Lily needed her help, she had now, twice, almost been taken in her dreams by some spirit. She was done with it. She had to know what Namu was hiding and how he knew all he did at such a young age, because the teachers wouldn't teach her how to protect herself until she had a strong enough foundation.

The solid gold bracelet on Molly's arm quivered as she ran up the stairs from the cafeteria. Lily had said that they would keep Namu distracted at lunch so Molly could sneak into his room.

Sometimes, Molly hated herself and how desperate she felt.

She could not wrap her head around the fact that she was doing this, but Lily needed help. Lily needed to know what project Namu was working on for an exam, and Molly was desperate enough to do anything to learn how to protect herself against spirit magick so that she could go back to her normal life. It was just like Kren had said: the first priority was making sure she could survive a normal life, since she was an empty vessel. Then she could go back and clean up the mess she had made.

Molly was happy she wouldn't have to go up as many stairs as usual when she went to her hall, since she was already out of breath. Her hall was on the sixth floor, one above Namu's.

The stairs, outlined in cool stone with dark hardwood in between, silenced her steps as her white tennis shoes pounded into them.

She debated turning back.

But no . . . Lily had told her that it had to be now. That they were running out of time.

Molly didn't know exactly why Lily needed to know about Namu's project so badly, but did it matter why? Namu and Lily were both second years, while Molly was only a first year. She was sure there was a reason, and Lily and Namu had, apparently, been friends for a very long time. Maybe Lily was worried. There were many things to be worried about at this school.

The rune for Namu's floor, which was an angular R, glinted a glossy black until it dulled against the gray stone a few steps above her, indicating that she was almost there. Molly had never been on this floor before. She hoped it wasn't as vastly different as some other floors were—like the floor she had seen with the spider webs—or her floor, which smelled of burning feathers.

The whinny of a horse echoed down the stairwell from Namu's hall. She paused for a moment until she heard banging that vibrated the stairs. Then she saw a shadow coming toward her. She backed up a step right as a horse—no, some kid—hit the wall to the stairs before they came barreling down at her. It was a kid maybe her size, with a horse's head in place of his own. He grabbed the head as he fell, rolling and twisting. The horse's ear brushed across Molly's leg as she jumped away just in time, clinging to the cold wood-in-stone banister.

She had never seen anything like this, even with all the magickal things that happened in this school.

The horse-headed kid landed with a terrified neigh near the next hall down. She wanted to help him, but . . .

She pulled out her phone. She didn't know if she should intervene; she probably didn't have time.

She thought about calling Ova for help but knew she couldn't. Ova would want to know why Molly was on that floor when she had no reason to be. And Ova was upset at Molly. Molly had chosen Lily over her.

A door slamming made her look back up at the hall she was supposed to be on. The kid who had fallen yelled out like a horse again. He was trying to stand up. His mane glimmered as he pulled at his ears, distressed. He sat up before he fell against the wall again from his too-heavy head.

The glimmer. This was transformation magick. But why?

She ran down to him, taking two stairs at a time, then did the one thing that Kren had taught her right away: called to her own spirit magick, letting it sit in her hand, then called to the horse's spirit magick, which was trying to pull away from her.

"It's okay," Molly said, scooting as she crouched closer to him with one palm out to pacify him. "It's okay."

He was panting and staring at her with the terrified black eyes of an animal.

When she was close enough to feel the transformation magick coming off him, she used her spirit magick to call to it and pull it to her. She could see the small transparent pink veil that indicated the magick used. Just like Kren had taught her, once her magick and the kid's transformation magick touched, she closed her hand into a fist and then she crushed it, disrupting any bonds. She watched the horse's head crumble around the boy, falling away, disappearing into nothingness until he was left with his normal head intact.

It was Derrin.

Derrin, who was panting and crying, had been too weak to keep a hold of that type of magick, so it had been easy for her to stamp it out.

He lay back and hit his head on the wooden floor, groaning.

"Are you okay?" Molly asked, coming nearer to him so she could touch his head. His black hair was soaked in sweat.

He groaned again.

"You need to go to the nurse," Molly said, pulling out her phone to check the time. She had been gone from lunch for ten minutes. She had to act fast before Namu came back up to his room. She had to give herself enough time to search his stuff.

He hit her hand away. "Ye . . . yeah," he said. He shook his head and grimaced, putting his hand to his now-normal head. "I will . . . Yes . . . Okay."

She got up and held out a hand to help him up, which he took. But as soon as he stood up, he yanked his hand away from her and held it close to his chest before examining her. "Did you . . . Did I . . . run into you?"

She shook her head, trying to resist the urge to look at her watch again. "No."

He nodded. "Well. Thanks." Then he glared up the stairs for a moment before moving down the stairs unsteadily. Molly watched him as he turned, gripping the banister so he wouldn't fall, and then headed down another flight of stairs. As soon as he was gone from her view, she ran up the stairs to Namu's hallway.

This time she didn't let herself slow down, even when she saw the annoying spirit sprites, which noticed her right away. There were three of them this time, coming out of the ceiling and up out of the floor. Their slender blue transparent bodies floated to her, and their fingers reached for her like they always tried to do. They were as annoying as mosquitoes, and the worst part was that there were mosquitoes at Lockdrest too.

She swallowed hard, then swore she saw black shadow-like fingers coming through the cracks in the gray brick wall, but ignored them while trying to disregard the spirit sprites too.

She tried to dodge one sprite when it tried to put its finger into her shoulder blade, but even when she picked up speed, it kept pursuing her. She wished she had been more prepared for this mission. If she had known, she would have spent more time banning the spirit sprites on this floor from touching her, but her mind was too unsettled to focus and do that now.

When she reached Namu's door at number 114, she realized another thing she hadn't thought of. She would need a key.

Namu's key. How was she supposed to get into his room? Why hadn't Lily thought of that? Molly knew that this was a last-minute thing, but how had Lily expected her to get in?

She pulled out her own key to try it, but it wouldn't fit. Then she felt a prickle of pain, causing her to cry out, and she swatted away a spirit sprite that had poked its fingers into the side of her neck. It yanked its fingers out, leaving a throbbing pain deep in her muscles. She hated how they poked and prodded her like she was some kind of interesting toy.

That gave her an idea.

She just hoped it would work.

Bending down, she slipped her key halfway under the door and used the glue spell that Mrs. Sleck taught her. She then walked back a few steps, relieved when the spirit sprites left her alone to dive for the key instead. She knew they loved to steal things with their long fingers, like she had seen them sneak into her room to do. Maybe it was their sprite magick, but, somehow, their bodies took form to steal items made of silver, gold, and bronze and even turn those things noncorporeal so they could hide them away in the walls, ceiling, and floors.

But the glue magick she used meant the key could not be budged. No matter how much the sprites worked together to pull it, it stayed still.

Then they decided to try the other side, like she knew they would do. Floating hastily, they rummaged against the keyhole in the door, putting their fingers inside it as they pushed their long ears against the wood, until there was a click and they could sit on the knob, turn it, and then pull.

Just like they did every day and night in the halls. Invisible ghosts to most, opening and closing doors.

But even as they dove to the other side of the door, they found they could still not pull the key free.

Molly slid through the crack in the door and then suppressed a giggle as she snapped the door shut. Two of the sprites had flown back to the hallway to work on the key from that side again, so she'd trapped one in the room with her. It buzzed around like an angry bee as Molly unglued her key and pocketed it. She could deal with one of them in the room with her but not all three. She just hoped the other two wouldn't try to unlock the door again.

She spun around and started looking for a book—any book that Namu might have that she couldn't find in the library of magicks or even in the non-magickal selections. She found a few issues of *Otherworldly Times and Places* magazine, but when she tried to pick them up, she cursed—they were glued shut.

The sprite flew around and then landed on Namu's desk, trying to wrestle free a silver pen that had been glued down too.

Of course Namu knew how to protect his things. He was a second year.

That meant that if he were hiding something, like Lily thought he was, it would not be at all easy to find.

Unless she used . . .

No.

No. She had been told not to use it. That using her cell-magick apps and paying bits of her soul to someone she didn't know wasn't good at all.

She pulled out her phone to look at the time and saw she had a text from Lily saying that Namu had gone to the restroom and would probably be heading up to his room next.

She had no choice. One more time. One little pixel. It wouldn't hurt. It couldn't hurt.

She could use the one that showed her magick residue.

Although everything was magick here and maybe it would be a stupid move, she was curious to see if there was a type of magick she couldn't spot or didn't know existed. Or if there was a tool or a book that he had hidden.

Molly opened up a glittering gold screen. She had used this app multiple times in her world to try to spot where magick might have been used outside her home. Many girls used it on items they were buying to make sure magick wasn't used to add luster. People also used it to check if someone they had met on a dating app was wearing magick to change their appearance.

Rexa had used it many times on dates.

Molly pressed her thumb into it, rolling her nail into an easy curve, then breathed out onto the screen, opening herself up to see all magick.

The room glittered gold all over, as if everything had been touched by lots of magick here.

She sighed. She knew that this was probably stupid and that she was wasting a pixel of her soul.

But then something interesting caught her eye—it had caught the sprite's eye too. There was a thin line of glittering gold that glowed brighter than anything else. The sprite was trying to grab it. Something in this room had an extra dose of magick.

Molly went to it. It was behind a small dresser.

She pulled the dresser out of the way.

There was a golden square outline on the wall with a golden handprint on the right side, as if it were a handle. She pushed her hand against it, but nothing happened.

She took out her phone and turned off the app.

Then she went to the web to search for openings that needed the palm of a hand.

It only took a minute of scrolling through images to find exactly what she needed. Many of these had been used long ago in castles, barns, and even in aircraft to hide stowaways, cash, and magickal items.

All it took was the right incantation, spirit magick, and the push of a hand.

The most common incantation was right at her fingertips to focus the incentive, *Opla inwar displa.*

She said it as she pushed her hand where the golden print had been. She exerted a little bit of soul magick and watched the wall fall away like sand.

Why was it so easy? Was this place wanting to be found?

The wall gave way into a little room tall enough for her to stand up in and lit by an unearthly violet glow coming from a door in front of her. The door was wooden, with a handle that alternated between gold and black metal every other moment. It was the perfect sized door for Kren but not for her.

Why was it here?

She heard something and turned to see that the wall had completely re-formed behind her; grains of sand were rising and meshing into a solid, dark wall.

Locking her inside.

Then she heard something clink and bang against the wall, as if the dresser had moved itself back in place.

Her muscles grew taut. The fact that her mission was failing taunted her as her hands shook and her mind numbed.

She turned back to the door that was staring at her. Inviting her. Wanting her to open it.

Taking out her phone, she went to the web again to try to research but found that she had no service.

That did not bode well.

And when she tried to hit text or call, the phone would not let her click on the buttons.

She sighed, utterly alone. She didn't know what to do. If the phone didn't work, she couldn't use it to figure out how to get back beyond the wall. She was stuck. Trapped. Trapped in a room she wasn't supposed to be in, with no legitimate excuse when she was found.

Lily knew she was coming here, so, hopefully, they would come looking for her at some point. She could wait here until she heard voices in Namu's room and start banging on the wall.

Or maybe she could just wait until Namu came and found her here. He had to know this was here. She was sure this was the secret that he was hiding. A door. But a door to what?

Did she dare look inside? Would Lily be upset with her if she went back and told her what she had found but that she decided not to open it?

Why did she care? She had learned that she needed to be careful in this school. But how could she see this door and not at least try to peek inside? What would Val and Rexa think of her if they knew of this place and knew this door was here?

She thought Rexa might be hesitant at first but that they would coax her to go inside.

She slowly took a few steps toward the door. The air was warmer the closer she got, and it smelled of smoldering flowers. All it would take was one twist of the handle so she could peek inside and then close it right away.

Then at least she would have something to tell Lily about.

She was already reaching for the handle.

With one little twist of the heated handle, the door opened ajar.

With a swallow, she bent down and looked inside.

It was a whole other land. Fields of grass invited her to play under a bruised purple sky.

Was this where Namu learned the magick he knew?

She slid off the bracelet Lily had given her and laid it next to the door to help prop it open. Her first thought was that she needed to make sure that the door stayed open if she went inside so she could get back to Lily, but she didn't care about Lily as she laid the bracelet down. Now she had her own curiosity.

It couldn't be too long until someone came back to this place, could it? Maybe they would see the bracelet and know where she went.

Molly stepped through the door into the world that breathed more magick than her own. It welcomed her. She felt it need her as a warm tingle festered in her veins, and the smell of burning pollen overwhelmed her.

Namu

Chapter Twenty

"Namu, what's wrong?"

He couldn't tell Lily. He could never tell them.

His world, his brain, were spiraling. His mind was breaking.

He couldn't tell them this secret. He had decided this ages ago. He needed to protect Lily. He needed to keep them from looking further into it. Keep them from going into that nightmare world, from turning into something like him, keep them from dying.

But why? Why was that place, that world, here? Why was it in his room? Why was it taking over?

When he had come upstairs to his room after lunch, with Lily following close behind, he had never expected to find it like this.

This was one of the worst things that could happen. What would happen to the students in the school?

He had to figure out how to stop it.

"Nothing," Namu stammered, brushing off the dust-like sparkles on his bed. He hoped that Lily didn't see them or that they thought that they were just dust particles, not the strange magick no one knew except for him.

The lamp was bruising into an unnatural shade of purple. A small circle deforming itself until it began to grow, taking up the whole lamp.

Smiling nervously at Lily, Namu walked backward away from the lamp, which was on the other side of the room, while keeping his eyes on his friend's coffee-colored eyes full of questions. His butt pushed against the wood of his desk. With one fake sneeze and a twitch, he brushed the papers on the desk all over the floor and then looked at them in false distress and horror.

Or maybe it wasn't false because he felt like his world would end soon if he didn't stop what was happening. Or if he was caught.

When Lily went over and bent down to help him with the papers, Namu darted to the other side of the room and switched off the lamp.

Bad idea.

Now he was seeing more than just sparkles of the magick-haunting dust floating in the air around them. He was seeing the true horrors of the place he was trying to keep locked away. Right over the bed was a starlit night against his wall. A hellish night that was expanding, the magick unable to be contained to one place.

But Lily's eyes must still be adjusting to the lack of light. They wouldn't believe what they were seeing. Or would they? They were smart.

"What the heck, Namu! What did you do? What's going on?" Lily demanded.

Namu could see Lily standing, abandoning their mission to collect the papers that lay across the now too-dark floor.

Lockdrest

The night sky painted itself farther across the wall. Lily gasped, finally noticing it just as it touched the wood on the desk, burnishing it before turning that part into metal—a black metal that might have disappeared in the darkness if not for the sparkle of stars lighting its way above it.

"Don't let it touch you!" Namu begged as Lily took a few steps away from the scene. The night started eating away at the desk before spitting it back out and transforming it entirely to that metal. The same metal that he had deep in his veins.

"What is it? What's going on? I've never seen magick like this before. How can it change the physical elements of things like this? How are you doing this?"

Those were the same questions that were once on Namu's mind, but the answers were ones he knew they would not like. No one would. He needed to understand why this was happening. Why and how this magick had gotten loose when he had never had an issue like this before.

"Something I'm working on. I want to blow the teachers away when the exam comes," Namu spouted out with a nervous laugh. Maybe too nervous.

He couldn't see Lily's face but could hear their disbelief. "This is stupid, Namu. Can you even control it?"

This time, he would not lie. Not if it could get Lily out of here. "Not always. Now is one of those times. So, maybe you should leave."

He made his way to the door.

"If you can't control it, why are you messing around with something like this, Namu!? You could destroy the whole school or severely hurt someone."

That, he knew.

"If it did that to the desk, what would happen if it touches someone?"

That, Lily didn't want to know. That was what he was trying to prevent.

"It's okay. For now, it's contained to this room, and it has touched me before. And see—I'm fine." He was not. "I just don't want you to get the magickal residue on you and spread it throughout the school. I can't have anyone knowing about it until the exam."

He was expecting Lily to move, to make their way to the door, but they didn't. He could see the outline of them just staring in his direction as the night grew closer to Lily, making the blood in Namu's veins constrict and the muscles in his jaw spasm. He needed to get Lily out. He needed them not to call his bluff. If they did, it might cost them their life.

"*Please*, Lily! You may not know this, but this is important to me. I want to finally surprise my parents. My dad! I could . . . could change the industry! That's right! I want to prove myself. This is my only chance! You have to understand!"

He knew Lily did. That was why he played this card. Lily was always seeking their parents' approval or finding ways to surpass their father's accomplishments. Lily might know where his true dreams lay, but with how different he had been acting this last year, maybe they would believe what he was doing was connected to something deeper.

Lily sighed. Namu waited a beat longer. If one more second went by and they didn't move, he was going to grab Lily and drag them out. But right as the sky from hell was about to touch their still frozen form, they moved away from it and walked to the door, which Namu opened for them to get out.

They stopped for a moment, holding it open and Namu's panicked gaze. "I request to be in the room when you take the exam. I want to see this. I want it explained to me."

Namu forced a swallow down his dry throat, then nodded once and went to close the door in Lily's face, but they blocked it with their hand for a moment longer to stare deep into Namu's eyes. "I'm only leaving so you can clean up this mess. My guess is that you will not do that unless I leave. I don't want it hurting anyone in the school. Fix it now."

Namu nodded and closed the door in their face the second Lily moved an inch. Then he turned the lock.

This was bad. Really bad. The dust was thicker now, threatening to turn his room into a night of fog that would make its way out and down the hall if he couldn't stop this.

Namu ran to the dresser that was now a burning black metal. He hissed, his palms blistering as he shoved it aside and stared at the square outline on the wall. He whispered the incantation to open it and pushed his bloody hand to the spot where there should have been a handle. The square fell apart as it turned to sand. The sand tried to force its way under his knees as he bent down and looked inside.

It was worse than he had thought.

A few feet in, deep in a room, was the door. The petrified wooden door with the loose golden handle that shifted between black and gold every couple of seconds. It stood only half his height, begging to be fully opened to free whatever was behind it.

A world of hissing dreams and long-forgotten nightmares.

The door was ajar.

Someone had found this place. Someone had opened the door.

There was a bracelet propping the door open. He recognized it instantly. It made his insides grow cold.

Someone must have gone inside and left the bracelet there to avoid being trapped.

A sickening feeling wormed its way from his stomach to his throat. If he closed the door, that person would be lost forever. But if he didn't, there was a chance they would all be doomed.

For the nightmarish night from the world beyond was leaking and seeping through the door, threatening to change everything in its path as it had changed him.

Forcing the bile back down his throat, he hit the door to slam it shut.

Trapping whoever it was inside.

Then he picked up the bracelet.

The bracelet that he knew.

Who had been sent in there? Whose death had he just guaranteed?

Molly

Chapter Twenty-One

I t was as if Molly's nightmare, the frozen world that she was forced to return to now and again, had been reversed. This world, the world beyond the door, was one of a bruised purple sky and a burning taste that lingered on the roof of her mouth.

Green specks dotted the atmosphere. They floated in the still air like pollen, carrying this world's magick straight from the yellow flowers set in rolling vibrant green grass under Molly's feet. Each flower huffed up green magick dust before erupting in heatless flames.

The first time one ignited, it had been so close to Molly's leg that she had expected flames to lick her skin, but they hadn't. They just caressed her leg like a cat's tail before they extinguished themselves, leaving the flower without a single burn on its petals. Yellow petals contrasted intensely against the shimmering purple sky as the dust particles formed their own kind of starry night.

The grass beneath her shoes shifted, swaying to a halt. Once bladed and flat, each strand of grass now stood rounded and full. Yet the flowers remained the same.

As Molly took another step, she realized the texture was different. It was less natural, no longer fresh, yet something new. Something synthetic.

She bent down to touch a blade. Its gummed surface gripped at her skin. It was rubber now or something close enough to it, suspended taut, refusing to bend.

Molly continued to walk. Her numb mind made her feel as if she were in a dream, yet her burning lungs and coursing blood made her feel alive. Looking back from where she had come, she found that she was a decent way from the door at a soft decline. With the door up on a hill, she felt as if it was promising that, if she wanted to return to it, she would easily be able to find it again.

There was a lake to her right on which large square chunks of ice floated in a syrupy kind of water. A few glossed over, momentarily becoming smooth like glass before they began to sink. The sinister feel reminded her of the place her tortured mind went to.

Goose bumps prickled Molly's skin, warning her to go in a different direction. She headed toward a cluster of trees close by. Some were dead and glistening black against the battered purple sky, the branches stretching crookedly upward, stone-stiff with green leaves of frozen gems.

When Molly reached the trees, the black metal called to her, singing a familiar song to the pumping in her veins, drawing her to it. Wanting her hand and the metal bark to connect and become one as if to grant her its magick.

She reached her hand out, and the bark greeted her skin with a sizzle and a scalding burn. She instinctively pulled away as searing blisters appeared on her hand.

Lockdrest

Hot tears burned down her cheeks as she looked up to the green leaves. She noticed they were now hard thin slits of rock sprouting from a deep brown creviced boulder, each standing erect toward the moonless sky.

Her breaths were ragged and pain pulsed from her palm and fingers as she bent them and watched them crack and bleed. Her heart was rushing in her ears. Each thump was a timer running out.

She needed to leave.

She needed to get to that door.

She knew nothing about this place. It was filled with mystical magick that was not for her. She wasn't sure it was for anyone. She wasn't sure how Namu could train in this place.

Prepared to run, prepared to find a way out of that room and through that wall, she went to wrap her hand in her shirt but then stopped. The fabric did not meet soft flesh but instead a firm casting like stone.

Suddenly, her hand was too heavy.

Her arm fell to her side as though weights had been hooked into her skin, and she almost toppled over.

She looked down to see her arm and hand shifting, turning into that same solid alloy that made up the black metal trees. She watched in horror as the material climbed up her arm, hardening around her skin before it climbed higher.

A faint warning ticked that there was no turning back.

She tried to run, but she fell.

Her feet were turning too. Trapped in heated, heavy, smooth metal with no pores to breathe. She could hear the cracking and crinkling as the metal cocoon that wanted to mold her worked up her legs, over her shoulders, and then around her chest, making it hard to expand her lungs.

Then she tasted her metallic fate as it worked over her lips, which she had clamped shut.

The last smell she inhaled was the igniting flowers that sprinkled dust into the sky; then the metal worked up over her eyes before she could blink.

It was forcing her to look out. Forcing her to see the world she would be cut off from. The world that kept her inside. Kept her there.

She could breathe, and she could move her eyes to see. The metal that layered her skin, keeping her in place, was warm. It wasn't sweltering inside.

She couldn't help but think it was better than drowning in the freezing purple lake.

She saw rather than felt the rubber grass shift again to its flimsy green. How many days would it take her to die here? How many times would she be forced to watch the grass change?

Molly wondered if Ova would look for her. If she would ask Lily where she was. Or if Lily would come looking for her. If Namu would know where to find her. If anyone was her friend. If anyone would care.

Or if everyone would eventually forget about her, like she was sure her friends had back home. It was funny because she had always been scared to lose herself, and now she was lost. She was living her biggest fear. All because someone had asked her to sneak into a boy's room. All because Molly couldn't help but be a follower.

Something she had been her entire life.

She didn't know how to live any other way.

Without following. Without having guidance, she didn't know how to make friends. She didn't know how not to scare people away. She didn't know how not to act weird or push people out. All because of the spirits that had constantly attacked her life.

Something heavy was on the outside of her metal skin that made her eyes flicker back and forth. It was climbing up her torso to her shoulder and then to the top of her head.

Another one was on her leg.

The torture of not knowing what was crawling on her sent nails down the insides of her mind, making her want to scream and squirm, but she couldn't. Her eyes strained, begging and needing to know what was crawling all over her layer of metal skin.

Then she saw it. At first, there was one head as big as three of her fingers put together. It was white and wide, slightly cute. Then three heads were peeking out from over her forehead down into her eyes. They stared at her with hungry black eyes, then began to crawl down her face, momentarily blacking out her vision. It was one creature. One creature with a white body that could easily sit in the palm of her hand and three heads floating on three thin necks. The creature made its way to her arm. She watched it sit there until one head bent down and went through Molly's paralyzed metal skin like a ghost.

There was a moment of pain, a pinch just like when the spirit sprites dug their fingers into her. She tried to scream as her soul sank inside her and pulled away.

Another head joined the first one to dig in. Soon, all three were digging into her, somehow able to slip inside her metal skin to her real skin and then inside that to what should be her soul.

But they came up angry. Vicious. The two eyes on each of their heads grew ravenous when they turned to her before she felt them crawling all over her again.

Then a few more creatures landed on her and started digging. Started pinching.

She wished she could scream.

But she couldn't. She was forced to stare at a petrified tree. Its life was trapped forever, withering and quivering inside, just like hers, as the white creatures ransacked and ravaged, trying to get at her soul.

Namu

Chapter Twenty-Two

Namu could only pace. He couldn't think about going to his Symbols One class. He could not think about school, classwork, students, teachers, or anything besides what he had just done. He didn't want to run into Lily. He didn't want to do anything but turn back time.

He restored his room back to its original state after using that one spell Mr. Vero had taught him to get rid of the dust. He had to have used it five times, which, normally, would have worn him out, but his adrenaline had kept him going. The last thing that went back to normal was his desk, which had now shifted back to wood and had left the dust that had changed it floating in the air.

He kicked at the desk, his foot going numb from the assault. Then he sat down on his bed and cried, his tears soaking and burning into his bloody, blistered hand that had been burned on the metal, as he deserved.

He had locked a student in that world.

What was he supposed to do?

If he went in there, he would be petrified again. He would be trapped there too. More of his soul would be eaten away. Just like it had been before.

But if he didn't do anything, that student, that person, that soul would perish. They would die. And it would all be on him.

His soul was already tattered and in ruins. He didn't think he could live knowing he had done that to someone else.

He had to get Mr. Vero now that he cleaned up his mess and made sure it wouldn't spread to anywhere else in the school.

He ran down his hall, the doors becoming a blur, then he grabbed the banister to the stairs and swung himself down, taking two stairs at a time. He didn't care what time or class period it was. He sprinted from the main floor to the grand staircase and ran down the hall until he got to Mr. Vero's classroom door, which was shut. He barged inside.

"Mr. Vero!"

Mr. Vero must have seen the panic in his eyes from the front of the classroom, for he took Namu in for only a moment before he raised his hand to his students. "Class dismissed. Please find your way out now."

The students, mumbling questions, started to leave as Namu knocked into a few, trying to get to the front of the class.

"What's wrong?"

"A student," Namu breathed. He felt like he was going to faint. His vision flicked to white every few heartbeats as he grabbed at a desk to steady himself. "I trapped one. Behind the door."

The silence drilled a hole into his heart.

He saw Mr. Vero in a blur walking around him to close his classroom door.

"You did what?" his teacher asked from behind once the door had clicked shut.

Namu spun around. "I went into my room after lunch—that world—the place—it was in my room. Changing things. Lily almost saw. Did see—"

"You trapped Pathon behind the door?" Mr. Vero was wide-eyed.

Namu shook his head. "I got Lily out. I don't know who I trapped. I checked the door. It was slightly open. I shut it. Someone must have gone inside."

"But how?"

Namu didn't have an answer. He had no idea how anyone could have known about the door. But he did know who may have had someone snooping around. He couldn't tell Vero that, though. He couldn't get that person in trouble. It was on Namu anyway for keeping secrets. He was a hypocrite. He had kept secrets, just like Mr. Vero had from him last year.

"I . . . I don't know what to do," Namu said, looking to Mr. Vero in desperation.

Mr. Vero studied him. "You *know* what we have to do. We have to go in there and get that student out. Like I did for you. Like Will did for me."

"But how? Their soul hasn't come out yet. And if we go in like you did . . . you said that the teacher who saved you died of some strange thing no one could figure out. We can't stay in there."

"I think I have a plan. I need to meet with the Transformation Drinks One teacher, Mr. Ferrer, and the others quickly and then I'll meet you in your room."

He turned to go out the door but then stopped. "And Namu . . ."

Namu stared at him, his heart wanting to be torn to pieces, his shuddering breaths threatening to do just that.

"It may take days."

Then he was gone.

An hour later of pacing, Mr. Vero met Namu in his room. He had on an odd belt buckled around his waist over his dark shirt; it looked as if it had come out of a generic role-playing game. It was tan, with holes all around it, holding a bunch of vials containing sloshing purple liquid. He held out a similar belt for Namu.

"What is this?" Namu asked, taking the floppy snake to buckle it around himself.

"We will do an astral-transformation spell like I did before to get your body. We will both go in to assess the situation and then make decisions from there depending on whether this student's soul has made it out of their body or not yet."

Mr. Vero moved the small dresser aside, then put a glue spell on it to keep it in place.

Mr. Vero then placed his hand on the correct spot on the enchanted wall and muttered the words that made the wall crumble away around his feet. The sand falling made Namu remember when he had come across the wall and the enchantment for the first time. He had been trying to rearrange his room, but the desk kept sliding back into place. After research and analysis, he had found the spell that Mr. Vero had done.

He still regretted that day.

Mr. Vero stepped over the piles of sand on the floor, and Namu followed him into the room.

They were silent as they waited for the wall to form behind them again. They would have to do the same, only in reverse, to get out. They would have to place a hand on the correct spot, mirroring the other side, then say the incantation backward. There was no other way out unless they were just spirits passing through, their bodies lying in this room or beyond this door.

Not even the transformation drinks, which would turn them into something like spiritual mists to help them roam more freely and stay away from those creatures, would help them pass through that wall.

Namu swallowed hard as Mr. Vero opened the door, took a vial from his belt, popped off the corked top, and downed it, making sure to splash a little on himself when it was done. The exact reasoning behind why he did that, Namu didn't know. But before Namu could think more about it, he watched his teacher disintegrate.

Namu did the same thing, copying the movements exactly as Mr. Vero did them so he wouldn't mess anything up. He had done this before with Mr. Vero in his private lessons, but Mr. Vero had never talked about it much in depth. It was a lesson he would learn later in Transformation Drinks and Remedies Three.

His brain began to fog and break away from itself, his eyes blurring as he lost all sense of self and started to fall apart piece by piece. It was unsettling for him, whereas other people, apparently, found it enlightening and addicting. It granted them a chance to fall away from themself after trying to hold themself together for far too long. But for Namu, it only made him feel emptier, more aware, and more desperate for his solid, full form.

"Are you ready?" he heard Mr. Vero's distorted voice say through his own foggy mist before his vision cleared. He was then able to see Mr. Vero floating in front of him. For a moment, he looked as if someone had taken their hand across a window of raindrops, creating a blurred image of something, maybe human, until Mr. Vero moved through the door, becoming more of a stream.

Namu followed. His own stream lengthened, trying to pull back into itself as he moved until he passed through the opened door. As a mist, Mr. Vero went back through the opening and then back into the world again, creating a slight wind current to close the door with him. It was then that Namu met the memorable twinge of pain scattering his insides as if needles were falling from the skies down through his misted skin.

"I know it hurts, Namu. We just need to assess the situation and then we can leave."

Namu nodded, even though he knew nodding was worthless in this form. A flower erupted in flames under him, and he dove away from it to escape the green dust. He knew the dust would burn his lungs and go deeper into his veins than it already was.

He kept an eye out for those creatures too. Mr. Vero had told him before that they could not grab onto this form, and Namu could see why now. Being in this form made him feel a bit safer, but he couldn't be completely sure.

Mr. Vero headed for the trees up ahead. By the trees, lying on the ground, was something that looked like a statue. A black metal statue shaped like a girl.

Namu couldn't breathe. He stopped moving and let himself sink. He had never seen another person like that. Had never seen someone as he had been.

"Namu, come on!"

The girl had those creatures all over her. They looked angrier than he remembered them being. They were tearing at her body as she lay still, trapped.

He had trapped her here.

"Namu!"

Namu watched as Mr. Vero's mist shivered, and his whole body appeared next to the statue and the creatures in solid form. Mr. Vero then took his brown shoe and put it against the statue for the first layer of the shoe to be burned away. He pulled back, with his finger to his chin.

But then Mr. Vero's arm started changing, a metal crust forming from his elbow.

"No!" Namu screamed, streaming for him.

But Mr. Vero unhooked a vial and downed it to turn to mist again, causing the small metal casing on his elbow to drop. One of the small white creatures pounced on it to dig into it with their heads.

Mr. Vero was next to him, coughing now, in his mist form.

"I know it's hard, Namu, but I need you to assess it, too, so you can see if I missed anything."

Namu couldn't. He couldn't go over there. He couldn't face the nightmare he had seen a hundred times in real life and in his dreams.

But he had to because this was all his fault.

He made himself float over there, even though everything in his body revolted against doing so. He made himself stand over the girl's body. He made himself look at her. He couldn't help every single emotion crashing down around him, especially when he realized that he recognized the metal face of the girl. It was the girl who had been at the fountain. The one who had asked him questions.

This was even more his fault than he had thought it was.

"Let's go!" Mr. Vero said.

Namu must have been staring for too long.

They both streamed to the door. Mr. Vero formed back into his physical body first, opened the door, and ducked inside. Namu went next. He grabbed onto the foggy line of transformation magick that glimmered with his misted hand and cut the connection, letting it disintegrate around him. His body was shocked at the impact of being pulled back together. A headache formed at his temples.

When the door closed behind them, Mr. Vero made a circle on the ground with a clear stone and then drew a few symbols, which he stood on. When he stomped his foot down on the circle, a light shined up, encasing Mr. Vero until all the dust from that other world had been eaten away.

Namu did the same.

"I didn't see her soul wandering around. Did you? Did you recognize her?" Mr. Vero asked.

Namu nodded. "A first year." He had not seen her soul either. "How are we supposed to get her out?"

"Well, we can't just wait for the cocoon to fall away like ours did and then have her transform or quickly pull her here. Her soul is in danger. We may have to try to pull the body with the metal casing closer to the door and then wait for it to fall away before we pull her through."

"But her soul might be dead by then!"

Mr. Vero went to shrug but then stopped. "I don't know what to tell you, Namu. That's all we can do. We can't bring the metal in here, not straight from the source. Not when we don't know what it would do, especially with those creatures on it."

"What if she turns into the petrified wood instead?"

A few bodies, including his, had turned into a wooden casing after the world beyond the door had released him for a moment before trapping him again. It had been in that moment that Mr. Vero had been able to turn back into a human and break his soul free.

"If she was petrified wood, she would be easier to pull, since she wouldn't burn away whatever touched her, but we still cannot risk pulling her inside. You know that. We just have to sit and wait. I'll go and collect what we need. I'll also cancel your classes and mine. I'll call in sick. As for Pathon . . ."

"I'll text them some kind of excuse."

Molly

Chapter Twenty-Three

They were back. Whoever had been there before, with the distorted muffled voices, they were back. She could feel their presence, the slight shift and change in the atmosphere, the sudden alertness of the creatures still trying to dig into her soul.

She didn't know if it had been hours or days since these people were last here. All she knew was that she hadn't slept.

A man. A man formed in front of her. It was one of the teachers. The one with the long dark hair she had seen working with Namu before. He had a long metal band that he laid on the ground in front of her before he disappeared.

There was a kick at her back. She rolled and then her vision went black. She felt the creatures scurry along her body, trying not to get crushed. There was another kick, this time in two places on her side, and she rolled again. Now she was not looking toward the trees but to the lake in the distance. She was facing the teacher, and the boy she recognized was Namu. Namu ran, possibly around her, as the teacher snatched up the metal band. She felt it tighten around her metal skin. The teacher scowled when he tried to ignore the creatures that only had attention for her. He was tightening the band somehow.

If her eyes could have widened, they would have. His fingers. She saw them shifting, changing into the metal.

"Vero!" she heard Namu yell.

There was a click and then a pop. She saw the teacher's throat bob as he chucked something down.

Then he was gone. He was a mist. Just like the mist she had seen before in her room.

But then she heard two pairs of feet scuffling in the grass and two people arguing and grunting as her body started to move. They were tugging, pulling, and trying to take her somewhere. But to what? Were they trying to get her to the door? Were they trying to save her?

She started counting to distract herself from the sudden panic she felt about not being able to help them. The two of them made three big heaves until one yelled at the other to drink. Then there were four more heaves until the metal snapped. Because, from what they had said, it had burned through.

Then they left her there. There was no more tugging and only silence. She was left alone with the creatures. One was gouging into her right eye.

It might have been the next day that they came back, only to fail again. It was the same process. She felt a metal band tugging at her waist. But the grass was rubber this time, slowing their progress and only allowing them five good pulls before the metal band snapped.

Another day. This time, she was half asleep. Her mind was not working any longer. Her body was growing weak, and her mind was eating away at itself.

She felt them connect the band around her, but then, suddenly, her body was as loose as sand.

Her limbs touched the prickles of the raw, live grass.

"Hey! Hey!"

One of them was yelling at her. She couldn't tell which. She could only feel them lift her head and tilt it back. Her head was unsteady.

"Drink this!"

Something touched her lips, but then it dribbled down her chin before a curse left their mouth. They were gone.

Another one was there trying again, but the liquid, whatever it was, would only sit in her mouth. She could not swallow it. Her body would not allow it. The smell, the burning smell of the world, was too much. She rolled over and puked acidic bile along with whatever they had put in her mouth.

Then she felt her body starting to change again. It was hardening into stone. A cooler stone. One that didn't burn.

There was more cursing before Molly was trapped in place. She was in the most uncomfortable position, on her side, with her hand at her throat and her mouth forced open.

Those things were crawling all over her again.

"Gods dammit! Get away!" she heard someone yell.

Then the band was around her again. She didn't care to look out from her eyes. She thought she was too tired to open them. Then she realized that they were stoned shut.

She was being pulled again, faster this time. This time, the band—or whatever they were using—didn't burn. It didn't break.

But then her body fell free again, and the metal tugging at her skin cut into her softness, causing a gurgling scream to erupt from her.

They stopped pulling, and she started sliding down a hill until they grabbed at the band again, which pressed her too tight, threatening to squeeze her in half.

Hands were behind her, stopping her decline. Those hands picked her up. She felt air all around her for once until they dropped her and she smelled burning flesh. Her face and her body hardened again.

She was left in the grass, alone, staring at the door.

"Do you really think she's still alive?"

They were back again. They looked as tired and worn as she did.

"Of course. Otherwise, those things wouldn't still be at her the way they are."

"But how?"

The teacher didn't answer.

A single strand of grass tickled the end of her nose and made her sneeze.

Hands grabbed her up. One, two, three, four, eight. She wasn't sure how many.

They pulled her through the door.

The door slammed shut.

There was a loud slap and a blinding flash of light before the itching and burning all over her skin and her eyes went away.

They didn't try to make her stand. Two of them looked down at her before she passed out. Her outer-self breathed a sweet release, while her inner-self ached.

Molly woke up in a bed. It had a stiff red cover that she pushed away from her cheek.

It wasn't her bed.

Over by the desk sat that boy. One of her saviors, Namu.

She tried to throw the covers off, but she was weak. She tried to sit up, but her head spun, forcing her to lie back down. She closed her eyes and put her hand on her sweaty mess of curly hair.

"Mr. Vero is going to get you some food."

The thought of food turned her stomach. She rolled over to puke. She tried putting her hand to her mouth to stop herself, but was too late. She vomited all over his sheets.

He grimaced and sighed, but did not turn away.

"We also destroyed your phone . . ."

Her hand grasped at her burning insides, first her chest and then her aching stomach. Her eyes squeezed shut.

"We did that because it was tainted from that world. Mr. Vero will get you a new one. But all your contacts and everything are gone now. He'll meet with Koz and take the new phone to see if he can reestablish anything that he can remember from before. That is, if you had given your phone to Koz, like practically everyone else has."

She nodded. Regret was beating the insides of her skull.

Opening her eyes, she saw Namu was still there, guarding her, regret growing hard like stone in his eyes. He took something out of his pocket and held it up for her to see.

It was the golden bracelet.

"Who gave you this?"

"Li . . ." It burned her throat to talk. She clamped her mouth shut and tried again, only to feel her pain coming out in tears.

"Lily," he said as if he knew, biting his bottom lip in disappointment. He nodded once and put the bracelet back into his pocket.

She wondered why he was upset. She wondered what that place was. Why she felt the way she did.

The door opened, and Mr. Vero came in. "Oh, good. She's awake."

He gave Namu something: a glass containing liquid. "Give her this. It's a calming drink. Her body will need it before it will accept any food. But make her sit up."

"Why do I—?" Namu stopped whatever he was going to say.

He went to the side of the bed, drink in hand, and, with a gentle caress, moved his hand over his pillow and under Molly's head to help her lift herself up. Mr. Vero was on the other side, his hands beneath her shoulders. He had moved the blankets to cover up where she had puked.

As soon as Molly sat up, she felt like she was going to faint. But the drink was in her hand, and she tipped it back, relishing how it wetted her mouth and healed her throat. It awakened her insides, cooling them down. The ice spread up into her head, quelling her headache.

She sighed with deep relief and drank some more.

When she was done, Namu took her empty glass. Then Mr. Vero held out her right arm, examining it. He made a few waves and twists with his fingers, then closed his eyes and breathed.

Then she saw his faint hint of a pure white soul coming out, trying to draw hers out.

But hers never rose.

He tried again, but Molly took her arm away.

"Odd," he said.

Molly tried to give him an awkward smile but couldn't. She could only stare down at her arm. She knew that her soul could come out partly, but she felt it deep inside her, hiding more than it ever had after everything.

"What's wrong? Why isn't her soul coming out for you to look at it?"

Namu seemed panicked for some reason.

"I don't know. I could try another area."

"You think they took her whole arm!" Namu latched onto the limb that Molly had been staring at. She tried to pull it away but was too weak.

"I . . . don't know . . ." Mr. Vero answered.

Namu let go of her arm and ran his hands through his hair. He looked as though he might pull it out. "I—I'm so sorry. I— What else is she missing!?"

"She was in there for a few days. I would say—"

But Molly cut him off. "I don't think I'm missing anything. Or if I am . . . maybe barely at all."

Hatred. Hatred stormed its way from Namu into her. "You don't even know what you're talking about. You don't even know what that place was! If you're trying to make me feel—"

"I'm an empty vessel," Molly spouted.

Namu's eyes did not calm, but he did look at Mr. Vero in confusion. Mr. Vero only sat back on his heels and looked at her as though she were something he had never seen before.

"What . . . what does she mean?" Namu asked.

"It's something most people don't know about. Something rare," Mr. Vero said.

"What does that mean?"

"No one knows exactly. It's just someone with a soul that is a little different. It hides in itself and is willing to lose itself for some reason. They are easy to take over," Mr. Vero answered.

"Then why wasn't her soul eaten by those things?"

"My guess is because it hid deep inside her. Can you even perform spirit magick?" Mr. Vero asked Molly.

Molly nodded. "I can. My soul just doesn't expel itself all the way."

"Interesting . . . When you feel up to it, I would like to study you."

Namu looked like he did not agree with that suggestion at all. He shook his head at his teacher, who ignored him.

Mr. Vero continued, "As for that door, you can't tell anyone about it for obvious reasons. We don't want any more kids getting stuck in there like you did. You were lucky. Anyone else would probably have died."

"But why is it here?"

Mr. Vero smiled. "That door is why our world changed. That is where all the disintegrated weapons went."

Molly was perplexed. "But . . . but why at a school?"

Mr. Vero chuckled, then got up to leave. "It's always the same questions."

He turned to Namu. "I'll meet you at the usual time tomorrow. When Molly is ready, send her back to her room."

Then he left.

"But . . . why a school? And what did he mean the same questions?" Molly asked.

But Namu waved off her questions to ask one of his own. "You asked me something before. At the fountain. Or you tried to. What was it?"

Molly was surprised that he would bring that up now. Suddenly, she felt uncomfortable and ready to go to her own room. She wanted to call her parents but realized she couldn't. She had forgotten that she didn't even have a phone and that they thought she was dead.

Loneliness sank into her. Did she have anyone to talk to? Obviously not if she wasn't allowed to tell anyone about the door. So, she couldn't talk about what had just happened to her, no matter how traumatic?

Except for him . . . She could talk to Namu. But why did Namu know?

"It isn't important," she answered. "How do you—" Suddenly, she remembered something. "Why is the door in your room?"

He brushed her off again, a stern expression in his eyes. "Your question at the fountain was important. What was it?"

She had already told him she was an empty vessel, so it wasn't like that was new. And if he was the only one she could speak with about the door, besides the teacher . . .

"Sometimes, spirits try to take me over because I'm an empty vessel. I saw you doing something. Mrs. Sleck refuses to teach me how to protect myself until I build a better foundation. I don't know what that means. I just wanted to know—"

"I'll train you," he interrupted.

She flinched in shock.

"I'll train you either during your first or second break. I'm sure Mr. Vero will lend us his classroom. Once you get your new phone, I'll give you my number so we can work things out on a day-to-day basis."

"Oh, okay." She had not been expecting that, but maybe if she met him on some days and he helped her, she could learn more about the door too.

All of what she had just experienced felt like a dream but a vivid dream that filled her head with questions. It had been terrifying but somehow less terrifying than being in the place of ice. In the world she had just been in, that petrified world, she still felt like herself. She never felt she might lose herself. Even though she feared she might die, she felt as though she would die as herself. In that world, she did not feel like she would be lost in a black oblivion of ice, never to be seen again, like she had felt since she was young.

"Is that a yes?" Namu asked her.

Molly nodded.

"Okay." He got up and returned to sit in his chair at his desk to watch her. "Whenever you're ready to leave, I'll help you."

It didn't take her long to be ready. It did take her a while, though, to become steadier on her feet. Namu helped her get out of bed and then led her down his hall, where they ran into Derrin, who gave them a weird look. Namu took her to the entrance of one of the restrooms on his hall.

She was a mess. Her hair was full of sweaty oil, her face thinner and paler than before, and her eyes looked lost and shallow.

She would have to shower once she found the strength, but she was too weak now.

Namu then supported her down the stairs to her hall. After that, she insisted she go the rest of the way by herself.

There was a surprise waiting at her door.

It was Ova. She was sitting on the ground in front of her door, almost half asleep, with her legs crossed and her body leaning against the wood. Ova didn't look up until Molly stopped and stood in front of her, staring at her saddened friend.

It was then that Ova's thin pink lips pressed down into a frown as she lifted her head, heavy with tight braids, to meet Molly's teary eyes. Shock stilled every muscle in Ova's body before she pounced up from the ground and wrapped her arms around Molly, almost dragging her down.

"Where were you? I was so worried! I called! I asked Lily! I asked the teachers! I begged for them to let me in your room!" She pushed Molly back for a second and held her out at arm's length. "You look horrible! What happened! Where did you go!"

"How long have you been waiting here?" Molly asked, her voice hollow and breaking with emotion.

"How long? Every chance I got. I do my homework here! My online classes. Waiting for you to reemerge from this door! And do you know how bad this hall smells?"

Molly couldn't help but to smile and hug her friend tighter.

She let Ova into the room, and they both sat on the bed. The worst part was that she could not tell Ova where she had been, and she told her so. All she said was that Kren had her go somewhere. Ova asked if that was the mini-troll. Molly said yes and that one of the teachers had taken her where he needed her to be.

Instantly, Ova knew that teacher was Mr. Vero, and then Ova filled in the rest of the story by herself. Molly wondered if filling in the blanks, even though she had to know those blanks were forged, helped Ova feel better. Ova decided that Molly had taken an insightful trip, maybe even one for Molly to try to find her god to follow.

Molly only nodded and didn't say a thing. It was such a typical conclusion for Ova to come to.

After that, Ova showed how much she wanted to take care of Molly. She took her to the bathroom, helped Molly get in the shower, and handed her things whenever needed. She brushed Molly's hair. Then, when Molly lay down to sleep, Ova prayed over her to her gods while pressing on the axe tattoo on her right forearm with two fingers. She set out a tarot spread on Molly's stomach and seemed satisfied with whatever answers she got. She then took out a leaf, put it on Molly's forehead, and told her to sleep. It smelled like daisies with a hint of mint. Then she kissed Molly goodnight on the cheek.

Namu

Chapter Twenty-Four

Namu was very lucky that Molly was an empty vessel. He had never heard of that before, which irked him a little, but under that irritation, he was relieved.

Somehow, she had survived without expelling her soul from that cocoon.

She was lucky. He was lucky.

He decided he would not let his luck go to waste. Or maybe it wasn't the chasing of luck that kept him going. Maybe it was the anger he still felt at himself for what could have happened.

And the anger he felt at his friend.

But he would deal with that later.

First, he was going to try to get rid of that door.

The desk his laptop normally sat on had been hard to get through the hole in the enchanted wall, but he had done it. Somehow, though, the small dresser that normally sat in front of the wall would barely budge when he pulled it. It was as if it had magnets that wanted to fix it in its normal spot near the wall or a glue spell that would not let it go over the threshold.

He tried running at it, kicking at it, tipping it, and even pouring some random transformation drinks on it, but nothing worked.

Exhausted and over it, he turned away, needing to take a breather and think of another tactic to try. Maybe a spell to make the floor slick somehow. But when he turned back around, he saw that the desk he had worked to get into the small room was sitting back in his room. How? And now the wall was back up and the small dresser was, where it always sat, in its rightful place.

Fine. He would destroy his room if it meant keeping other students from harm. He didn't mind getting kicked out of the school. Not at all. He could guilt-trip Mr. Vero to keep helping him when it came to filling up the missing parts of his soul if he had to. The parts that those creatures had eaten.

But then something stopped him. What if the only way to get those parts of himself back was by getting it directly from those creatures? Was that possible? Was that worth a try? How would he know, though, if he caught those things, what parts were his and what belonged to others? They might have eaten many people's souls over the years.

No. It wasn't worth it. He was going to let the room burn. With one single lovely spell, he would burn it to the ground. Anything to keep people away from that door, away from the fate he and Molly had been forced to face.

He took the quartz wand he had in his drawer, then began to draw the symbol for "ignite"—a circle around a twisted flame— all over his desk, the ground, and the walls. Then, with a whisper and a rub of salt between his fingers, he flicked the grains at each symbol and watched as they flickered to fire. After he lit each one, he left the room, closed the door, then leaned against it, wanting to feel the heat.

But no heat came. And soon, he realized no smoke was escaping his room near his feet.

Shoving in his key and ripping open the door, he found no flames and no symbols.

He pulled out his phone and saw he didn't have time to try anything else. He needed to meet with Molly like he had promised. To train her. It was one small deed to make up for almost taking her life.

"Have you been in there before?" Molly asked.

She was clean today. Her curls sprang up on all ends, and her brown eyes filled with questions. She also had some color to her cheeks. She was asking about the nightmare world that he never cared to talk about. But it made sense. She had every right to have questions.

"I was locked in there before, just like you," Namu answered as he set up Mr. Vero's room for the both of them. Today's lesson would be short. He just needed to become familiar with her soul, just like Mr. Vero had with him during their first few lessons.

"How did you get out?"

"I expelled my entire soul." He didn't look at her as he set one of Mr. Vero's favorite items down on a desk: a black marble slab for Molly to lay her hand on. "I know you said you can't expel yourself, but can you bring your soul out just a little?"

"I used to—I think I can. I just feel it's not really there since those creatures . . ." She trailed off.

His heart skipped a beat. He bit the inside of his cheek, trying to erase the thoughts of what those creatures did to her and him from his mind.

"If you didn't have a soul, I'm not sure you would be alive." He wasn't entirely certain that was correct, but it was his best guess. "So, it has to still be in you."

She only shrugged her freckled shoulders.

"Well, put your hand here, palm up."

She did. Her skin was very pale compared to his. He almost wanted to put his hand on top of hers to compare, but he didn't. There was something more important he needed to compare.

"Tell me what you want in life," he said.

Since he was a novice when it came to teaching, he needed to know more about her to get his soul to call to hers. He knew there might be little things that would work. Mr. Vero had proven that. Namu had seen him pick up things by casual conversation or, sometimes, even from someone who had not spoken to him at all, but Namu didn't work like that. He couldn't examine people that deeply.

"I don't know . . ."

"You have to know."

"But I really don't."

Maybe it was too deep a question, especially from someone she barely knew. Maybe he was delving too far to get her soul to come out. He had just figured that the deeper the question, the stronger his hold on her soul would be.

"Okay. What's your favorite color?"

"I . . . I don't know."

"How do you not know your favorite color?"

He felt bad when her fingers flinched at his tone. He just didn't understand why she was keeping these things from him if she wanted him to help her. The questions weren't that hard. They were things he thought about every day and night. He knew what he wanted for his life. Didn't everybody? And didn't everyone at least have a favorite color?

"I just don't."

"Favorite food?"

She shrugged.

"Seriously?"

She pulled her hand away, and he let her. The black marble was now bare without her warm flesh. What else could he ask her, then? Was there a different approach to this? Was there any way they could connect?

What about her need and want to train? Was it like his?

"*Why* do you want to learn from me, exactly?"

"I'm sorry. I just don't know that much about myself. I . . ."

Oh. She thought he was reprimanding her. Asking why she was even here if she wasn't answering his questions. "No. I mean, what exactly will you gain from it?"

She looked at the marble circle that her hand had been on. "I just want to learn how to protect myself . . . from spirits."

It wasn't exactly why he worked with Mr. Vero, so he pressed deeper. "What happens?"

"They see me all the time. They try to touch me and then I go to this place of purple ice. I then drown. I . . . almost lose myself."

That was it. He had it.

Just like him, she knew what it felt like to lose her own essence. She had the fear, like him, of not knowing if her real self would ever return or if it was even still there. At least, he hoped he was right.

"Put your hand back on the marble slab," he instructed.

This time, he dug into that part of himself, the part he hated looking into. The pieces that were missing. The fact that he would never be whole because he had lost bits of himself along the way on this journey.

With ease, his light-blue soul lifted a strand of hers. It took several minutes to bring forth anymore of it. Her breathing hitched as she tried to calm herself, until finally, he expelled some of her soul's essence in the shape of half her arm.

It was perfect. There was not a single hole. Not a single bite.

He let her soul slip back inside her physical arm and tried to swallow his anger. He knew it was not fair to be mad at her. It wasn't her fault that she was different. He knew that. But she had been in that world for days and seemed not to have lost a single ounce of her soul. That irked him. It irked him even more that, as much as he had studied spirit magick, he had never heard of an empty vessel before. He would have to do some research on it. Why hadn't Mr. Vero ever brought that up if it was something that could help him?

Molly took her hand off the marble again and rubbed her arm. "So, all the weapons, when they disappear, they go there? In that world? Is that what that dust is?"

"I don't know if that's what the dust is, but, yes. And now, some of those metals, whatever they call them, are in your veins, your body, and in your magick." He wondered if she felt it roaming through her like he did. That slow and steady burn that was close to anger.

"But, isn't that bad?" Molly asked. "Now you and Mr. Vero have that in you too."

"Mr. Vero had it in him before."

"He had been in that world already?"

He didn't answer her. He thought it was obvious. Instead, he went to put the marble slab away. He had learned what he could from her for the day. He would have to figure out how to help her another time. And he would, after he had dealt with what was burning in his pocket and he had researched what exactly she was.

"What do you do with it? With the chaotic metal in your veins?"

He didn't face her.

"I live with it."

The marble slab clanked when he opened the long gray cabinet above one of the long tables on the side of the room.

"Is that why you had to get rid of my phone?"

She had a new phone now. Mr. Vero had put Namu's number in it. "Yes. It messes up phones and then the chaos spreads into this world a little."

Namu already had to deal with that last year.

He waited, but Molly didn't say anything else. "I'm going to let you go now. Enjoy the rest of your break. We will keep meeting like this and get to the point where you build a better soul-magick foundation."

"But . . . we didn't do much of anything today."

That was because there was too much on his mind. He had just wanted to know for sure that she was fine before he worked with her. If she hadn't been, he would have worked on them finding a way to heal themselves, but she didn't need that; only he did. So, now, he knew he would have to put himself to the side and figure her out. He would work out how to give her what she needed and how to destroy that door. Those were his two tasks now.

"I'll see you tomorrow," he said, leaving her in the room.

He went outside to the courtyard. Only half of break had passed, so he had time to confront Lily if he found them.

And there Lily was, observing the students as they were pretending to read a book about gnomes.

They hadn't talked in days. Lily had tried to approach him, but he had given them the cold shoulder. Lily had apparently approached Mr. Vero when Namu was trying to rescue Molly, but he had told Lily that Namu was sick. Lily had tried to come to his room too.

He wondered if they had realized that Molly had been gone also.

Lily's wide shoulders stiffened for a moment as Namu approached. They put their hands behind their back and smiled. "Finally willing to talk to me?"

"You're lucky. You know that?"

"Why would you say that?" They wore a lopsided smile and tilted their head to the side. He knew it was their defensive position. A position to get him to let his guard down.

He took the gold bracelet out of his pocket and showed it to Lily. They accidentally let their cool demeanor slip for a second as their eyes widened, but then they smiled again. "What's that?"

"Don't play with me, Lily. You know exactly what this is. I've seen you use it even before we came to this school. You used to brag about it. Why would you give this to Molly?"

Lily looked away. "I see you know her name now. Completely susceptible, is she not?"

"Is that why? She was one of your young and dumb things to play with? For what reason?"

"Is this seriously why you've been so angry at me? Is this why you haven't talked to me in days? Where did you even disappear to?"

If he wasn't prone to second-guessing himself, he would have said that, when they turned to face him again, Lily had tears wanting to form in their eyes before they blinked them away. "Before, you wouldn't have cared what I did with that bracelet."

Except this time, you almost got someone killed, Namu thought.

"I just want to know why."

"I just—" Lily paused. "I knew she was special and I know—*I knew*, sorry—that you were hiding something. I just thought that if she could find a way into your room, it would prove that. I didn't think . . ."

"Didn't think what?" He wanted to push them. He needed to push them.

"I didn't think that the two of you would disappear and I would have no clue where either of you went!"

People were looking at them now. Lily took notice and started storming off toward the forest. Namu followed.

"I wouldn't have had to disappear if you hadn't done that. If you have to know anything, know that you almost got Molly killed, Lily! You almost killed her! A poor, clueless, innocent girl."

One who didn't even seem to know herself.

"But how? Why? How does sneaking into your room do that? And what did I see in there before, when I followed you in looking for her?"

"Why does that matter?"

"Because it does!"

"No. What matters is you trusting me when I say that I can't tell you!"

"No! What matters is you telling me everything, Namu! You've been there for me through *everything*. Through my pronoun changes, all through non-magickal school, throughout the bullying, throughout moving and going to bigger and better places, and even through the first half of this school! You've always been here. Until now! Until last year! I just don't understand. I don't understand why you're leaving me behind."

"I'm not leaving you behind."

"Yes, you are! You know how important it is for me to succeed. You know how important you are to me. And somehow, you're surpassing me when you never cared before. And while doing that, you're leaving me behind. Keeping me in the dark. You're taking both things that are important away from me!"

Lily kept walking, their hair angry threads battling in the breeze, but Namu stopped following. Honestly, with everything that had been going on, he had not known that he was that important to Lily. That keeping something from Lily, even though it was something that could save them from themself, was killing Lily inside. Didn't they realize that he wasn't surpassing them, that he was drowning, sick, and angry? That he had an emptiness that he was trying to fill? It had nothing to do with them.

But during everything, this whole time, this whole thing, he had only thought of himself. He had thought Lily was okay. That Lily was more than okay. That they were on the right path, while he was on the wrong one. When, really, Lily was fighting a never-ending battle. One he should not have missed. They were trying to be as successful as their father.

It was something he should have known they always wanted. They always talked about their dad, and ever since Lily's life had changed, their perspective on life had changed too. It was then that they began tackling bigger things and had a desperate need to learn and be closer to their father. He remembered the long nights of Lily complaining about how their father was never home and how Lily only had Namu to keep them company, only had Namu who understood them, only had Namu who they felt comfortable around.

And Namu had taken all that comfort away from them to only focus on himself. He had taken himself further and further away from Lily, leaving a giant hole between them.

Lily reached the trees and then spun around. Their eyes were wide, and they threw up their arms. "AND NOW YOU WON'T EVEN COME AFTER ME!?"

Namu couldn't help but laugh, cross his arms, and stand there and wait for Lily to come back to him. He watched Lily huff and stand still. Finally, after at least five minutes, they came storming back up to him. "What?"

"It had nothing to do with you, Lily. I'm sorry. I just needed some time for myself to figure something out."

They shook their head and would not look him in the eyes. "Something you can't share with me?"

He didn't grab Lily's arm. He stayed back and waited for their gaze to come close to his face. He didn't care if it didn't meet his eyes. "Lily, it's private. I will share it if I'm ever ready and if it's ever the right time. Now is not the right time. You have to trust me. I'm sorry I didn't think about us at all while I've been trying to figure this thing out. I'm sorry that you've been having as hard a time with it as I have and that I didn't see it."

They looked to his lips and would not let their eyes travel up from there. "You're asking me to level up our friendship?"

"I guess . . ." If that meant trusting him and letting him keep a few things from them.

They sighed. "I accept that. I'll try to trust you, although I cannot accept not knowing what you're talking about. It will continue to eat me up inside. But because I care about you so much, I will let it. For you. It is just not in me to *not* care about what you're hiding or to not think about it. Which you know."

He guessed that was fair. He wrapped one arm around Lily and took the golden bracelet out of his pocket to place it back on their left arm.

"There's another thing I know you normally don't do that I need you to do this time. I need you to apologize to Molly and tell her what this was for."

Lily looked taken aback. "Why?"

"For growth."

He did not say it was for Molly's growth as much as it was for Lily's too.

Molly

Chapter Twenty-Five

"We're going to try the same thing we did yesterday," Namu instructed.

He had Molly sitting at a desk with her arm out. She didn't understand why it was always her arm they messed with.

"Are you ready?"

She was not. She hated this. She hadn't thought that his training would involve him shoving her back into the ice-cold world of her mind to drown her. Did he even know what he was doing? Yesterday's attempt had been a disaster. He had to carry her to the nurse because she wouldn't wake up after hitting her head on the floor. That's why she was sitting in a chair now. The whole thing scared her and made her not want to return today. She thought they were supposed to be building foundations, not forcing her into the one thing that broke her.

Molly wanted to text Kren to tell him someone was trying to teach her to protect herself, but it had been days since Molly

Adora Michaels

had a new phone, and she still did not know how to get Kren's number. She was too shy to ask anyone if they had it. She also realized he didn't have any social media accounts. She would have to make him one and make herself a new one. She had rarely used hers before and, since she had been at Lockdrest, never touched it at all. She didn't want anyone knowing she had made the decision to leave. Not yet. It was better for the non-magickal world she came from, including her parents, to think she was gone for good until she was able to protect herself and go back.

She could only hope that if Kren hadn't heard from her, he would come to the school to see if she was okay or demand to know why she wasn't answering him.

Maybe then she could tell him about the door.

"Molly? Are you ready?"

"No," she squeaked and accidentally jerked her arm away from Namu's touch. "I mean . . . I just need a second."

His eyebrows drew in, agitated. "I'll pull back when it becomes too much. This isn't like what happens to you out in the real world. I'm not going to take you over."

But then why did it feel the same as when a spirit tried it?

"We'll try this for a few more days to see if it gets us anywhere. See if you can somehow not drown."

"Sink or swim?" Molly mumbled.

"Exactly," Namu breathed.

She still did not like the idea. "What happened to the basics? To building a foundation first?"

"I'm working with the materials I have, like building something. The basics you need may be different than what I needed to get where I am. We need to see exactly what you're made of and what you can do. Then we can go from there."

Now Molly really thought Namu did not know what he was doing. During the first few days, the most he had done was ask her questions about herself that she could not answer. Then, in the days after that, he had asked her the same questions again, as if she had thought about those questions and would have different answers to give.

He didn't seem to understand that she didn't know certain things about herself. There were just some things she had never cared to dive into.

Then he had her do a few spirit magick spells to show him what she knew so far before he dove into questions about her being an empty vessel, like where exactly she went when spirits touched her and what exactly happened. He also had her try to draw the ice world of her mind.

Now they were here. He wanted to take her arm with his spiritual hand and plunge her into depths that she might never escape from. He wanted her to trust him when she had never trusted anyone with this vulnerable piece of herself.

His spirit expelled of his arm. He was ready, whether or not she was. He gave her a look, his brown eyes wide with impatience, as he nodded to the table and her arm. She knew it wasn't easy for him—or for anyone—to expel their spiritual essence, even just a little. It expended lots of energy, and he still had classes for the rest of the day.

She did as his eyes told her to do. She kept her arm still but bit her lip tight and closed her eyes.

Then she was there.

There was never an icy wind in the world, just an eerie frozenness that lingered and sliced into her skin on all sides of her. She didn't know if a wind would have been better or worse.

She tried not to gulp when she looked down at the sheet of purple ice with water underneath. She was waiting for him to pull her under. She knew it was coming soon. Too soon.

She could feel his ice-cold grip on her arm. Dread was leaking through into her insides, hardening the only places left of her that were still warm and alive.

The worst part was the waiting. She didn't know how it worked. She didn't know why sometimes the ice was already broken and sometimes there wasn't even a crack. But she could faintly feel the weakening of the sheet beneath her.

Her breathing quickened. She hugged her arms, hoping they wouldn't be cut by the ice shards when she fell through.

A crack. It started as a little fissure beneath her big toe and worked its way out and then around to crawl beneath her little toe.

Another crack was forming beneath her heel. She could feel its unevenness. She wanted to step away, but she knew that pressure would only make it break faster.

Another splinter. This one was on the side of her left foot. It trailed away from her, traveling fast into the unknown.

Watching, waiting, she stared down at what would soon be a jagged hole as one more crack formed, this one thinner than the rest.

Then a gloss of silver trailed the thin line, chasing the splintering ice right under her feet.

A glossy silver that was warm.

She moved her foot to get a closer look. That was the wrong decision.

The ice broke, and she fell with it. She just had time to see that the silver that had layered itself on the ice had turned black.

Her head hit ice before the water rushed over her.

She couldn't kick. She couldn't swim.

She could only sink.

But then she felt something new. There was a heaviness on her arm, and it lifted the tiniest bit, allowing her access to her body and her limbs.

She took the chance and fought to the surface, even though the entire world wanted to weigh her down.

She tried to grab the ice that hadn't broken, but her hands kept slipping along it. Her fingers were too wet, and the ice had no give.

It let her loose, and she dunked back into the water, flailing her arms and trying to grab the ice again. She needed it to hold her. She needed it to hold steady, or maybe she could just find a crack and dig her fingernails into it.

But then something warm touched her hand. It helped her hand hold its place.

She threw her other hand up and found another spot of warmth.

She held herself steady, her body still immersed in the water. Her arms were bent at odd angles as she held onto the ice like some creature. She needed a moment to breathe, to collect herself. Was Namu doing this? Had he found some way to keep her afloat if she fought hard enough for it? Had he found some way to change the ice?

Her muscles almost gave up, but she refused to let them. She squeezed and strained, trying to lift her body out. She would not let go of the one thing she could feel that wasn't cold. She did not grab onto anything else, fearful of losing the one hold on life she had.

It was a little easier to pull herself up once she got her knees out of the water, even though the ice broke in a few more places until she scooted to a thicker layer of ice. She had a moment to breathe, but she expected another crack. She never let her hands leave the circular black metal plates that had melded themselves with the ice.

She felt Namu let go of her completely, then a gasp escaped her lungs as if squeezed by a fist. She was back in the room.

"Didn't pass out," Namu commented, seeming satisfied. "I loosened my grip on you a little this time."

So, that was what he did to let her move more freely. That had helped her swim back up.

His face tensed with concern. "What's wrong?"

She must have looked panicked or stunned. "I . . . I didn't drown. I saved myself."

"That's good!" Namu's brows relaxed. "Why don't you seem happy, then?"

"The metal was there. On the ice. It became a part of the ice in spots. It helped me crawl out of the water."

"What metal?"

She looked down at his chest, then back to his brown eyes.

"The stuff from that nightmare world?" he asked. There was silence for a beat. "Were you able to control it?"

"I . . . I don't know." She couldn't remember if she had asked for it to save her in some way.

"Do you want to try again?"

Abruptly, she stood before tripping out of the hard desk seat. "No. I . . . I don't think I can. I don't want to anymore." At least not for a while.

He looked confused. "But we're getting somewhere."

Before, when she had the incidents all throughout her life, they had been spaced few and far between. She had never had to face that place for days in a row. And now, she was being asked to drown more than once in a single day? Did he not realize how traumatic it was for her? To get torn up, for the ice to freeze itself into all her muscles until she couldn't move or breathe and had to wait to lose herself? Had she not made it clear to him when she had explained how it felt?

"I just can't today. Or for a while." She needed a break.

"You have a chance to finally get to do what you've been wanting to do for a long time. You told me that. You have no idea how lucky you are that you're actually making progress within a week! And now you want to stop? I thought you wanted to figure this out!"

"I do—I ju—can't right—I just need a break. It's a lot."

"Isn't it a lot *more* knowing you can't protect yourself and almost losing yourself whenever you run into a spirit? You told me it sometimes even happens in your sleep."

It was. It bothered her every day, but her body, her mind, whatever it was that was affected by going to that place, could not deal with going to it again right now or tomorrow. She couldn't do it multiple days in a row. Even the thought of it . . .

Panic stirred in her, making it hard to breathe. Normally, she could remain calm. She had taught herself to do that. She had to teach herself to do that in order to not make scenes in school or around her friends. But Namu was pushing some kind of button she didn't know she had.

"Do you want to lose pieces of yourself?" Namu kept pushing. "You went into that nightmare world and came out unscathed. Some of us did not get to do that. You get to do that and then decide to just lose yourself here?"

"It isn't like that."

"Yes, it is. If you aren't willing to work to save yourself, you're willing to lose yourself."

She forgot she saw him practicing things every day. Molly closed her eyes in frustration. He just didn't get it. "Why do you practice? What are you doing with Mr. Vero?"

He looked away. Anger had her gripping the desk, with blood pounding in her ears by the time he answered.

"I would rather not talk about it."

Why did he get to push her and ask her questions constantly but then refuse to answer hers?

"Okay. Then, I would *rather not* do this again."

"What's wrong with you?"

"What's wrong with *you*?" she snapped back at him.

"I'm so sorry that I'm used to being around people who actually work hard and people who actually know themselves."

He was being sarcastic. She could almost taste the bitterness of his words.

"I just assumed that, since you're facing a life-and-death situation, you would try harder."

"Try harder? Where you take me, I drown! I bleed! I suffocate! I'm paralyzed! Do you really want me to try harder doing those things?"

"No. I want you to try harder not to lose yourself. I want to help you find a way to not have to go through those things."

But she had to go through those things every time she went back there. It never got easier. Even if it ever became easier at some point, even if she found a way to save herself from drowning, there were still too many memories and emotions tied to that place that she knew would never leave. She would rather never go back again.

"Did you think that maybe I lose a piece of myself every time I go back there?" Molly whispered.

Namu shut up at that and held her gaze. Then he looked down at his own hand and squeezed it shut. "How bad was it for you in the cocoon?"

The cocoon? Why would he want to know? But fear was dilating his pupils. That cocoon must have been his most traumatic experience. His most traumatic place.

"The cocoon was horrifying. Another horrifying place I would rather not go to again. But it's nothing compared to the place I go to in my mind. I would rather not visit either. I would rather erase them both."

He didn't look back at her. Instead, he pressed his palms against his eyes as if trying to stamp out the fear she had seen. "I understand."

Molly was going to tell people she was an empty vessel. Working with Namu, someone truly knowing that part of herself that she had always hidden, there was a power in that. There was strength she had never had access to before. Just like there had been strength in standing up for herself by saying she never wanted to go back to that place.

She needed more of that strength.

She was tired of hiding a small part of herself. The part of herself that she actually knew. The part of her she had confidence in because she had been through so much in that place. And someone knowing about it somehow made it lighter.

It was nearing the end of break, and Molly didn't want to be late to her next class. If she had the courage to do this, she had to do it now. Especially since she was still buzzing with adrenaline from her confrontation with Namu.

She found Ova near the library, grabbed her arm, and started tugging her up the grand staircase.

More people needed to know, and she could only think of two other people who she had come close to conversing with. Koz and Rem who could also be friends at some point.

"Molly! It's almost class time. Where are you taking me?" Ova asked, but Molly ignored her. She wanted to be spontaneous. She wanted to make this decision for herself.

She wished she could find Lily, too, but she hadn't seen Lily anywhere over the past few days. It was as if Lily was avoiding her. Or maybe Molly had been too busy and hadn't looked hard enough.

"Molly! It took me forever to help you catch up on all your classes! You can't miss another one! I can't either!" But for some reason, even in all her complaining, Ova let Molly keep tugging her up the stairs. They had maybe less than ten minutes.

"This is important," Molly insisted.

She took Ova to the technology room and dragged her through the door.

"Why are we—"

Koz and Rem were in there, as usual. They were packing up, preparing for their own classes.

When Koz saw her, he stopped midway through putting a laptop in a bag. "Hey, Molly. Something wrong with your new phone?"

"I just want all three of you to know that I'm an empty vessel," Molly announced. Her lungs exhaled the words. Her shoulders sagged in sweet relief. It felt so good to let that loose. Now more people than just Namu, Mr. Vero, and Kren knew. Now she had people she could talk to who knew that tiny piece of her.

Koz paled, and Rem flapped her hands and squealed, perking up like Molly had never seen her do before.

Ova just looked confused. "A what?" she asked.

"It's just like in that game! In—" Rem enthused.

"Rem!" Koz interrupted her before backing up into the desk that held all the computers along with who knew how many phones. He pushed a button on one of the phones and lights sprang up all around the room, dancing on the walls with exhilarating music.

Molly didn't know what was happening. She could only laugh. She was elated. She was relieved she didn't have to hide anymore.

Namu

Chapter Twenty-Six

N amu couldn't believe he had pushed Molly to go to that place in her mind again if it was worse than when either of them had been trapped behind the door. He had just wanted her to do what he couldn't do for himself. And he was so used to Lily and Mr. Vero. They would have kept pushing themselves no matter how hard it got. Molly was different, though. She had more reasonable limits. She had dealt with trauma her whole life. Way longer than Namu had ever dealt with his.

So, why had Namu pushed her when she had said no?

He was an idiot. He had been wrong to do that to her, and he would never do it again. Everyone worked differently, and that was something he needed to respect.

But he had a pressing desire to figure Molly out. To understand why she was the only one who hadn't been destroyed out of everyone who had gone beyond the door. It might be because she was an empty vessel, but what did that mean?

He had tried researching it on his phone but couldn't find anything.

It was like the problem he had been having with the holes in his soul all over again. Any solution he tried or research he tried to look up didn't work. There was always something pushing back at him. Something not willing to give in.

He didn't blame Molly. Not anymore. Not after her outburst, which he had not expected from her. He blamed the door.

And that brought him back to needing to find a way to destroy it.

If he couldn't block it or eliminate it from the outside, he might have to slip inside and somehow destroy it from within.

Without dying.

But how?

It was his allotted time to work with Mr. Vero, but he had told his teacher that he needed a break instead. He was sticking to what he had decided the previous night. He would put his own problems aside and figure out what needed to be done. A whole class period and lunch were enough to give himself time to research.

He was going to scour the school's library. He knew that the door was too hidden, too new, too secret to have anything written about it yet. But empty vessels . . . He thought those were worth a try. He figured the chances of them being ancient, even if they were rare, was high. Which meant that there might be at least one book kept about them at the magickal school.

Namu heard a commotion coming from the near-empty library: Mrs. Yitter was screaming at the books on one shelf, and something was gushing and leaking and forming a puddle around her feet. A clear liquid was ballooning out of the pages and the bindings of the books that Mrs. Yitter was yanking off the shelves and dropping to the ground with multiple splats. Her striped pink-and-purple romper was swimming in the expanding puddle, and the light-blue rose she wore near her heart looked as though it were weeping.

"What's happening?" Namu asked, ducking when Mrs. Yitter threw a book his way on accident. At least he hoped it was on accident.

"The computers! Trying to make a system for these books and input them. The technology messes with them sometimes!" She only had a few more books to clear off the continually soaking shelf. It was as if there was some water system traveling through it that had sprung a leak.

"Can I help?"

"You can step back. I'll be with you in a moment. Just be glad none of these caught on fire or became slugged like last time. Slug slime is impossible to clean!" She tugged the last two books down, held them in her soaked arms, then dropped them to a table as she ran to the one computer that was turned on. "I have the hardest time with the history books, especially if we get a new one I have to put into the system," she explained as she typed, continually hitting the delete button.

"You don't want to know the type of things the system causes for those," someone said from behind him.

Namu jumped. It was the religious coordinator, wearing a light-blue dress with long flowy sleeves.

"Oh dear, Daphen!" Mrs. Heard yelled, walking over to Mrs. Yitter while she continued to type. She pulled Mrs. Yitter into a hug, squeezing her tight, and Mrs. Yitter looked over her shoulder at the bookshelf. Namu looked too. The waterworks had stopped. "If you wanted a bath, I could have drawn you up one! You didn't have to go that far today and get all the books wet!"

Mrs. Yitter pursed her lips before letting them slide into an annoyed smile when Mrs. Heard let her go. She looked at the religious coordinator with adoration, then looked down at the wet books with disgust. "I hate techno magick."

"And apparently, it hates you!"

Mrs. Yitter laughed.

Namu stood there awkwardly, hating wasting his time, but he understood the frustration. Since techno magick had been put into the school, there had been many hiccups in the system that ended up requiring more magick, spells, and energy to clean up. It was because the magickal incentive that writers put into books was reacting to the techno magick and not blending the way it should. It would take Mrs. Yitter the rest of the day to dry out those books.

He admired the smile that Mrs. Heard was giving her wife and couldn't help smiling himself at her suggestive wink when she looked down at the librarian's soaked clothes. Maybe it wouldn't take too long with the two of them working on it together.

Mrs. Yitter realized she had forgotten about Namu. Her cheeks flushed, which made Mrs. Heard howl with laughter.

"What can I help you with?" Mrs. Yitter asked, avoiding Namu's eyes while squeezing each of her fingers as if trying to regain her calm.

"I was just wondering if you had any books on empty vessels."

The pulling and squeezing of her fingers stopped. Her cheeks returned to their normal color and then her cutting brown eyes took him in. "I've never heard a student ask that before. Why?"

He could feel Mrs. Heard's scrutinizing gaze on him. "Hey! Aren't you that boy who works with Mr. Vero? The one who skipped a Spirit Magick class. The one who . . . Oh, never mind. I think that's why, Daphen."

"Oh." Some memory sprang in Mrs. Yitter's eyes. "I'm afraid we don't. I've only heard of empty vessels by word of mouth. I have an older brother, though, who has his own personal library and has collected many highly sought-after books that he has only let me glimpse." She let out an agitated sigh. "I could reach out to him and ask."

"If he would even tell you," Mrs. Heard said.

Namu felt annoyed. "Well, thank you," he replied, turning to leave them with the mess so he could try to accomplish something by the end of the day. "Please let Mr. Vero know if you do happen to find one."

He disappeared behind some shelves farther away from the librarian and Mrs. Heard, then put his hand on one of the shelves, waiting for one to light up down the line.

Nothing.

He did it again until he found a section that might help.

There were no guns anymore, no bombs, nothing like that in this world. But could magick make something similar? The world he despised held all the disintegrated metals from those weapons. This world ate them up right before everything disappeared behind that door. Could he produce something that could disrupt that process? That atmosphere? That world? Something that could maybe destroy those creatures and that entire place?

Almost like the mix of techno magick and the old magick in the library, there had to be something he could mix to cause a reaction in that nightmare world that would be a disaster.

He then could close the door, leaving no one to fix it.

He wished he had someone to talk over his ideas with and ask for help. But he didn't. He knew what Mr. Vero would say. Mr. Vero thought the door was essential. He couldn't see how much more important it was to stop the killings and the eating of students' souls.

He couldn't let Mr. Vero know what he was trying to do.

And Molly . . . Molly didn't have the anger that he did about it. She hadn't been eaten alive. She hadn't watched someone almost be killed.

He took a book about multiplying metals off a shelf.

Molly

Chapter Twenty-Seven

Every time Molly was in the technology room for class without Rem or Koz there, it felt odd. Everyone else in class seemed to feel the same way because other students kept glancing over at the two empty chairs and computers in the corner of the room.

She did not understand how Rem and Koz understood techno magick on the level they did when they were so young. It barely made sense to her. Her Technology class was a nightmare. Apparently, some symbols could be interwoven into coding to do certain things. There was also interchanging of spirit magick into technological devices to give and get in return. Then there was coding to create some kind of vacuum for the technology to gain or retrieve specific energies. They were discussing all the different types of energies now, along with why certain devices could only take on so much energy, how energies were transferred, and how they were directed by code.

It was all linked to old magick and how old magick worked with incentives, direction, and the flow of energy. But the energy for new magick was in another dimensional world.

Molly was happy that this was an elective class and that it didn't have any more levels. She was frustrated at Kren for signing her up for it. He'd probably never taken it himself since it was so new. She was sure she would fail unless she asked Koz and Rem for help.

But she felt bad even thinking about asking because Koz had been awkward around her since she had told them she was an empty vessel. She had Rem's attention, though, and now she didn't know what to make of her rash decision. Had it been right or wrong? Because, ever since then, it felt as though she were trying to force Ova, Rem, and Koz together.

They didn't fit particularly well. Whenever Molly dragged Ova into the technology room, Ova got frustrated with Rem for not paying attention to her. She and Koz refused to answer her religious questions.

Molly found it pretty funny, but she could tell Koz was annoyed, especially since they were taking up their gaming time. Molly was scared she would annoy them even more if she asked for their help now.

Namu: Tomorrow?

Molly sighed. She had canceled on Namu today. She was tired and didn't want to deal with him or anything to do with spirit magick. Her last class had already been enough. They had to make their spirits go in and out of a few trees outside and say what they felt from them. Since the incident behind the door, Molly had been unable to get her spirit to expel at all, other than the one time Namu had done it. So, she had not gotten anything out of that class but frustration.

Molly: Maybe.

She hoped he wasn't mad at her. She knew that Ova was getting irritated with her. After Molly had told her what she knew about empty vessels, Ova had become way more persistent about Molly finding a god or goddess to follow. Molly still didn't want to. She didn't want to face all the choices and pick the wrong one. She didn't have time to look up the most popular ones, and she didn't want to go by Ova's opinion because a small part of her wanted to make her own decision and not be influenced by someone else.

Her classmates were getting up from their desks. They must have been dismissed. Molly hopped up with relief, leaving her book of diagrams and coding, which she knew she would never understand, on the table for the teacher to collect.

Lily was waiting outside the room for her.

"Oh! Hey," Molly said. She tried to smile but found herself too nervous to do so. Lily's nose was scrunched up as if they were angry about something. Was it because Molly hadn't looked hard enough for Lily? There had been so much going on, and she had figured Lily hadn't wanted anything to do with her after days had passed. "I haven't seen you in a—"

She felt her arm. The bracelet wasn't there. Her cheeks caught fire. She remembered Namu tucking it into his pocket. He had taken it. But Lily didn't need to know that. They could think that it was in Molly's room unless Namu told them otherwise.

Lily stared down at Molly's arm leaning against the glass wall of the classroom as the teacher passed them. They looked like they might be contemplating Molly's demise. "I wanted to—I was told to tell you that the bracelet I gave you was a trick."

"What?" Molly's one word felt too small.

"Those bracelets, they can be charmed to work on people like you. I gave it to you so you would do things for me."

"People like me?"

"Yes. Susceptible people. Don't you know that about yourself?"

She was susceptible? Susceptible to what? Wanting a friend?

Molly's eyes were about to betray her and show Lily just how naive she had been. They were growing wet with tears.

"Well, anyway. I'm sorry." Lily turned to walk away.

"Wait!" Molly staggered after Lily but then stopped herself. She had thought that Lily was so cool. That Lily liked her. Molly had thought that she could be liked by someone who knew who they were, someone who fought for their beliefs the way Molly had always dreamed of, someone who was an inspiration and, in a way, a hero. Someone Molly could never be. "You . . . you didn't want to be my friend?"

Lily shook their head. "Susceptible. No, Molly. I wanted to use you."

Susceptible? She thought she knew what it meant. She knew the gist of the term. But she had to look it up on her phone to get the exact meaning. To learn that she was *liable to be influenced or harmed by others.*

Lily had used her? Lily had cornered her and had given her that bracelet because they had known that about her? Just in a couple days? They had known that by barely talking to her? By not even being her friend?

They had known—knew how desperate she was?

Molly slammed the door to her room shut and decided that she would not go to her last class. She also had a text from Ova that she would not answer. They were supposed to meet for break, but she threw her phone on the floor, hoping it would shatter into a million pieces.

Who knew if Ova was using her, too? Maybe she was trying to gather followers for a certain god. She sure acted like she was, with how she pushed her beliefs on other people.

And at some point, Molly might have fallen for it because she was susceptible.

Liable.

Allowing.

Permitting.

A follower.

The questions that Namu had asked her roamed in her head like a snake, coiling, squeezing, and biting until she threw herself on the bed, screaming and thrashing around.

Namu knew it too. He knew that Molly didn't know herself. That she was a nobody. He knew that she was susceptible. That the reason she had gone into that petrified world and almost died was because she was stupid and naive. That was why he had kept the bracelet. She was sure that he had been the one who told Lily to apologize to her too.

But why? Because he felt bad for her? Sorry for her? All her life, she had tried not to make a scene and tried to stay hidden, and somehow, she was more than easy to read. Somehow, people understood her better than she understood herself.

Somehow, they told her things about herself before those things had even crossed her own mind.

First, the empty vessel, and now this. Two things she hadn't fully known about herself had been shoved in her face.

Was it because she was an empty vessel that she was ignorant, mindless, naive, and dull, or was it because she was all those things that she had become an empty vessel? Had she been all those things her entire life? Since birth?

Would she ever even know? Did she have the capability? Was she a joke? Was she just trash?

Fingers lining her scalp, nails ready to bite and pull, she looked around her room. There was nothing there. Nothing. Just like her.

Then she felt it. She felt something by her ear. The small little earrings that Val had convinced her to get. No. That Molly had happily gotten so she could be just like Val. Had she even liked them? Had she actually wanted to get her ears pierced at all? How many decisions had been swayed because she only wanted to please someone? When, if ever, had she made a decision for herself?

She had always been so scared to lose herself, but, apparently, she had never truly known herself at all.

She ripped the earrings out and was happy to see blood.

That bright red blood was hers. It belonged to her.

She got up, her brain fighting the urge to fall into a trance, and went to her drawers. One by one, she jerked them open, pulled all the clothes out, and tossed them to the floor.

The ones with colors that made her rage inside, she ripped up. The ones that reminded her of her friends' styles, she promised to burn. The ones that she had decided to get only to please, she tore at with her teeth.

She would wear only one outfit now. Day in and day out until she was sent out to get another. The plain blue shirt and jeans she was wearing now. The one with the blood. The one with the memories. The one that would remind her that she needed and wanted to change.

She would no longer be susceptible to anyone else.

Namu

Chapter Twenty-Eight

Namu stormed into the technology room during lunch. He had made up an excuse to bypass Lily, Molly had bailed on him again, and he wasn't in the mood to eat.

He had stayed up most of the night with the few books he had found from the library and ravaged the internet.

He had a solid idea now. Something that might move the nightmare world behind the door off-center and push it over. It could even make the nightmare world too busy to worry about anything else that slipped through the door. But he needed Koz's help. Koz, who he had never approached before, even though many students went to him to solve their technical difficulties.

Namu wanted to ask Koz to build something into his phone. Something specific. Something infinite. Something that might not be possible, but Namu hoped it would be.

It looked like Koz and some girl with big blue eyes and messy hair that fell to her shoulders were setting up for the hour-long lunch period. He had heard that Koz preferred to eat in this room and spent every one of his breaks in that exact chair.

"Can we help you?" Koz asked him. His eyes were tired. There were no dark circles, but the gateway to his soul looked worn for the day, like he needed to sleep and recuperate.

"I wanted to ask you to build me something. An app."

Koz woke up a little at this. He looked over at the girl, who smiled a too-big smile and then plopped down in a chair before grabbing a purple tablet that Koz had set out.

"Build you something?" Namu could see his desire for a challenge. "What were you thinking?"

Namu had learned yesterday that through magick one could transfer metals if one needed to build something, but that it took a lot of work, a lot of energy, and usually took more than one person to do it. He had also learned that creating fake metals was something that they used to do in the past that had gotten banned. The metals had not been as strong as non-magickal ones and had caused all kinds of problems in the non-magickal world. A division of the magickal community had to go and clean up the mess.

"I recently learned that certain things can be created through techno magick," he said. It was a new study. Something about nano-bits, electrons, and techno magick made it possible, but it only lasted so long. "Metals can be created, right?"

Koz's chin lifted as he grinned. He looked impressed. "Yes. Those things *are* real, in a sense, but for only a moment. Same with the feel of it. You can physically feel the item but barely. It isn't as strong as the real thing, since it is a trick of the mind, using spirit magick linked to memory magick held in revers, with the added touch of the nano-bits and other things in our world. But—" Koz stopped himself and smiled. "I won't bore you with the details. Go on."

"What if you could make them infinite?" Like the fountain bubbles that had exploded a few days ago when Molly had first tried to talk to him. "What if they kept growing? What if they could keep being produced out of the technology through techno magick?" There had to be some kind of code.

Koz's face lit up, and he dug his hand into his cargo pants to pull out his phone. He began tapping things that Namu could not see, but his smile kept on growing.

"That's brilliant! I never thought of that! I actually have an app that does something similar. It creates water—but not water. Like what you were saying. It takes the elements I mentioned and a few more to combine them to temporarily make an imperfect material that then goes away. See!"

Koz put the phone down on the desk and pressed a button that was taking up almost the whole screen. It was blue with swirls of green on it. Immediately, water started raining up from the phone like a fountain. Some drops hit Namu. Some even disintegrated before they hit any surface. They were wet for only a moment, or maybe it was just a tickle, before they disappeared as if they had never existed.

"I can slow it down," Koz explained, putting his hand through the water spout to push a button on the screen. The spout grew smaller and slower. The drops were larger, and the spray was not reaching as far, but the water stayed longer before it disappeared. Some water lay on the desk now, never quite forming a puddle. "The less energy used up at a slower rate, the longer the imperfect-techno-material stays."

It was almost exactly what Namu had envisioned. "Can you make something like that with metal—like coins?"

Koz hit the middle button on the app, making the imperfect-techno-water turn off. "Yes! I could do that in a matter of ten minutes, since I have this system already set up. I just have to transfer and tweak a few things. I'll do it on my phone before putting it into my database. Then I'll transfer it to your phone. It will take me no time at all."

Koz almost missed the chair when he went to sit down. "You may want to sit, though."

Namu remained standing.

"Is this for a game or something?" Koz asked, turning his focus to his computer.

It took Namu a moment to realize he was asking him why he wanted the app. "Oh . . . yeah . . . Kind of."

"I don't know why I've never thought about what you suggested. I thought about other possibilities, of course, but I've never thought about metals. And the fact that you asked for coins . . . With the correct outlining and coding numbers, I could, of course, create little bits of anything or everything to a certain degree. At least things that can't move, right?"

He looked up at Namu as if assuming Namu understood, but Namu had no idea what he was talking about. Namu only knew as much as he had researched the previous night. When Namu didn't reply, Koz looked back down at his phone.

"If we could perfect this, it could really have an impact on gaming. After many years of testing, of course, to make sure it isn't dangerous. Mentally, like in the psychological sense, or physically." He reached down to pull out his laptop from his bag, then opened it on his lap.

It seemed like Koz knew a lot about a lot of things. It made Namu want to ask him more.

"Do you know anything about empty vessels?"

Koz's eyes were glued to his computer when Rem answered from behind him, "There's a veil in the ghost game Koz designed!" She had abandoned her tablet and was staring at Namu.

"A what?" Namu asked. He didn't know what she meant.

Koz thumped his head back against his seat to glare at Rem. He seemed caught off guard. From the thin line of his pressed mouth, he looked annoyed, his spark from only moments before gone.

Namu tried to fix his mistake. He didn't want Koz angry if he was helping him build what he needed to finally end things with that door. "If it's a secret game, you don't have to tell me anything about it."

"It isn't!" Rem beamed. "The veil represents an empty vessel! It was so smart!"

So, Koz did know what empty vessels were.

Koz sighed. "Souls work differently than most magick when it comes to spirit magick or just existing in general." That was something Namu knew. He worked with them all the time. "Souls can spread themselves out like a veil. They can be thick or thin. The more they spread out, the thinner they are. If they're older, they have more layers, which gives them more substance. But if they're younger, they have a harder time existing and can be very, very thin. It's almost like they're not there at all."

Why hadn't Namu heard any of this before? He guessed he had never really studied the anatomy of a soul. He had only studied spirit magick in general. Even though parts of his soul had been eaten away, he never thought about the insides of a soul or what it was made of, only that it sometimes looked like the body of what it came from. But why would a technology geek like Koz know this? How had he found out? Was it for a game?

"I don't understand," Namu said, wanting Koz to elaborate.

Koz sighed again and shook his head. "An empty vessel is a newer soul. It's a soul that hasn't been reborn many times and hasn't grown many layers yet."

"They're like thin veils you can barely see!" Rem added.

"In a way. It's more complicated than that. That's a personified explanation, not a scientific one." Koz typed a few more things before reaching over and digging into his bag for a cord that he plugged into his phone and then into the device he had on his lap. "They are newly made souls that either have never been reincarnated or have been reincarnated only a few times."

Namu stared at him as he worked, wondering what that even meant. It was the most he had heard about empty vessels. So, Molly was a newer soul? New enough that her body felt like it was empty? Was that why she was able to hide from those creatures? Had she been able to fold into herself because her soul wasn't thick? Was that why spirits tried to take her over? Because her soul was so new and easily swayed one way or the other, like a child, making it easy to force down?

Koz closed his computer and unplugged his phone. He set it on the desk face up and opened an app to a black screen with a small golden coin in the middle of it. He rubbed his hands together, then hunched over his phone and pushed the button before backing away.

One golden coin with hints of silver popped out of the screen, landing on the desk with a clatter before vanishing. Then came another and another. It was slower than the fountain had been. Each coin stayed visible for maybe a second.

"You can tell they're fake." Koz didn't look satisfied with the results he had produced. "It will need some upgrades, but will this do for now? The speed can be increased but not as much as the water. There's a lot more going on here. There's more for the techno magick to lace together."

He waited until another coin popped out before pushing a button near the bottom of the screen that made two coins pop out at once and then three before they were gone, and the phone released three more. Those coins didn't even touch the desk and made no sound before they were broken away, back into the nano-bits that had made them.

"It's perfect. Thank you," Namu said. It was close enough to what he wanted. He just hoped that it would work. That it could do something in that world. Anything.

Koz moved his hand toward the screen, brushing the coins aside that erupted out of it like they would from a video game. They bounced off his hand as they sprang loose, making a clinking noise before they faded. He pushed the button to turn it off.

"And that will go on forever?"

"As long as the battery is alive and the phone is still working," Koz remarked, holding his hand out for Namu's phone. Namu unlocked his screen and handed it to him.

Koz grabbed it, swiped a few times, then halted. "You have no magickal apps on here at all."

Namu didn't feel the need to respond to something he already knew. He was ready to take the phone and leave. He was pleasantly surprised with how fast he had been able to get the app that he had been hoping for from Koz. He now had time to see what it could do.

Koz handed him the phone back. For some reason, it felt heavier in his hand, warmer, more alive.

"Have fun with your game," Koz said.

Namu tried not to grimace and nodded instead. It was his game against fate. He just hoped he wouldn't lose a piece of himself this time.

It was good that he had stored some of those transformation drinks they had used to help Molly in his dresser each time Mr. Vero had gone out to get food and more transformation drinks. It was the only thing that made him feel safe enough to return to that nightmare world again alone.

He slipped his phone into his pocket, hoping that it wouldn't start acting chaotically before he was able to use the app. He hoped that at least a few coins would come out. He needed to see what it could do—if it disturbed that world at all. If it did, he would go and buy more phones if he had to. He would then ask Koz to put the app on each one, go into that world, and place them all over until he overwhelmed the place.

This was his game against the door like it always had been. Since the moment he had gotten trapped inside.

The idea was that, since Namu couldn't actively make weapons without those said weapons disappearing, he would use this app to continuously make coins filled with the intention for them to disrupt and ruin the world that had destroyed him. The hope was that techno-made coins would produce faster than the world could make them disappear and that they would overload the world. He thought they might even confuse it, since techno magick didn't seem to pair well with this place.

He slipped on the belt that Mr. Vero had let him keep and put another transformation drink into it that he would use to get back. He would have to figure out how to make more of them if he was to go back and try this again later on or at least figure out how to get more. He didn't have too many left.

He moved the small dresser, said the incantation, let the wall fall away, then crouched to get into the open room where he could stand. Where he was facing the door and his possible doom.

What happened if the phone did worse things than he expected? What if it went absolutely chaotic? Should he run as soon as he put it down?

The vial in his hand, which was already slipping with sweat, reminded him that he had a plan. He would drink the other drink and get out of there as quickly as possible, no matter what.

Lockdrest

He turned the handle. As the door opened, he drank the drink in his hand and then slipped through the door as a mist.

The needles began right away, pulling and tearing at him. He couldn't tell if the world was physically hurting him or if it was all in his mind. But he did know that this nightmare world hated him. It hated everybody.

He looked around. First at the bruised purple sky, then at the glass-ice lake, and then at the trees and the burning flowers. Where should he put the phone down? Over by the trees where those creatures always were? Or were they only there because the trees were something that anyone coming into this world would be drawn to, like he and Molly had been?

He decided the trees were his best bet, if only to try to do something to those creatures. He figured they would be there at some point.

He pulled himself back together, dissolving his mist and the magick that held him with a squeeze from his deteriorated hand to solidify. Then he pulled out his phone. The screen was already misting and blinking with static from black to lime green.

He opened the screen. He had to wait a moment until the green flashing brightness passed and his heart thudded before he was able to press the button for the app. Then he set it down gently in the grass and stepped away.

One coin emerged, slower than it had for Koz. It was gold mixed with silver, then it turned black. It hit the grass just as it twisted into that green dust and floated off into the purple sky.

He wanted this world destroyed, and he wanted to watch it burn. Was that what fed the coins here? His anger? He was making this metal, this app, into a weapon with his mind because he wanted to use it for destruction, like all the weapons in his world had been made for. His plan was to give this world a constant, direct supply of weapons it would have to eat up. A supply it could not keep up with. A fake meal with elements it would not enjoy.

A few more coins popped out all at once. Four of them. The world took them, devouring them in greed.

Metal, warm and alive, began growing on his shin.

More coins were spewed up out of the phone as the screen flashed. Golden coins flipped to black before they spilled along the grassy ground.

Namu unhooked the vial from his belt and held it to his lips as his metal casting grew to his thigh. He watched as another green flash from the screen reflected the anger from this world. This time, countless coins sprang up, spurting like a fountain. They were speeding up. Something was wrong.

Namu drank the concoction, turning himself to mist. He soared away over the grass, which shifted and turned to black metal until each blade pointed straight up to his face like knives. He needed to get out. Things were changing. There was lightning for once in that bruised sky, as if a bleeding cut had sliced across it.

He made it through the door, unhooked the astral spell from his body, slammed the door shut, and performed a spell to get everything off his skin.

He only had a moment to feel relief. He only had a moment for pride to seep into his heart before there was a loud BOOM! The door flew off its hinges into his face, and the world beyond the door came gushing out into his.

Molly

Chapter Twenty-Nine

An alarm started blaring overhead as Molly sat with her classmates in the technology room. The alarm was piercing, making everyone cover their ears before the teacher told them they all needed to assemble in the basement outside the library so they could check on everyone.

Molly and the others fought their way to the door. In the scrambled mess of student bodies, she realized why the alarm was blaring.

There were students screaming and running outside the classroom. A few were crying. Some students had pieces of shiny black metal in their strands of hair. One student had metal growing over the left side of his face.

Whoever had opened the door to their classroom froze, stopping everyone else from getting out.

"Hivick, open the door so we all can move CALMLY to the basement!" Mrs. Fissh yelled over the frustrated and panicked students, who were starting to push. "We need to make sure this is not coming from the outside!"

In the midst of the chaos, Molly stared out the glass wall into the group of students who were almost trampling each other as they tried to fight their way down the stairs outside the classroom. She swore she saw particles of green dust.

She knew what this was . . .

She needed to get out of this class now and find Namu.

Usually, she would have been worried about upsetting someone, but that fear tickled in her mind for only a moment before she found herself pulling people aside by their shoulders and then shoving some behind her out of her way. She would brawl her way through them all if she had to. The fear of what might be happening curdled her insides, and she let it. She was over letting her mind guide her. She would let her feelings lead her now, like she had decided to last night. Her feelings were her feelings and no one else's.

"Get out of my way!" Molly yelled, making her way to Hivick, who was shaking. She ducked down under his arm that was holding the door handle and then shoved him away when she was between him and the exit. Satisfaction shot through her when she saw his hand rip away from the handle. When she took possession of it, it turned.

The students behind her came flooding out of the classroom, and she came pouring out with them, almost getting knocked over. She steadied herself and tried to figure out where she should go. Would Namu be downstairs?

Long, cold fingers wrapped around her arm and began pulling her to the stairs. "Molly, the stairs are this way." It was Mrs. Fissh. "We don't know what's happening, so we need to be listening to directions."

Molly wanted to fight her, so she did. She yanked her arm away and then stared at her teacher's watery blue eyes, which did, in fact, look similar to a fish's. "I can go on my own. Thank you."

Her teacher nodded but did not leave Molly alone. She held out her hand, waiting for Molly to take the lead. Molly did with prickles of goose bumps growing all down her neck, stemming from her anger. She just hoped that Namu was down there so she could figure out what was going on.

She was surprised to see that not many students had assembled where they had been told. Maybe some teachers had left the kids they knew were okay in their classrooms. Maybe Namu was still in his class. She couldn't see Ova either.

Mrs. Fissh seemed to realize the same thing. She pulled at her graying blonde-blue hair and approached another teacher. "I know the hall is also being used, but where are all of—"

A mist, an astral mist that Molly instantly recognized, soared right to them and then appeared as a teacher. It was Mr. Vero. He looked exhausted and was breathing heavily. All the teachers gathered in a group around him.

The gathered students were too busy standing around talking to each other to notice that the teachers were having a meeting. A few students with sparkly green dust and metal growing on them were being dragged out of the crowd by Mrs. Heard to sit away from everyone in a group. The larger group was unsettled by this and leaned in to hear what Mrs. Yitter was saying to the students who had been pulled aside.

Molly was more interested in the teachers.

"I haven't had a chance to check the source, with trying to keep the creatures off students and round them up. I need more of this—lots of it. As much as we can make in a short time." Mr. Vero held up vials of a transformation drink, which one of the teachers took and then ran off toward the classrooms with. Another teacher followed.

"How much has it spread?"

"It has reached the main floor. It will be here soon. I didn't have time to check the two upper levels," Mr. Vero said.

"Why in the world would we have the students come down here?" one teacher asked.

"What is happening? What is the source?" another asked.

Mr. Vero ignored the first teacher. "We needed our own resources, and we had to make sure this wasn't an attack from the outside." He pulled another vial from his deep pockets, about to drink it. "I have to go and try to catch those damn creatures and keep them off the students. I'll be back for the vials."

But Molly grabbed Mr. Vero's arm before he could lift his drink. He seemed shocked at first but then pulled her to the side.

"What're you doing?" he asked.

"What's happening?" Molly asked.

"I'm not sure. I tried to make it to Namu's room to check on the door, but . . . those creatures . . . and the students . . ." He looked over her shoulder to the stairs. "I need to help them. I can't have anyone's soul . . ."

She knew what he meant.

"Where's Namu?"

"I don't know," Mr. Vero said, shaking his head and then slamming the drink down his throat before turning to mist once more.

He was gone.

He didn't know? He hadn't had time to check Namu's room? She understood he couldn't risk those creatures eating away at anyone. The students' souls were most important. But were the creatures truly the biggest threat? Wasn't it more important to close the door where those creatures were coming from?

She needed to go upstairs to check on the door herself. She just hoped Namu was in one of the classrooms. She didn't see him among the few students standing around waiting for the teachers to tell them what to do.

"Molly! Where's Namu? He isn't in class!"

It was Lily. They had come running from another direction, the direction where the teachers had run off to make the transformation drinks. Lily must have snuck out of their classroom.

"I don't know," Molly mumbled, heading past Lily toward the stairs. The teachers and students would, hopefully, be too busy to notice her slipping away. They all looked too panicked, trying to figure out what to do.

"Where are you going?" Lily asked, following her.

The top of the wooden banister was starting to turn a burning metallic black. Molly knew that color too well. She had stared and stared at her arm, which had been that hue when those things had dug into her. But where were those things now?

Lily noticed the metal too. "That's just like what happened in Namu's room. What's going on? What has he done?"

Lily started running up the stairs past Molly.

"No, Lily, wait!" Molly yelled, fear choking her.

Lily was almost to the top when they turned. "Why? What's going on? I need you to tell me now!"

Molly didn't know what to tell them. She knew she wasn't supposed to say anything about the door, but it was already out, and Lily was smart. They had proved that with the bracelet. They would probably figure it out themselves at some point.

"Namu is in trouble." Molly felt it in her gut. "He might be in his room."

Lily ran up the rest of the stairs, and Molly followed, but they both stopped when they reached the top. Patches of the black metal from that petrified world were growing along the hardwood floor. It was strange, like a feverish nightmare. In some spots, the metal was disappearing and reappearing as if the world were having a hard time sustaining itself, but when Molly stepped, trying to avoid the areas that she knew would burn her feet, she saw the second stairwell that led to the halls. It had transformed into a mix of petrified wood and black burning steel. She then knew it was only a matter of time before that other world found a solid hold on this one.

"Owww! What's this?" Lily asked. It had burned through their shoe. Molly wondered why the metal that layered itself over a living thing didn't burn when it took over the skin. Molly remembered the warmth that had trapped her in the cast of metal.

"Don't touch it!" Molly yelled, trying to make her way to the stairs.

"And your plan for that is . . . ?" Lily asked, coming to stand right next to her.

Lily was talking about the stairwell. The impossible stairwell that they wouldn't be able to climb. Molly didn't have any of the transformation drinks to help them.

Heat sizzled right on the outside of her foot. She pulled it away from the metal that was crawling toward her.

"You don't know, do you?" Lily asked. They grabbed hold of their hair over their shoulder and drew a symbol right above where their finger and thumb encircled it. A white light formed for a moment, making a white line that split and separated all the hairs in that exact spot like a cut. Lily held the insanely long ends of their hair in their hand.

Molly watched as Lily did soul magick to expel a part of themselves from the separated ponytail. Their spirit was pink, like Kren's but deeper. Lily then used transformation magick by pushing their thumb against their white teeth, while trailing the pink wisp to their mouth, before flicking their thumb away from the edge of their teeth and snapping their fingers. Their limp hair turned to solid, straw-like rods. They broke those sticks into four unequally large pieces that were stuck together and then used a quick glue spell on the bottoms of their shoes to keep them there. They handed the other two to Molly.

Before Molly glued the two pieces of the straw-like board onto her tennis shoes, she watched Lily draw something on theirs. The symbol they drew, which Molly couldn't make out, glowed red for a moment. Molly still couldn't believe that Lily had chopped their hair off to shoulder-length in front of her.

"Quit looking at me like that! It's just hair!" Lily said as they made their way to the stairwell and then tested what they had made by putting their foot on it. Smoke formed, curling around their ankles. They pulled their foot off and then asked for the bottom of Molly's shoes.

Molly obliged. The bottoms burned red briefly before they calmed back to their original color.

"It won't last long, so we have to move fast!"

Lily ran up the stairs.

Fehu Hall was no longer golden but a dreary dark black when they ran past it. Uruz was no better, with black metal spider webs suspended in various places glinting silver. The next hall was Thurisaz, where Lily dove, panting, pulling Molly in with them. Nothing was wrong there.

Molly checked the already half-worn, burned bottoms of her feet. "Why is this hall okay?"

"This is the one they said to go to if you were close to it. This hall always protects its occupants. Don't you know that?"

Molly thought she remembered Kren saying something about that but felt a sting pierce her back. She turned, ready to see the growing metal she had seen on the others.

"Why is it touching you like that?"

It was a spirit sprite.

Molly didn't care to explain, especially not to Lily after everything that had happened with the bracelet. "Let's just go," she said, swatting at the blue menace. She hoped it wouldn't follow them.

They got up and continued to run up the stairs. Although the smell from Lily's burning creations made Molly nauseous, she was thankful for them because she felt no heat. She was also grateful that the spirit sprite refused to leave that particular hall, probably scared of the burning metal.

They reached the next hall, Anuz, and Molly almost grabbed onto the scalding banister before she caught herself. There was a student there. They had been running to the stairs but were now a statue, one hand covered in black metal reaching out for the banister.

"What the dimensions?" Lily whispered until the smoke rising to their nostrils from their feet made Lily cough. Lily pulled Molly up the stairs with them.

Once they made it to Namu's hall, the floor itself didn't burn as much. It took Molly a moment to notice why. The carpet was rubber, like the grass in that world had been. But it also had patches of shaved metal in it. Midway down the hall, Lily squatted to get a closer look. Molly continued to go to them, watching her steps, but then let out a gasp when Lily jumped two feet in the air. They were staring at something in the wall. Molly ran up to them and noticed the glint of blue-black metal eyes glaring at them through a crack in the wall. Unmoving. Paralyzed.

"I hate this hall," Lily mumbled.

Above them, a spirit sprite was stuck halfway into the ceiling. Its bottom half was turned to metal.

When they finally reached Namu's door, they saw it was open. Sheets upon sheets of black and silver metal had poured out over the threshold like a tidal wave.

"Namu!" Lily tried to yell over it.

There was no response.

Lily got on their hands and knees to crawl over the burning hot metal to enter the room. They let it scorch their skin. Molly heard them fall to the floor on the other side. "Screw this stuff!" Lily yelled. "Namu!"

There was a silent pause. Molly, who had been opening and closing her fists, waited for some kind of reply. When there was none, she tore across the metal like Lily had to get inside. The metal welcomed her with flashes of burns and the smell of her cooking skin as she climbed over it.

The room distracted her from the pain. It was a disaster. Everything had changed. Parts of the bed had turned into rubber. Some areas on the walls and the floor were stained purple and green, with glittery dust all around. Metal spikes protruded out of the dresser, the bed, and the floor. Random waves of wood were growing from various places.

Lily was standing in the room through the opening in the wall, their back turned to Molly. Molly went over and gasped, her hand finding its way to her teeth. The door had been torn away and was lying on the floor on top of a body.

Molly ran over as Lily continued to stand perfectly still, paralyzed.

"What is . . ." Lily asked as Molly ran by them.

They were looking out into that other world. The petrified world that was mixing with their school.

"A dangerous place—we have to get Namu." Molly heaved the door off him with a clatter and then burst into tears when he cried out. The metal handle had burned its way into his side, melting his shirt into his skin. His feet were encased in metal and his thighs too. Had the door protected his head? The other parts of him?

"Namu! What do we do?" Molly yelled at him as he stirred. They didn't have much time. She could see that the atmosphere of that world was thickening through the opening. She had been in that world. There was no emptying it. Would it just continue to grow and completely fill theirs?

"Mol—the door . . ."

"It's ripped off."

Lily was next to them, getting on their knees and lifting Namu's head. "We need to get him out of here so he can explain everything later. What—what is that? Why is it—"

The metal on his thighs was thickening, not spreading out, but thickening across his limb like wadded gum. Namu yelled out.

"I have drinks—those drinks in my drawer. Give me one. Take some. Let's go!"

Molly knew what he meant. She ran to his dresser and started pulling out drawers, beginning from the top. By the time she reached the bottom drawer, tears had escaped her eyes.

There were five vials. She pocketed two in her shorts pocket, then ran and handed Namu one. With a shaking hand, he took it from her and tipped his head back, emptying it into his mouth.

He turned to mist in Lily's hands.

"Here!" Molly yelled, shoving one into Lily's grasp and then taking one herself.

She had never taken one before. Her world splattered around her, extending as her thoughts turned white and everything slowed down, leaving her with nothing. Then everything gradually came back, but she was left with no feeling, sense of self, or ability to grab anything. She started floating toward the opening into that other world. She couldn't do anything to get herself to float the other way.

Then she felt someone or something mesh with her.

"What are you doing!?" a distorted voice yelled.

Whatever it was started pulling her with it, showing her that if she pushed, almost swam, extending and condensing the particles that made her, she could head in a specific direction.

She could head into Namu's room and then out the door into his hall.

Soaring back down the hall and the stairs was less painful than it had been coming up since Molly couldn't feel or touch anything, including her burns. But then she passed through something or someone that made her lose all sense of self. She sneezed, making her particles scatter.

"Namu!" she heard Lily's distorted voice yell.

Molly didn't know why they had stopped and why she was left floating until she saw that same boy they had seen earlier. That statue with the extended hand . . . It had a creature on it. One of those white creatures with the three heads and three toes that were digging into the boy's metallic skin.

Mr. Vero must have missed this one unless more creatures were coming through.

"What is it?"

But Namu didn't answer. She felt and then saw his mist. It was shaking, shivering, becoming more of a fog.

"What's wrong with you?" Lily asked.

The creature took two of its wide white oval heads out of the boy's extended arm and then jumped up to the boy's head to dig in again.

Out of nowhere, Lily was their full self again, trying to hit and shoo the thing away. The creature ignored Lily, worming around their hand to find another spot to continue its feast. Lily's feet were smoking again from the shoe protectors they had made. The straw planks must almost be worn through now.

"What is it? I'm so sick of no one answering me!" Lily yelled.

"Fro . . . m . . . th . . . at . . . wor . . . ld . . ." Molly tried to answer, but she felt like it came out garbled.

Lily sighed, took the remains of the smoking straw hair off their feet, then wrote a symbol in it with their nail before digging for something from the back of their ear and flicking it at the straw, bursting it into flames. They threw it at the creature.

It landed on the ground next to the statue's feet.

Lily then did something that Molly had never seen before. They put their hands across their eyes for a moment, standing on one foot while the other continued smoking and then, after pulling a bit of their soul from their palm, wrote another symbol with it and blew it into the flame that had landed on the ground. The whole boy in metal erupted into fire.

Molly found herself streaming for him, needing to save him.

"Molly, don't," she heard Lily warn as the creature scurried away. "It's vision magick mixed with gnome magick for effect. The flames aren't real, but once the real ones die, then those will die too. Let's go!"

Molly couldn't help but to admire Lily and view them as a warrior as they ran down the stairs two at a time, not screaming or wincing but leaving a trail of blood from their injured feet. Molly could feel Namu following close behind.

When they got back to the library, Molly heard one teacher tell another that most of the students had been sent outside to get them out of the building. All, apparently, except for Koz.

Koz was still there, typing away at one of the computer desks, with his laptop sitting on top of another computer that Rem was balancing for him as he ran back and forth.

Rem looked horrified, her eyes wide and glossy, moving from one person to the other.

Mr. Vero was instructing Koz about something, shaking the many vials into his face whenever Koz had a chance to turn to him.

But they all stopped when they saw Namu appear holding his bloody side. The metal on his legs must have fallen away when he had turned, but Molly hadn't noticed. Lily was sitting on the ground, blowing on their bleeding feet. And Molly was trying everything she could think of to grab onto herself to turn herself back, which was impossible when she could not feel herself at all. It was like working with a sleeping hand.

"Where's Molly? What happened!? Namu—what—where—" Mr. Vero stopped himself.

"Molly is somewhere," Lily informed, waving their hand around. "I don't think she has used an astral-transformation spell before."

Molly watched as Mr. Vero squinted and then walked toward her. He snatched her from the air. All of a sudden, she grew heavy and fell to the ground. Her body tingled all over.

"What happened?" Mr. Vero tried again. "Someone get the nurse in here!" he yelled to a few of the teachers who were running around pulling books off the shelves and storing them in boxes and containers.

Someone ran off.

"The door opened," Namu said, clutching his side and wincing in pain.

Mr. Vero seemed to have no sympathy for him. "How? Magickally?"

"Of course magickally! We live in a magickal school!" Namu spat but then took a deep breath and looked around. He saw the few students tucked in the corner of the library, the ones who had been infected by the world that had leaked through. "What are you doing? You know those creatures are roaming around. They need to be stopped!"

"I already stopped them. They're in my room. I collected them all," Mr. Vero said.

"There are more!" Namu challenged.

Mr. Vero's eyes widened.

"One was eating that boy who turned into a statue near the stairwell in one of the halls."

Mr. Vero grabbed a vial and started heading that way, but Lily yelled at him, "I handled it!"

The nurse came running in, her long black hair pulled back into one thick braid that was six times the thickness of Molly's wrist. She fell down to her knees next to Lily with a medical case and drew a circle around her, then started pulling out ointments.

"I wish I could bring that child down here, but I can't. I don't have a way to figure that out right now," Mr. Vero said to Namu. "My hope is that he will turn back after we figure out how to get rid of all this and send it all back into that place."

"How?"

"Well, first, I'd like to know how it happened!"

Molly noticed that Koz was listening as he took one of the vials and poured it into some kind of machine that looked like a computer box. His ear was tilted to the side, his eyes downcast.

Namu started pacing. "I did it, okay! But it was an accident! I was trying to destroy that place! Nothing else was working to destroy that door, so I had to do something!"

"For the last time, Namu, *what did you do*!?"

"I put my phone in there with an app that creates nonstop metal coins."

Koz dropped one of the vials. It broke, spilling its contents all over the carpet.

"How would that do anything like this?"

"Because I made it into a weapon by wanting it to destroy that nightmare world."

Mr. Vero turned his back on him and walked away. "So, instead of listening to me, instead of ignoring it, instead of doing your duty, you do this! You release catastrophe into this world! You release chaos! You know that it's a realm with dimensional magick we don't understand, right? Magick that seems to have a mind of its own because of the metal we have stored there. Released, over time, it will kill off this world and make it its own! It will kill everyone!"

"Then, why put it in a school!" Namu screamed. Blood was pouring through his fingers.

"I don't know why they put it here, Namu! My guess is because they assume we have ideas on how to stop it! Because they know we can work more diligently than some can. Because, like I told you before, we *do not want power.* We want safety for all of you! Why else would it be made in the first place?"

To stop all the school shootings and all the war. Molly knew that. Why didn't Namu?

"Who would decide to put it anywhere near them if they didn't want power?" Namu muttered under his breath.

Mr. Vero turned back to him, grabbed Namu by the shoulders, and looked him in the eyes. "Who cares that that door was brought here and that a very few select people have to deal with it? That a very few select people have to know about it. That even fewer people have to protect others from it. Who cares, if it means others can live in happiness and live free? I'm sorry I failed to help you see that, Namu. I'm also sorry that in a way I caused all this to happen!"

Namu shook his head. "It doesn't matter. I still hate it. It should be somewhere else."

Seeing the way Namu was still holding onto his hate brought questions to Molly's mind that had never been there before. Who had made the final decision to put that door in their school? Why had they decided to put it in a student's room? Why not a teacher's room or at least an adult? Who knew about it being there? Did Kren?

Mr. Vero shook his head too, giving up on his student. "Some things can't be destroyed once they are made. Some things must be put elsewhere for those responsible enough to take on the burden. I have no idea why the school chose you."

He let go of Namu and returned to Koz. "How is it going?"

"I'm almost done. But won't it be dangerous having all the students do this? Molly just proved that. She had no idea how to come out of it and how the students could mesh together and become one."

"It's only for the infected before we do the light spell. We will put them in separate places in the library and then have the teachers pull them back together."

A flash of red and purple from upstairs set off most of the lights, throwing the room into darkness. That flash was followed by a deafeningly loud clap of thunder.

"Was that lightning? In the school?" someone yelled.

"Why is it so dark? Why? Why is it so dark?" Rem yelled.

Green emergency lights came up, and the computers started turning back on. Koz cursed. Molly looked to the stairs. The black metal was now halfway down the stairs and traveling like frost.

Mr. Vero noticed. "We need to hurry! I don't understand any of this, but the first thing we need to do is heal those students and then get them out of the building."

"No. The first thing we need to do is turn off the phone I put in that world," Namu interrupted.

"It's still on? Are you sure?" Mr. Vero asked.

Koz was the one to ask the next question. "When did you put it in . . . wherever you put it?"

"During lunch."

Koz looked down at his phone. "It's still on," he confirmed.

Mr. Vero didn't ask how Koz knew. "Well, you can't go, Namu. I need you to help us with a few larger spells to get everything back through that door."

"But I need to—"

Lockdrest

"The answer is no, Namu! Maybe we can get one of the other spirit magick teachers."

Molly spoke before she realized. "I'll go. I'll take one of those vials again and go in there. Just tell me where it is."

"Also, no."

Molly wasn't having it. She wasn't about to let someone tell her what to do. Not when she wanted to do this. "I'll go. You know why I'm fit for it! I'm the safest in there! Just tell me how to undo the astral-transformation spell and how to shut off the app on the phone. And tell me where it is!"

Namu grabbed her hand and dragged her to the stairs. The nurse followed, trying to apply cream to Molly's burned. It might have been soothing, but instead, it was too much at the moment with her nerves.

"Do you have the other vials?" Namu asked.

Molly nodded. The nurse moved away, arms crossed, waiting for Namu to be done so she could attend to him.

"When you are in that astral-transformation spell where you can't feel yourself, you only need to tell yourself you can," Namu said. "It sounds ridiculous, but it's all about incentives. It's your brain floating and playing mind tricks on you. There's a button on the app. You should be able to just push it off. If that doesn't work, find a way to destroy the phone. It's by the trees."

Molly nodded again as she listened, taking everything in. She could see Mr. Vero approaching them, regret all over his face. But she downed the drink before he could have a say in her life. Before anyone could try to stop her.

She had to do this. For Namu, for the school, for all of them. She would go back there. Back into that world. Back through that opening to fix Namu's mistake. A mistake that she didn't even blame him for making.

She saw in his eyes that he felt bad about it but held firm in his belief that he hated that place. She could see his pure wrath about it. His want for that aspect to change. It was like how she wanted to change the part she hated about herself. Even though she saw the goodness in the door, the benefit it had brought to the world, she didn't know what it had done to Namu. It wasn't her right to judge. She had to believe that what he was doing was for the good of others. To keep others from slipping through the door like she had.

She could only admire his strength in standing up for his beliefs, even if it went against anyone else, including his teacher. Just like she had made mistakes in the past with following her friends, he had made a mistake too, and she was sure he would never do it again.

Mr. Vero reached them both, but Molly had already floated up and away over the metal stairs where he couldn't grab her. He would be wasting his time, energy, and any chance at saving the school if he went after her now. They could bring her back again like they did before. They could go in and get her out if anything happened.

The school was truly turning into a nightmare. The ceilings now were deep purple with swelling bruises. The floors had turned completely metal, and the stairwell . . . the metal on the stairwell was growing, merging, almost blocking the way up.

She slipped into the stairwell where there were a few of those creatures chillingly staring at her. When she made her way past them, they gave her no notice at all.

She made her way up the stairs, past the boy who was now only barely flaming, and then to Raido Hall and into Namu's room.

Then she flew as fast as she could straight into that world, and it made her cry out. It felt like she was back in the world of her mind right when she fell through the aching ice, and it ripped at her skin. Except here, ice shards were tearing all through her. Every piece of her.

She didn't remember it being like this when she had last been here. Maybe it was because she was in the form she was in now, and the world didn't agree with it.

She made her way to the trees over spiked metal grass. Sure enough, lying on the ground, sprouting black coins that shifted to a green residue that got siphoned up into the air like a small tornado, was a phone flashing black and green as if it contained its own lightning. When she got closer, she saw that the screen had a few cracks in it.

She did as Namu had told her. Although it felt silly to tell herself that she could actually feel herself when she couldn't, in a way, it almost felt like the shift of her mind recently. Like telling herself that she was done following people and would only live for herself when she did not truly feel that way deep down. She was grasping at nothing but making herself do it anyway.

It was then that she felt her hand. Bits of it, as if it couldn't take form but wanted to. She guided it to grasp onto the spell that made her into this astral floating being. Heaviness returned to her limbs, erasing the stinging pain she felt in every nerve, although there now was a different kind of toxin in her lungs from the air.

Lightning flashed as she put her hand into the fountain of coins. It resisted her touch. The coins stung her with heated flares as soon as they shifted to that black metal, but her finger found the screen that thrummed against her as more coins kept emerging from it. She hit it and hit it again, but the thing would not turn off.

At first, she thought it was a coin burning a finger on her other hand, creating a warm throbbing heaviness. But when she looked down, she saw a metal casting starting to grow.

Adora Michaels

Panic seized her. She only had one vial left, and she came in here to do this one thing. To get rid of this one thing. To help. To prove herself to herself. Had she made the wrong choice?

No. She could not think of it that way. There was no wrong choice when her heart, her very being, wanted to help. When she had chosen to listen to herself for once. She just had to find a way to stop this.

She dug the last vial out of her other pocket with the hand she had used to try to stop the phone. She uncorked it with her teeth. Then she slammed her metal fingers down from her other hand into the phone with a fist, breaking into the already cracked screen. She did it again. And again.

The screen flashed black and then laid there, dead. No more coins were being produced. No more waves of green sand or dust were being eaten by the sky like a storm.

She downed the vial, and the metal casting released her hand. She made her way back to the opened door.

Namu

Chapter Thirty

Namu yelled out as the nurse used pliers to peel parts of his melted shirt out of his skin. When he clamped his mouth shut, he accidentally bit his tongue.

"I'm sorry. Faster this way," she whispered, scraping along his raw flesh. At least she had stopped the bleeding with magick.

Lily's burns were tightening as they dried with the ointment put all down their legs. They were not glistening wet anymore, and some of the outer edges were returning to their normal skin.

Namu couldn't believe that Lily and Molly had come looking for him.

The thought of Molly going back to the nightmare world made Namu bite his tongue harder in guilt. He hoped she would be okay. He knew she was the best choice because of what she was. Out of everyone, she had the best chance of her soul being okay if she was wrapped in a metal cocoon again. He just hoped that nothing else would happen to her and that stopping the app would be easy enough that she could get back to them. Then, hopefully, they could solve the problem of that world taking over the school. The problem he had created while trying to save everyone else.

Once the app was disposed of, hopefully the affliction would slow down, and they would be given more time.

He tried to tear his thoughts away from the students being scattered by the teachers around the empty shelves in the green glow of the library, along with the one student he had seen upstairs, who was now a frozen statue. If the teachers couldn't stop the growing metal on their bodies, the ones in the library might turn into statues also. And if they did turn to statues, if the teachers failed, Namu would have ruined their lives. It was a punch in the gut to know he had destroyed the life of that one student upstairs just as severely as he had ruined his own the day he had first walked through that door. He didn't know what to do with that guilt. He didn't know what to do with the heaviness of having all the blame on him for once, instead of deflecting it off to someone else, like he had Mr. Vero.

That boy . . . that boy would blame him . . .

In trying to save anyone else from slipping into that place, he had, instead, brought that place here. He was an idiot. Maybe even more so because it did not change his want to find another way to be rid of that door for good. He could not seem to find a middle ground when it came to that. If the door hadn't been there, none of this would have happened.

"What do we do now?" Lily asked.

"We hope this works," Namu answered.

Koz had found a book in Mrs. Yitter's locked-away library in her office handwritten by a woman named Oplin Betrist, who had a passion for creating magickal concoctions. She was the one who had invented the astral-transformation spell.

Koz had inputted it into the classification system and went into the techno database to find the connection from the system to the shelves. By inputting a code and pouring a couple of the vials, he planned for the shelves to spout the liquid like the shelves did when they glitched after trying to input a new book into the system.

They would see if it would help all the affected students perform an astral spell all at once. Koz said it should be safe, that the library system of old magick actually did something that replicated the configuration, as if it taught itself and knew what to draw from to make more. In this incident, with how easily Koz had found the correlation, it was almost as if the school was encouraging him to save the students and itself. If the school system kept producing the astral-transformation spell, maybe it could help the school break away from the metal too. Or at least begin to until they came up with another plan.

At first, Namu wondered why they didn't just give each student a vial, but then he learned it was because they could not make enough of them. This way was faster. They needed to use the drinks that they already had for the students who could not make it down here or for the teachers who needed to act fast. They could not risk the teachers getting turned into statues. They needed them to finish up spells to try to fight this whole thing off. They also wanted the astral-spell solution to flood the school, maybe seep into the wood, into its foundation, and do something.

It was worth a try.

It was odd seeing students with little bits of metal growing on them, some at a faster rate than others. One student had an entire arm that was now metal. One had a blotch of metal growing off his neck like a mass. It was interesting how differently the metal acted at the school than it had in the nightmare world. He remembered the metal on his thigh thickening and clutching onto him instead of layering all around him. But then that boy upstairs in the hall . . . The metal had layered over and completely enveloped him. Maybe the magick was unstable here. More chaotic. But what would happen if at some point it wasn't anymore? Would students turn to metal statues immediately like he had and have no chance to get out?

He heard the rip of a bandage before he felt it pressed against his skin. The nurse had cut a square in his shirt to give her room to work without him having to remove it. It felt nice to be completely covered again with the bandage. He felt less vulnerable and less naked.

"Working in this green light . . ." she mumbled, shaking her head. "Anything else?"

His head hurt from the door hitting him and knocking him out. He wondered if he had a bruise on it, but he didn't say anything. He wanted her to go away. He shook his head.

The nurse ran off to help other students. Namu then got up painfully with a grunt and walked to where he could get a better view of what would happen. There were thirty-something students spread around the library shelves waiting, with a teacher by each one's side.

Koz pushed a button.

Purple liquid came spraying and leaking out of the shelves. It started at a shelf near the back area, the remedies and transformation drinks section, then began sparking its effects all around.

The students held their mouths open to drink. One by one, the students turned to mist, and whatever metals had been on their bodies dropped to the ground. The teachers then solidified each student's bodies and dragged their drenched selves out of the spray.

Once every student was done and gathered, three teachers led them in a line to the classroom with a hole in a wall leading them outside.

Namu stayed behind.

Mr. Vero came over. "How long will this run for?" he asked Koz.

"I'm not sure," Koz replied. "Maybe as long as the computers aren't destroyed, maybe not long at all. These glitches are new. I know techno magick, but I know less about techno magick mixing with old magick. I'm surprised putting that solution into the computer system worked the way it did. It probably wouldn't have if the school's essence wasn't also fighting against this thing."

"Let's hope it continues to run long enough for the school to get some of the solution. I need it to seep into the concrete or wood or whatever is partially alive so that the metal will have less of a grip."

"Will that really work?" Lily asked. "Seems insane to me."

"It's the best idea I have right now. Everything has a spiritual essence, so astral spells can work in different ways on many things. I have studied it in blocks of wood before." He looked down at the carpet and then over at the concrete by the stairs, which shifted to metal the moment he did so. "Let's just hope it works for concrete too. We need to save the school and stop the metal altogether. Otherwise, it might keep spreading through the opened door and attack everything in this world. What do we do if it gets into the water off the island? If it gets to the cities? We have to go!"

"But Molly . . ." Namu said.

"I'm sure she'll find her way out. If she doesn't, we'll get her when all this is done."

Lily did not look so sure about Mr. Vero's suggestion.

Mr. Vero led them through the basement, where the metal was moving faster, threatening to nip them at their heels. They then went through the classroom with the giant hole at an upward angle leading to the grassy outside. Koz grabbed Rem's hand, his laptop still in his other hand, and helped her climb out, keeping her steady. He went next after shoving the laptop into the pack he had strung over his shoulder and chest. Then Lily went, then Namu.

They all stood in a drawn white circle as Mr. Vero cast the spell of light that would rid them of the residue and dust from that world so they wouldn't spread it. Each student had to go through a flash before being sent farther outside away from the school building.

Namu had to give it to the teachers; they had been very proficient in making sure that anything from that world had been contained using novel ideas he never would have dreamed of.

"Hey!"

Namu looked down into the hole in the wall they had climbed out of. It was Molly. He couldn't help but grin as he reached down to help pull her out. She looked exhausted.

"Is it done?" Mr. Vero asked outside the circle, lighting it up again before letting Molly go beyond it. She closed her eyes as the light struck her and waited for Mr. Vero to nod to tell her she was in the clear.

"Yes. I destroyed it," she said, stepping out. "And it felt as if the petrified world calmed down somewhat afterward."

Namu saw a girl trying to run out of the crowd of students waiting together and watching the school, but a teacher froze her in place. Namu ignored the slight commotion and looked at the boxes of books the group had brought outside. Would they need to search through all of those? Did one of them contain the information they needed to stop the spread?

"Ova!" Molly yelled, making him jump. It felt as if a knife had been stabbed into his side.

Molly was running to the girl who had been frozen. Namu watched as Molly threw her arms around the frozen girl and begged the teacher to let her go.

Lockdrest

"What now?" Lily asked, watching Molly alongside Namu. Mr. Vero was talking to other teachers.

Namu turned back to look at the school, now completely covered in that black metal. It was as if it had its own cast. Namu ground his teeth at the thought that the school's own soul was trapped inside.

"I don't know . . . I guess we wait for the teachers to figure something out."

"Don't give me that, you lazy bum!" Lily shouted. They shook their head. "Now tell me about that door! If you already had, I might have figured this out by now. What exactly is it?"

This was the moment Namu had been waiting for. The time to tell Lily what he had been keeping from them for too long. "It's where they stored the disintegrated weapons from that giant spell. Apparently, they had to store it in another dimension and leave the door to it in a school." His anger burned as hot as that metal.

"Makes sense," Lily nodded.

"How does that make sense? Putting kids in danger makes sense? The door is in my room! I didn't even know about it. Kids have gone in there and died! I almost died!"

"Well, you didn't die. And apparently, they were stupid, and so are you. Why go through a door you know nothing about?"

"You can't tell me that you wouldn't have. I didn't tell you about it because I knew you would have."

Lily shrugged. "I can admit that I'm sometimes stupid too. At least this teaches us that we need to learn to protect ourselves before we dive headfirst into things."

Namu shook his head. "Sometimes you can't protect yourself at all."

"You didn't die," Lily pointed out.

"I was lucky about that, but I have holes in my soul now. Holes that won't go away. That I've been trying to heal."

"What?"

Namu expelled a part of his soul to show her. His arm. Lily swallowed hard, staring at the spiritual essence with three missing chunks, then looked him hard in the eyes. "That's why you've been working with Mr. Vero."

"Of course."

Lily shook their head. "You're such a wimp."

"What?"

"You had such a big problem like that and wouldn't tell me? And now you'll let this thing beat you and destroy the whole school and world! What's wrong with you?"

"What's wrong with you, Lily? How is this my fault? And I'm not letting it beat me. I'm letting the teachers do their jobs!"

"How is it not? You did this! So, *you* help me figure this out. Stop whining over what happened to you and figure out how to fix this. You lived. Learn from it and help me."

"Why? So you can get all the glory?"

Lily smiled. "Of course."

Namu sighed. Lily had him worked up just like they used to in non-magickal school the day before a test, when Namu told them he knew he would fail. Lily would then call him an idiot and the stupidest person in the world, so he would stay up all night studying just to prove them wrong. Then they would say he had only passed because of them.

They worked well together that way.

He studied the school before them again and began to talk as his thoughts flowed. "When I was in that other world, I was trapped. Like that boy upstairs. The metal surrounded me to . . . I think to cage my soul. It paralyzed me for days. Those creatures—"

Lily stopped him. "So, the metal is trapping the school's soul. Okay. Does whoever go into that world get trapped in metal like this?"

Namu nodded, appreciating Lily for stopping him. He didn't want to relive what he went through right now.

"Those creatures ate parts of your soul. The chunks I saw out of it that can't heal." Lily was piecing things together. "That's why Mr. Vero prioritized capturing those creatures so they couldn't do that again."

Namu waited. He loved seeing their mind work, even though they were biting their lip, almost making it bleed like they did every time they tore apart processes like this.

"But then why send Molly back in there? Why is Molly different? When you and Molly disappeared, she got trapped in that world, didn't she? And you guys got her out. But then you let her go again just now. She said that she was the only one who would be safe. And she arrived at school with that mini-troll. What's with her? How is she different?"

"She's an empty vessel."

Lily's brows furrowed. It was obvious Lily had never heard of that before. It was something Lily couldn't figure out or put together, just like Namu couldn't until Koz had told him exactly what an empty vessel was.

"Apparently, it means that her soul is new. Spirits easily take her over. She came to this school to learn how to protect herself. When she was trapped in the metal, her soul folded in on itself, and the creatures couldn't get to it, unlike—" Namu stopped.

They looked at each other in silence. Then smiles widened on each of their faces.

They had an idea.

Lily ran to Mr. Vero first, waving their arms. "We need to make a new school!"

Namu stopped running mid-stride and bent over to laugh. That was not exactly how he would have stated it, but it would work.

"What?" Mr. Vero said.

"Namu, help me explain!"

Namu shook his head, still laughing. "This is all you."

Lily huffed. "The school. That's an old soul, right? The metal is eating it. New souls are souls that things want to take over, right? Like empty vessels."

"Umm . . . No. Not exactly, I don't think."

Lily ignored him. "If we combine visionary magick, gnome magick, and I don't know what else"—Lily was an expert at combining visionary and gnome, except they always said that it wasn't enough. That they needed to go further, like their dad had, and implement new magicks to make something extraordinary—"then we could try to draw that metal to the new school to overtake that one instead."

"It wouldn't work," Mr. Vero said. "The metal will just keep growing. It will just take over your fake school *and* your old one."

"You have that astral stuff in there," Lily pointed out.

"Yes. But that doesn't mean anything. That might not do anything at all."

"Come on, Mr. Vero. You're smarter than this!" Lily begged. "For everyone else, that astral spell made it difficult for the metal to cling onto them. I'm sure the metal will want to search out something else if it has a hard time clinging onto the school. Help me. Think! Soul magick! Do you think the metal has a soul or soul essence? I would think so, right? Since almost everything does. Why can't we try to do a type of soul transfer—but with the metal? We can get it to leave the school and move to a fake one."

"A soul transfer is not a thing, Pathon. Not exactly."

"How isn't it?" Namu spoke up. "Isn't that what we basically do? When combining souls with mine to try to fill up my holes? Isn't that what we did with that tree?"

Mr. Vero sighed and shook his head. "But to do that to something fake, it wouldn't connect or even latch."

"Nothing is fake, Mr. Vero. You should know that. Nothing is fake if it can be conjured up in the mind as real!" Lily said.

"Fine. Let's say that we can somehow do that. How would we get the metal to only attack that? And what purpose would that be for? What are we supposed to do with it afterward?"

"What purpose would that be for?" Lily asked. "To trap it so we can collect it and put it back."

Namu looked to Koz. "And as for how to get the metal to only attack what we want, we can use that app Koz made. We can ask all the students to stay in the middle of the fake school with their phones and bait it. We can have them plan for it to destroy the metal and then it will make the techno-made metal disintegrate. It will cause that metal to grow and maybe to head toward them. Like calls to like!"

"And risk the students' lives?"

"Not if the fake school is like a shell and the students are like the new soul, like the empty vessel folding in on itself to hide so the metal can't get to them."

Something sparked in Mr. Vero. "A shell!"

"Isn't this school known for runes and symbols?" Lily asked. "What could you do with a husk of combined magicks?" Lily was on to something.

"Many things," Mr. Vero said enthusiastically. "Many, many things. A shell or a husk is a type of shield. And if we make a shield . . . Well, a shield is one of the most corporeal things that holds incentive when it came to magick. Everyone has the same idea when it comes to the use of a shield and what it is made for."

"Exactly," Lily said. "And if all the teachers did a shield spell with a collective incentive—"

"Then, we can trap the metal, work to put it back, and close the door."

He turned and yelled for the other teachers to join them.

They were lucky that the teachers were resourceful and that there were so many different kinds of teachers in the one school. Maybe Mr. Vero was right that putting the door in the school had been smart. Except, like Mr. Vero told them all, the real test would be to see if the school could hold up. If the school's old soul, created by Freya's essence, could help them fight off the metal if they loosened it. They had already given the school the drink. Now they would have to provide it with the means to fight.

Mrs. Heard had been handing out bags of her religious materials and praying during this time. She dug into a few bags and grabbed a horn that looked like the one in the statue of Heimdallr in the courtyard.

Namu remembered seeing Mrs. Heard change the terrain of the courtyard once last year to something very odd, like ice during a heated day. This time, she went over and turned the courtyard terrain to lava stone with a blow of the horn. A black canvas. The teachers started setting up their supplies and began drawing symbols suspended in the air. The lava stone would make the symbols and runes last longer and expand the spells, instead of condensing them like when the students used some other terrains. This one was only to be used by the teachers. They planned to blast their symbols and spells to the fake school that they would create in the grass in front of the old one.

The teachers picked out a few select students to help with the more challenging parts of the spells that had to be cast. They set those students up around the courtyard and also around where the fake school would be that they had lined out.

The metal was starting to grow along the grass outside the school, now reaching for the sidewalk, carrying the green dust with it. They had to be quick if they were going to succeed.

Many students didn't know what was happening. Namu heard some teachers explaining to some of them, but then others were telling the majority of students that this was all a test or a drill but a dangerous one. They then asked for volunteers. Many students seemed hesitant at first until an older group with a serious demeanor about them said they would do whatever anyone needed. Then a few younger students joined, although half of the younger students decided to stand off to the side and observe.

After Namu had explained to Mr. Vero how the app had worked in that world, he said that the students had to stand in the middle of the fake school with their phones, which is why he wanted them to volunteer. They didn't know whether the phones would actually work if the students stepped away from them like Namu had. There had to be a big enough incentive for them to want the metal destroyed, and it sounded as though Namu's phone had glitched when he had used it. That was what all of this banked on: the giant spell put into place twenty-three years ago that affected the whole world and made it so any weapon would disintegrate and feed into the world that had escaped from the door.

Molly, Ova, and Rem were set up inside where the fake school would be with the other students who had volunteered. Their phones were opened and at the ready. Koz, during the setup, had gone into his database and automatically put the app into each phone he had worked on in the past. The students only had to open the app and press the button to start creating their own coins that would hopefully draw the metal to them.

Not just because like called to like but because with this many students thinking of the coins as a weapon, the metal would hopefully take notice and want to devour them.

Lily and Namu were on one of the stations on the outside, prepared to do the visionary magick mixed with gnome. Namu was to work on visionary magick, since it was easier, along with a few other students, while Lily and others would do gnome magick. All Namu knew about gnome magick was that it was all about the mind and how it made others feel. The problem with visionary magick at this large of a scale, though, would be getting everyone to envision the same thing, which is where the teachers came in. One would flash an image from a courtyard spell for a few seconds of what they needed to envision in their own minds. It would still be hard, though, since everyone perceived things in different ways. No matter what they did, he knew the "new" school would be weak, even with the added spells and magick the teachers threw at it to give it body.

Namu bent down and tore out some grass, ready to write whatever symbol he needed to suspend what he saw and bring it to light so others could see it too. The gnome magick would come in to make it feel and look more real. There was already a barrier spell around the students inside the school to protect them, just in case.

An outline vision of the school flashed. It was a small visual, which made it easier to hold in his mind. Namu wrote the symbol and tried to keep what he saw in his mind, wanting it to stay right where he had seen it flash moments ago.

It came to life. When he blinked and blinked again, the vision he had made would not go away, but it was like a distorted mirage. The school wasn't structured right. The part of him that loved construction could see all its flaws, the weaknesses that made it look as though it would fall. He could only hope it would work.

Lily drew their finger up their leg next to him and then drew a symbol on their thigh. The outline of the building flashed and then stone started to grow where the illusionary stone had been. Namu saw that, like their visionary magick, the gnome magick was flawed because of the momentary phantasm that kept flickering, allowing him to see the students inside the school before they vanished from view again. But they had done a good job regardless. The new school looked real.

Some of the students in the middle started to push the buttons on their apps. Silver and gold coins began falling onto the ground but did not last very long before they disappeared. Some students focused harder on the old school, but some looked like they thought what they were doing was useless, and Namu could tell they were giving up. It took another minute until some of the coins started turning black before disintegrating to green dust. When that happened, a few students dropped their phones, the coins flying all over the place, hitting some students on their heads but, thankfully, leaving no marks.

Namu was surprised that the app seemed to be working because the metal was growing toward the smaller new school. It was reaching for it, crawling along the ground. Namu and Lily backed away along with the others. His heart was in his throat as the metal climbed the fake walls.

But the fake school held. The barrier held. Namu just wanted the teachers to act fast. He could tell that the spell's structure and the school they had conjured up were frail.

He looked over to the teachers. Some surrounded the original school, drawing out some essence from it. Some were shooting spells from the courtyard to the growing metal now enclosing the new school.

But then Namu noticed that parts of the metal were slipping through invisible cracks. It was starting to break through the walls of the new school. With one more push, it broke all the way through. Like a wave, this giant mass of metal was traveling down to the barrier protecting the students.

Namu ran for them, but Lily grabbed his shoulder, stopping him, making him fall. Something he couldn't quite make out appeared out of an astral mist and threw up a spell, stopping some of the metal that was working on breaking through the barrier at the students' feet. There was now metal crawling at them from the ground all around them. That thing from the astral mist disappeared as more students screamed from the other side. They all scooted in closer to each other. Namu got up and ran over to that side and saw the same thing happening again. Something was stalling the metal. Something was giving the students more time.

But then the barrier holding the growing burning metal away from the students started caving in. A few more spells blasted at the barrier, trying to hold it up as the students screamed.

They shouldn't have done this. They shouldn't have risked any more lives.

The coins started dying out. Namu realized it was because most of the students could only think about their upcoming deaths. They didn't want to hurt the metal anymore. They only wanted it to not hurt them.

"Namu, look!"

He did. The real school was almost all clear, while the fake school had almost completely been consumed, but the spells the teachers had in place were failing at keeping the mass of metal from crushing the students. Was this how it was going to end?

They had to do something. Why weren't the teachers making the shield? The shield made of magick would be able to catch all, reflect all. Namu knew that the metal was surrounding the students on all sides, but why wasn't someone making a path to run in there and get them out?

There was one last scream before the barrier completely splintered and all the metal fell to the ground.

Namu fell to his knees.

But then he saw something flicker on the ground. It was a light. A shell. The rounded oval that the metal was now stuck to. It had come way too late.

Namu watched. All the teachers' faces were pale, lost, broken. The massive reflective shield of magick flashed golden three times. He didn't want it now. It was too late. He didn't want it to take all the metal away. He didn't want to see the smashed bodies underneath that he knew were there. That he knew were his fault.

The shield, shaped like a shell, started lifting with all the metal attached to it. It was easy to control by more than one person. A shield was always meant to do the same things: to cover, to protect, to reflect, to repel. Some of the teachers came running and wrote symbols on the ground that condensed the giant shield to trap the metal to it.

The other teachers rushed to attend to the students, if any were still alive.

But where they had been was a giant hole in the ground. Not from the giant mass of metal crushing them but from what looked like a creature. Something was crawling out of the side of the hole, panting and sniffing, with a small pointed pink nose and giant flattened hands with five long yellow nails. It took Namu a moment to realize that the creature had the bottom half of a person. A boy.

Apparently, that student had dug the hole. He had drunk some kind of transformation drink, turned into a half-mole creature, and had dug a large enough hole in time for the students to crouch down inside. His name was Derrin.

Namu walked with Mr. Vero through the real school now, alongside a floating, cloud-like metal band that looked like a river through the air, which they knew began at the shield and would lead to the door. They had left the other teachers and students behind. The school was still filled with green dust that they would have to flash light through once they fixed and closed the door. Hopefully, it would now hold.

Once Mr. Vero gave the word that it was closed, the teachers planned to use the continually growing metal on the shield to hurt or destroy something. That way, it would be a weapon and therefore disintegrate and go back through the door.

At least they had control of it now.

They made it to his room. All the metal up the stairwell and down Namu's hall was gone, along with the rubber carpet and the metal sheets that had gone through his door, almost knocking it off the hinges. His room was back to normal, and the wall was still open, with the small dresser toppled over on its side. Was that how to get it to not move back to the wall?

They entered the other room. The metal band flowed toward the door, which still lay on the floor, where it became just a trickle of airborne particles. Mr. Vero and Namu picked up the door together, Namu avoiding the handle this time. Even though it had never burned him previously, now it made his side throb. They fit it back into the opening where the green dust floated through.

The hinges clung to each other and turned darker than black for a moment, burning hot. Namu knew it was from the heat. They pushed it to make sure it was closed entirely for good measure.

"What a scare," Mr. Vero commented as they walked up the stairwell and down his hall to his room. Namu wondered what the teachers were doing now to get rid of the metal mass, which must have stopped growing since they had shut the door. After they got rid of the metal, he knew it would be just as taxing, if not more so, to try to get rid of the shield that they had all built together. It had so many combined magickal energies that it would take a while to disintegrate and was too powerful to keep around. He imagined most of the teachers would be up all night and there would be no school tomorrow.

Now, Mr. Vero and Namu's job was to release the creatures that Mr. Vero had captured back through the door.

Namu thought about the kid now passed out, free of being a statue. They hadn't been able to attend to him yet. The nurse had been sent to him, though. He wanted to speak with him once they'd closed the door dealt with the creatures.

"I'm sorry," Namu said. Not just to the kid and everyone else in his mind but to Mr. Vero too.

"You know what?" Mr. Vero said. "I'm still sorry, too, for the mistakes I've made. I honestly feel sorry for you because you will always carry it with you."

Namu didn't say anything. He knew he would. He was lucky no one had died today, unlike the students who had died when Mr. Vero had made his mistake when it came to the door.

Mr. Vero filled the silence. "But you came up with a decent idea."

"It almost got those students killed."

"One student saved them all."

"What if he hadn't been there?"

"Maybe someone else would have."

Namu shook his head. "I'm just tired." He was tired of feeling empty, angry, and upset at himself.

They reached Mr. Vero's room and went inside. On the desk was a cage almost as large as the desk containing those squealing white creatures. Namu hadn't known they even made noises. In that nightmare world, they had seemed so content.

"Can't we just get rid of them some other way? For good?"

"And throw off the balance of that world again? We know nothing about these creatures. They may be there for a reason, and that is their home. Help me lift this." Mr. Vero grabbed one side of the cage. Namu's hands shook when he went to pick up the other side, and he was surprised to see that his fingers did not go through to where the creatures could touch them. There was a barrier spell placed around it. That was when he noticed the runes placed inside the cage.

"I know they hurt you, Namu. But, like you, they were just doing what they know best. Just like you were doing your best in trying to protect the students here at this school."

Namu hated being compared to those creatures as they walked with the cage. But he kept staring at them and their many eyes on their many heads as they tried to maintain some balance and clung to the cage walls. They reminded Namu of himself: just clinging on as life dragged him from one place to another.

They returned to Namu's room right under Mr. Vero's. They set the cage to the side, opened that door and then scooted the cage to the opening. Then Mr. Vero did a spell to release the creatures.

"Did you get that other one?" Namu asked, watching them go. He didn't know now if he truly hated that world or those creatures anymore. He didn't know if he could actually hate them. Not if he thought of those creatures as something like him. Something placed here to do the best they could until something like him had to ruin their plans, just like they had done for him. They were similar in many ways, it would seem.

"Once we clean everything up, I'll catch it and send it back like the others," Mr. Vero said and patted Namu on the shoulder.

Molly

Chapter Thirty-One

During everything the day the metal from the petrified world had tried to take over and, most of all, when she had been inside that false school made entirely of magick, Molly wanted her family and friends from her other life to be with her. She shivered, remembering how she had carried that feeling on her shoulders when the metal had slinked toward them and then when it had started climbing the walls. The feeling had grown even heavier when the temporary school built around them broke, and she could tell the barrier could barely hold. Then that feeling became unbearable when the giant sheet of metal had fallen, almost crushing them to death.

She could still feel hands on the back of her head as students grabbed whoever they could, and she did the same once they all noticed that the dirt at their feet was falling away. She had thought at first that she was imagining it, but then she had seen the half-human creature digging around in the dirt under them, loosening it, making the hole.

They had all taken the opportunity to use that hole to save themselves just as the hot steam press layered on top of them. Molly hadn't thought it would actually work, but somehow, some other kind of barrier spell lit up, sealing them inside the hole. The heat had then faded, besides the breath of the warm earth, and then the metal had been lifted.

Later, they discovered that the boy who had saved them had been Derrin. That he had multiple transformation drinks on him and had taken one that turned him into part mole. He wouldn't say why he had chosen that one or how he had learned to make all those transformation spells. But everyone was thankful for him, especially Molly.

After all that, after they had been saved, after she had watched the teachers take the metal that clung onto the magickal shield they had made and try to destroy the school to disintegrate it all, she had found that the feeling she had before of wanting her old family and friends had faded just like the heat. She still wanted to see them at some point, but she didn't yearn for their presence, because she knew they wouldn't even know who she was anymore.

No one in that old life would recognize the new her.

She fell into that new self now as she fell asleep in her cool, safe bed.

But then that old self took her over the moment she arrived back on the bright purple ice.

"No, no, no, no!" She scrambled around on hands and knees, the ice slick and wet beneath her palms.

Why was she here? What was trying to take her over?

She thought that this wouldn't happen again. She thought that she would be safe, at least for tonight. That she could settle into her new self and not be dragged back here and forced to lose herself. The new self she had just found and still wanted to make strong.

The ice didn't crack this time. It completely broke through, plunging her into the cold water. It was its own freezing cocoon of ice, the opposite of the metal but still paralyzing. It was a prison that would trap her inside until it stripped her of all she had.

Until she couldn't breathe.

She felt a sinking not only in her gut but of the world around her as she lost herself to the dark depths of the water.

It enraged her now because she had been so close to finally finding herself, and something or someone was trying to take that away.

Her veins and lungs burned as her body worked for oxygen. Or was it anger that was creating this heat? Could it be the metal that she had faced the last few days? The metal that had helped save her the last time she was here, even though every other moment with the metal had been terrifying. The metal that had swaddled her and starved her almost to death. The metal that had almost crushed her. The fog of her brain was overtaking her now, reliving those moments, making her tremble inside.

She knew those moments were not as terrifying as this. Not as terrifying as now.

But still, all those little memories in her head, being trapped, being almost crushed to death, drowning. Why did she have to go through all of them? Why did she have to relive them? Why did she have them floating around in her brain? How was it fair that she would be tortured her whole life with those feelings and images?

Those scattered moments were taking control and overtaking her now. The screaming, the ducking down, the burning metal overhead laying a shadow over them all. The creatures, the crawling, the digging, the band around her waist almost cutting her in half. Those creatures in her hall, in her room, plucking at her insides. All the spirits grabbing her arms, her legs, anything they could reach.

How was it fair? How was it right? How was it that when she was about to be lost to this world, this was what the world wanted her to relive as some sick joke? As a reminder that maybe her trauma was all she had. Was all she was.

The bottoms of her feet hit something solid.

Was this her end? The place she had never reached before? Was this where she was going to live forever? In the memories of her horrible past.

The solid surface beneath her was warm. But suddenly, she was rising. The water was being pushed away. It was being pushed out from all around her.

She didn't know what was happening, but when whatever was beneath her feet started burning, she had an idea. And when she resurfaced out of the giant hole that had driven her deep, she saw she was right.

All around her was metal. The entire body of water was now the burning hot metal of her nightmares, taking over everything. If she wanted to, she could walk the expanse of it and see what was on the other side of the lake or ocean that had always tried to suck her deep.

But she couldn't because she woke up in her bed with a thick hand on her arm that was not her own and sweet-smelling shampoo making her sick.

Trennly was staring at her in shock, his green eyes full of disbelief and his violet mohawk longer than the last time she had seen him.

He let go and took a step back. His chest came up to the top of her bed. He then pulled something out of his pocket. A vial. And he went to take a drink.

But no, she was not about to lose him now.

She grabbed his thick arm and did a glue spell on her own hand, melding her skin with his just as he drank the contents of the vial and turned to mist. But he was stuck, left to float there around her arm. He couldn't go anywhere. Molly grabbed her phone from the other side of her bed off her dresser and made a call.

"Namu! Get Mr. Vero to my room now!" Then she hung up. Mr. Vero was right down her hall. He should be here right away.

It was then that Molly tugged and let the magic fall all around them, bringing Trennly back down to his physical form.

He landed with a thump on the ground, almost dragging her out of her bed.

"You've been doing this to me!" she yelled down at him.

He didn't look sorry. Anger stretched a sneer across his face. He didn't say a thing.

Her door flew open. Apparently, it had already been open, like the other nights when she had almost been taken over. She saw a spirit sprite leave. Was that how he had been getting in?

"Molly! What is—"

Mr. Vero immediately did a spell to paralyze Trennly, whose snarl was fixed as Molly unglued her hand.

It didn't take long for them to take Trennly away. More teachers came in to bring him into another room. They told her that authorities were going to arrive. They also said that they had contacted Kren and that he would be at the school in the morning. Molly was so relieved she could cry. She had caught her own over-taker and would see Kren again, the mini-troll she had somehow grown attached to and had been dying to talk to. She knew he would understand and accept the new her. She wanted him to be a true friend and someone she could talk to, because he was one of the only people she had met who had her best interest at heart. She was thankful he had placed her here.

She still couldn't believe that she had done it. She had finally learned how to protect herself. She had kept herself from drowning in that world, even though someone was trying to hold her under. Somehow, going into that world beyond the door had granted her the ability to do so. But in a way, it wasn't enough.

She was happy she had a way to save herself. Happy she knew now that she didn't have to die if she ever returned to that place. Now she could start building on her new self and never completely lose herself. But she did not like how she had to do it.

She shouldn't have to relive being petrified and almost being killed in order to survive. There had to be more to it than that. She should not be forced to go through a traumatic episode every time in order to live.

She would find another way.

A part of her wanted to return to her old life, but she would stay. She would visit her old home soon, after the end of the school year, since she could protect herself now. She would show her parents her new self, her unforgiving self after she had grown more. The self that maybe she was always supposed to be. And she would tell them about this school and about her magick. But she would tell them that she would have to stay here a while longer and attend at least another year.

She was scared of their reaction. Worried that they wouldn't let her come back. But she needed to find a better way to survive. A better way to save herself that didn't involve hurting herself all over again.

She was beginning to love herself too much to do that.

There was another knock on the door after all the adults had left. She smiled when she saw it was Ova and then burst into tears when her friend took her into her arms.

Lockdrest

She was happy that she had someone. That she had someone to at least talk to through the night.

Namu

Chapter Thirty-Two

There were no classes today, but Mr. Vero still met Namu during their usual time slot, only because Namu had begged him to. He had wanted to know what had gone on with Molly after that phone call in the middle of the night. Molly was lucky that Koz had given Namu one of his many phones and linked his old number and information in case Namu saw another one of those creatures. He didn't want to think about what might have happened if he hadn't.

Mr. Vero had just finished telling Namu what had happened with Molly.

Namu could not believe that the mini-troll who had tried to take over Molly's body was the same one he had seen in his hallway talking to that first year, who had ended up saving all the students. He felt lightheaded trying to piece everything together, including the fact that particular mini-troll had been the reason why Molly had come to the school in the first place. And how another mini-troll named Kren, who had picked up

Molly this morning, had signed her up at this school to protect her.

But Molly had not been protected. Namu had seen the mini-troll named Trennly. He had seen him in *his* hallway and had ignored him.

"But how did Molly stop the mini-troll from taking her over?" Namu asked. He was dying to know how she had survived that. The last time they had practiced together felt like ages ago, and she had just given up.

"She said it was something that you taught her."

Something he taught her? Did it have to do with that metal she said had helped her before? But Namu had loosened his grip on her when they had practiced together that day. He had tried not to completely take her over.

He would have to ask her exactly how she had done it when she returned from wherever Kren had taken her.

"Why would a mini-troll want Molly anyway? He isn't a lost spirit without a body."

"Maybe he is, in some ways."

It still seemed odd to him. Unless maybe this troll's soul was damaged like Namu's was. But how would taking over a body fix anything? Wouldn't the old soul fit right inside the new body? Nothing would change. Unless the troll just wanted a new body. But why?

The thought made Namu worry for Molly even more. She had been through so much in a short time. How did she deal with it all?

"That boy," Mr. Vero said, "the one that was the metal statue in the hallway with the creatures . . . He's going to need you. I talked to him. His name is Terrance. He's pretty traumatized."

"I don't blame him."

Mr. Vero's eyebrows lifted. "Oh, really?"

Namu paused. He wasn't sure why he had sparked Mr. Vero's interest. "Yeah."

Mr. Vero said his following few words slower. "He's already having a hard time reconnecting with his friends."

"Anyone would after that. Does he have any holes?"

Mr. Vero nodded and added, "I found that last creature and sent it back."

"Good." Namu felt horrible that he had caused the one thing he had been trying to prevent to happen to an innocent boy who had done nothing. "I'll talk to him and do whatever I can."

"I'm sure he'll appreciate it. I did not tell him about your past situation. I'm leaving that to you. But I'm sure it will help him to know that he's not alone. You both just need time to heal."

More like time to start all over, but that wasn't possible unless he threw away his old soul and became a newer soul like Molly was. But if he did that, would he even still be him?

"Is it possible to just discard your soul?"

Mr. Vero stared at him, startled, his blue eyes more serious than they usually were. "Why would you want to do that?"

"To start all over."

"I think you mean to heal. You want to heal, Namu. Not throw yourself away. You have a lot going for you."

Namu couldn't think of anything that he had going for him.

Sighing, Mr. Vero patted Namu on the shoulder. "Why don't we approach your situation differently? Think about this boy that everything has just happened to. You don't expect him to return to the way things were before, right? It's nearly impossible. He has changed. The events have changed him. So, instead of expecting him to regrow his soul and get back to normal, wouldn't it be better to expect him to come to terms with his new life, meditate while reflecting on his new self, and let those holes fill in slowly, making new pieces of himself? Newer parts of his soul that he's missing?"

What was Mr. Vero saying? That it was possible, instead of forcing growth, to let it happen through acceptance? That one could heal by coming to terms with the fact that everything had changed? For some reason, when Namu thought of himself having to do that, he didn't want to. But when he thought about the boy named Terrance, he didn't want him to suffer the way Namu had when trying to force things back to how they were before. Namu had learned that was impossible. It was a lost cause to return to your old self when something traumatic had taken pieces of you.

But it didn't mean that those pieces couldn't be reborn and become something new. Something stronger. Could Namu cure himself that way? By building pieces of himself back up from this new beginning? This new foundation? By acceptance?

Would he be more willing to do that for himself now that he had someone else to guide?

Molly

Chapter Thirty-Three

"You sure no new clothes first?" Kren asked. He was holding his nose and cringing while looking her up and down as they stood up to get off the plane. Molly wasn't even embarrassed. She looked down at the clothes she had been wearing for the last few days. They were tattered, bloody, and disgusting, but they showed her growth, what she had recently been through, and where she had come from. "Not yet. After. But I'll pick them out, and when I do, I don't want your opinion."

"What happened old clothes?" Kren asked.

There was no need to lie to him. "I destroyed them."

Kren's eyes grew wide. "Why?"

"For good reason, I promise. I won't do it again."

He left it at that and guided her into the airport with a few other students who had traveled with them by plane. After everything that had happened, the students had been offered a few days off at home, and many had gladly taken it.

But Molly wasn't going home. She would spend a couple of days with Kren, recuperating, after they visited the prison. Kren had offered to take her home afterward, but she refused. She would gladly go back home at the end of the school year. Just not yet. She needed more time away. She didn't care to tell him exactly why.

When he'd picked her up this morning, he had seemed more unsettled than usual. He hadn't asked her how her classes were going, anything about the events with the metal overtaking the school, or anything, really, except questions about Trennly the whole plane ride. She could tell he was worried about his old friend. Honestly, Molly was a little concerned for him too. Although a part of her felt like he should be locked away, another part of her could not help but feel bad for him and his story.

Molly followed Kren as he hurried through the airport to a car already waiting for them on the street, a slick midnight-blue vehicle she had not seen before. When the door opened, she saw that the white bench seats were long enough to fit four people across and that they faced each other. Kren cringed again as Molly scooted inside.

"It will clean itself," he said as the car took off.

"I've never seen a car like this," Molly remarked. It was eerie how clean and quiet it was. She also did not like how she could not see the driver in the front because there was no window.

"It takes us to prison. Some other facilities too. Walitt owned."

Molly didn't know if that was a company or a last name like the airlines or both.

They didn't talk as they drove for miles, leaving the city and then traveling across open roads to a tunnel.

"Will get dark," Kren warned, looking out his window to the tunnel they were heading toward.

Lockdrest

It was even darker than Molly expected; she had figured there would be the yellowish lights that usually lined road tunnels. But instead, everything went pitch black and continued that way. Molly felt disoriented in her seat and had to grab onto the door to try to steady herself and not become sick. The stink from her unwashed clothes was not helping either.

But then everything became bright again, and Molly had to shut her eyes against the glare. They left the tunnel and came out on a gravel road.

"Was that a normal tunnel?" Molly asked, looking up the road to a giant menacing steel-blue building with no windows. It had to be three stories in height and had only a single silver door in the middle. It looked more intimidating than Lockdrest.

"Yes and no," Kren answered. His face fell as he looked at the building.

The car parked itself, and Kren opened the door and scooted out. The air smelled musty, and the sound of gravel crunching beneath their feet rattled Molly's already unsettled nerves as they walked up to the unwelcoming building.

Kren knocked on the door with his large fist.

Kren was the one who had wanted to confront Trennly and had wanted Molly to come with him. At first, she had been for it, wanting to hear Trennly's side of the story and maybe get an apology so she could make her mind up about him, but now, after arriving at this place, she was a little freaked out.

The silver door opened.

A tall, thin, pale man peeked out and down at them. "Visitors." He opened the door more, revealing his black suit and long thinning beard to study Kren. "I presume for the recently detained."

Kren nodded, gnarling his hands together, refusing to look the man in his beady eyes.

"The . . . other mini-troll was brought into the back this morning. For attempting a body-snatch? Correct?" The man stood aside so they could enter, but Kren didn't move. He didn't even nod.

Instead, Molly answered for him. "That's correct. I was the body almost snatched." Then she carefully pulled Kren's hands apart and gripped one of them into hers to lead him inside.

"Interesting. And why do you wish to see him?"

The room they came into was narrow, like a foyer, but was decorated like a fancy living room, except everything was silver. The walls, the couches, the carpet, the tables, the silverware, and a machine that looked like it might be a coffee maker with silver cups were all gleaming, purely coated in metal.

"We just wish to talk to him," Molly answered, mesmerized by the hauntingly modern, chrome-like display around her.

The man waited a few more beats, but when Molly said nothing else, he seemed to accept her vague explanation. "Fine. Let me get the key for his cell, and I'll lead you there. Make yourselves at home."

"Can . . . can I use?" Kren pointed at the machine on the table that made some kind of drink.

"Of course," the man said, opening a second silver door next to the table holding the machine before slipping inside and shutting it, leaving Molly and Kren alone in the room.

Kren dug deep into his brown suit pockets and plucked out a few bundles of herbs that he, apparently, carried around. He set two bags on the tall table, then put his hands on the table to try to lift himself, but his hands were too slick with sweat. Everything rattled.

"I can do it," Molly said, taking up the flowery-smelling herbs. "Just tell me what to do."

Kren sighed. "Open top."

Molly did. She peeled back the lid to reveal a clean silver bowl.

"Put inside. Close. Then push button."

Molly followed the steps, and there was a click. She grabbed a cold silver cup and put it under the hole just as pink tea started pouring out of a spout.

It didn't take too long for the cup to fill. Then Molly handed it to Kren. He took a sip, and his shoulders relaxed and eyes drooped.

The door creaked open.

"This way, please," the tall man said.

They followed him through the door.

There was a long beige hallway with solid walls and nothing else, except at the very end of the hallway, which was a brown door with a small window in the upper center. The tall man opened it and led them through. It took them to a set of black stairs that they climbed. The tall man was faster than Molly could keep up with, but she didn't even try. She stayed behind with Kren, who was going extra slowly since he was trying not to spill the drink he had brought with him. The man was waiting for them at the top by the time they arrived, then he opened another brown door. It led to a hallway that looked exactly like the previous one.

Molly didn't understand the point of the solid blank beige walls until the tall man hit a key card on a particular bare spot on one of the walls, which then fell away as if it had never existed. Behind the wall was a cell, complete with bars.

Was that what was behind all the walls?

Trennly was startled inside the cell, cowering for a moment with his hands over his head. But then he turned toward them. When he saw Kren, he shook his head and looked at one of the walls outside his cell. His eyes drifted to Molly. His face fell, and he clenched his jaw before his gaze sought out the floor.

"I will leave you be," the man said, walking off the way they had come. Molly listened to his footsteps on the hardwood flooring, then heard the door at the end of the hall open and close.

Molly looked between Kren and Trennly. Trennly wouldn't make eye contact with either of them.

Kren's face fell further. It hurt her inside.

Finally, Kren spoke up. "I came all way to see you."

"I don't know why," Trennly responded, plopping himself on the floor before he began dusting off his black shoe to no avail.

"I looked all over. You closed up shop."

This got Trennly to look up at him. "So did you."

Kren shrugged and took a drink from his silver cup with shaky hands.

"You have a drinking problem," Trennly remarked, watching Kren gulp it down.

Kren shrugged again, wiping his mouth with his sleeve. "You have getting in trouble problem."

"Always have."

They were silent for a while, leaving Molly standing there, not knowing what to do or say.

Kren looked to the door at the end of the hall. "Should I leave?"

"I would rather you not come here at all."

"You knew I would. You know I won't stop."

Snickering for a moment, Trennly got up from the ground with some effort and made his way over to them. He put his hands on the bars that separated them. His hair did not smell as nice as it usually did, and the color wasn't as vibrant. His skin was not as shiny or perfect either. And there were small purple scars on his arms and hands that she hadn't seen before.

Lockdrest

"Garlic bread, again? Really, Kren? It makes your breath stink, especially mixed with whatever herbs you're drinking."

Kren ignored his comment. "Apologize."

"To who? Her?" Trennly still wouldn't look at Molly. He looked only at Kren.

"Name is Molly. You feel bad. You won't look at her."

At one time, Molly might have been self-conscious that he was refusing to look at her, which sounded silly to her now, after everything. But that was when she had despised herself. Now she knew that the reason why he wouldn't look at her wasn't because of her; it was because of how he felt about himself.

"Apologize," Kren said again.

"For possibly finding a solution and trying it?" She could see Trennly growing angry. At himself or at Kren, she didn't know.

"I found a way, Kren. I found a way that could have worked. And once I was inside with her soul"—he squeezed the bars—"I could have studied empty vessels, unlike anyone else."

Kren shook his head. "Not possible. Whatever planning, not possible."

"I'm an expert at drinks," Trennly sneered. "I was and still am smarter than you, Kren. I could have figured it out. I have. You don't understand. I have nothing! This was the only thing that could have worked for me. For those like me in the future."

"You would have killed her."

"No! I found a way to make sure her spirit stayed. That it wasn't lost and wouldn't drown. I would have found a way to save her. I am not a troll, Kren. I said I will redeem myself from being one."

"A way? What way?" Doubt flickered in Kren's eyes.

"A token that follows the rule 'like calls to like.' It would have kept her human spirit in her body. Would have kept it from dying until I figured things out."

Molly remembered the token she had found briefly that one time in her room when she had escaped the place her mind imprisoned her in. How, when she had looked again, it was gone.

"Where did you find token?" Kren crossed his arms.

Trennly looked around first before leaning in to whisper, "From the deep magick market. Someone had taken pieces of destroyed souls and worked to put them into these coins to see if they could make a whole soul, at least enough so it could pass as a soul to bypass certain things . . . Like calls to like, Kren. So, another human spirit would have kept her soul there. Would have kept it from drowning."

"You don't know. That's a risk." Kren shook his head.

"It's not fair for me to be trapped like this," Trennly said. "Not when this isn't what I was meant to be. I'm tired of being forced to live like this and face the trauma life has dealt me every single day."

Molly's heart stopped. Her mind paused. Trauma? Living with himself was as torturous for him as it was for her being in that place of ice?

"All I want is to be something respected, not a griffon or another creature but one I identify with. You wouldn't understand. You relate to being a troll. That's you. Not me. What was I supposed to do? No one ever listened. I've—we've—been ignored when it has come to this our entire childhood. Turned away by everyone. Even by Lockdrest!"

Molly started to back away. Trennly was struggling. He had been struggling. He didn't feel right with himself. Worse than she had ever felt with herself. Was he really the bad guy in this story? Could he be a bad guy when he only wanted change that the magickal world would not offer him? He had not planned to hurt her. Not really. He had hurt no one. Only saved them. But the way he had gone about everything had been wrong.

Desperation had taken his hand when everything and everyone else had turned away.

Trennly's next words stopped Molly backing away.

"You know what . . . I'm done. I'm done with this world. Done with everything. I'm sick and tired of no one listening to me or understanding. We have magick. If more people cared and took their time, we would find a way. Just tell Derrin I won't be meeting with him anymore."

He let his hands fall away from the bars and hang limp at his sides. "He doesn't know what happened to me, and he is traumatized after the incident, I'm sure."

Kren tsked. His eyes narrowed. "Why mess with other student?"

"I was helping him." Trennly squeezed his hands into fists. "Well, helping him *and* using him. He wanted to impress someone at home, so I offered to help. I used his room to sleep in while he was at class and taught him what I knew."

"Derrin . . . Derrin was the one who saved us," Molly breathed.

Trennly had taught him. How?

"I know." Trennly turned to her and actually looked at her for the first time. "I was there."

Kren nodded as if he were not surprised. As if he knew deep down that Trennly was good and that he was just a little lost. Yesterday, Molly had thought something was floating around them in the fake school built on visionary and gnome magick. That something had been shifting to fight off the growing metal that was reaching for them. But she had been too freaked out to pay too much attention to it. She had been too focused on the growing mass above them that was breaking the barrier. But it did make sense. Trennly must have used an astral spell. He also must have given Derrin the one drink that helped save them all.

He had been helping another student this whole time. He had also risked himself when he didn't have to in order to protect the other students. He had saved others and let a student take all the credit for what he had done. Did that prove he was actually good?

Molly walked back up to the bars. She trusted Kren and his opinion. If Kren thought deep down that Trennly was a good guy, then she also wanted to.

"I want to find a way to help you," she said.

Trennly sneered at her. His eyes were full of anger, unfairness, and doubt. "Good luck with that, princess."

Molly met his eyes. "I will find a way to help you. You're good. You just have been dealt a bad life." She knew how that felt.

"I'm not good."

"You saved those kids, and you didn't have to. You didn't even have to put yourself in danger for them." Molly would find a way to save his soul that was lost like hers used to be.

"I tried to overtake you. I'm not good." He shook his head. "Kren, tell her."

Kren didn't say anything for a moment. "I'm sure you thought could save her soul. You did her wrong. It is her to decide."

Trennly rolled his eyes and sighed. His cheeks burned red.

That did it for her. She was going to help him no matter what it took. She would find a way.

He had done a bad thing. She knew that. She also knew that he had been fueled by loneliness and desperation, so he had taken matters into his own hands.

But he had not hurt anyone. He had not planned to hurt anyone. He had planned to study empty vessels, and maybe he would have found a way to help her.

And it was her life, her soul, that he had wronged. So, it was up to her to decide. It was up to her to understand and to sympathize with him. She might not forgive him fully. That would take time. That would take him proving himself and showing that he would not hurt her again. But she wanted to believe.

Without him, she would never have gone to a magickal school. She would never have learned to protect herself. She would never have found herself. He had saved the school. He had saved them. She owed him something. She owed him healing.

He helped her heal in a way she never could have, so she would also help him heal.

After she found a way to help him out of this prison first.

Then, together, they could both try to find a way to make the magickal world listen and traumatized people be seen.

Author's Note

So, I brought you a story with a few things left to be answered. Let me say to you that the answers will come. I have realized that the more I write, the more I plan out a story well in advance, saving things for later to give readers a more significant 'aha' moment. For example, Ova's red marks will be brought up later and will be important in her character arc. Also, the reason why Koz had the reaction he had toward Molly being an empty vessel will play a part in the story later on. I like to stay true to the characters, so to me, there was no way for Molly to know the whys behind Koz and Ova, especially since both of those characters would be private about their certain circumstances. Also, if you didn't get enough of the cell apps plotline, that plotline belongs to the overarching plot and will be tackled a big deal in the second book and then finished off in the third. So, I hope if you continue on this ride that you enjoy some of the slow burn, and more than anything, I hope you enjoy the story as a whole.

With that, each book in this trilogy will be diving into and visiting one of the three schools mentioned in this book. This will open a little more of the magickal world. The next school that the characters will be brought into is Opendrest.

This story came to me when two ideas collided. The first idea was from a draft I wrote when I gave myself a writing exercise after watching *The Magicians*. Something happened in that show that made me want to write a quick scene where the main character was panicking and knew what was happening, while the reader did not know. So, I wrote the scene where Namu finds that the door is open and his room is changing. At that time, I didn't know about the door or why he was so upset about it. Then, sometime later, I started a writing class. In that class, we were supposed to produce a short story or a chapter. I decided to write a first chapter and let my mind run wild and free. It was honestly so much fun.

After that, I decided to find a way to put the two ideas together. I made the story two points of view and focused the world-building on two things that I wanted from our world. First, I wanted to create a world with no weapons, especially guns. The second thing I wanted was to focus on healing from trauma. I was in therapy at the time dealing with my PTSD and *hated* how I was being forced to relive my trauma to heal from it. I wanted to write a book that tried to find some other way to heal. So, each one of the books dives into different ways that people can heal from trauma. Molly represents myself when it comes to her trauma and trying to fight against having to go back to the same place each time.

I will tell you that the hardest part of making this story was having to go back and change/make sense of the magick system since that wasn't what I built the world around. I was able to do that and everything is laid out on The Lockdrest Universe website. I hope all of you have fun with that.

The last thing I want to and need to talk about is Trennly's arc. I know you don't get much of him from this book, but expect more later. I hope you don't hate him because he will be going through a redemption arc. I feel this character is very important to the story for reasons you might be able to figure out, which will be addressed more in-depth later, especially in the next Author's Note in the Negligent Magick Trilogy.

Thank you so much for reading through this and being on this journey with me. I have been creating a quiz for Lockdrest that I hope you enjoy when it comes out. I have also already finished the first draft of the second book in this trilogy. After this is released, I imagine that draft will be going through the editing process. Our next release is November of this year and will be an LGBTQIA+ fantasy about a witch who is a demigirl. That book will be the first of a duology. I hope you give it a try. As for the second book in this trilogy, the projected release date is April 2025.

Please leave a review if you have the time because every bit helps. Also, if you find you are a Moonshade Reader and want to stay up to date with everything, please sign up for our monthly newsletter!

Acknowledgments

It's insane how much can go into an academia book when you want to really dive into each little piece that forms a magickal school. We had a lot of artists we collaborated with on this one.

I would love to thank Carlos for the door design, especially when I thought I had a great idea for a design and then only a month before this book went to formatting decided to change it.

Our concept artist Julija Gumbryte was so fun to work with. We LOVE our cast of characters she created. She also made the art for the back of our hardcover. We have a couple more fun ideas coming up with her that we hope you enjoy.

Our cover artist Maja K. who has now had my back twice, is absolutely amazing. It took us more than a few times to get this cover right and she kept me uplifted the entire time, which I am thankful for. This is our second time working with her and I hope to continue to do so.

Eli Cuaycong is another artist I would like to thank. He is so reliable and always blows us away. He created the keys you see at the beginning of each chapter and at the beginning of the story as a whole. He also made keys for the main characters which you can find at the beginning of this story, on The Lockdrest Universe website, and on the back of the hardcover and paperback.

Alana Tedmon is yet another artist we loved working with. I met her at a conference so long ago. A funny memory is that we ended up washing dishes together in a hotel room bathtub haha. I was so happy that we kept in touch and that I was able to reach out to her for her to make the beautiful and haunting inside title page!

As with every book, there comes editing. The beginning of this manuscript went through many changes and has seen many eyes. I would love to thank one of my awesome teachers Ananda Naima Gonzalez, who is the reason this manuscript exists. Also, Emily Forney who had excellent suggestions for the first chapter.

I need to thank Amr Saleh for checking over the beginning of this book multiple times and assuring me that it was good after attending a group together where even more changes were made.

I want to thank our developmental editor, Nick Hodgson. It is because of them that readers received more time with Koz and Rem in the story.

Our amazing beta readers are the best. Alyx Ramos (alyxreads), Lilith Henry, and Tessy Dockery gave awesome suggestions. I'm thankful for the time they took to read this. I highly appreciated Tessy Dockery's enthusiasm, which is always such a need to keep me going.

Our copy editor Olivia Valcarce was such a gift to this story. She was able to catch so many mistakes that flew by everyone who read it beforehand and she streamlined so many things. Also, she gave me suggestions to help me grow as a writer overall. I laughed so many times at her suggestions and comments. I don't know what I would have done without her.

Thank you once again to our amazing formatter and proofreader Samantha Pico for putting everything together for us and once again making one of our books come to life. It's a dream to get to hold a physical book in our hands. I'm also thankful for her guidance.

And lastly, I want to thank my husband who has gotten me to the point where I am starting to accept and love myself. It has been amazing growing with him these last thirteen years. I don't know many people in my life who would stay up with me past midnight to perfect things as much as we can for our readers. He loves me through all the stress and has been there to pick me up during PTSD episodes and talk me through them. It's he who drew the layout of Lockdrest. He also put together our Moonshade Press hardcover designs under the dust jacket. I truly could not have tackled this without him. The fact that he is always ready to jump in with me when it comes to the next book is such a big gesture to me, especially with how stressful and busy our lives are. He means everything to me and I'm so happy to have pieces of us combined forever with each book we create.

LOCKDREST

ART BY JULIJA GUMBRYTE

Newsletter
&
QR Code

This is the QR code to our bio link for easy access
to our online collective. I hope you enjoy!

adoramichaels.com

The first book in *The Passing Realm Series* will be released in
November 2024.

About the Author

Adora Michaels is a Ya/New Adult Fantasy author. She grew up surrounded by people who were not like-minded. It wasn't until she returned to therapy in 2021 that she started gaining the courage to allow herself to be herself. Although it is still a battle, she works on expressing who she is every day while grieving the Adora she missed out on and could have always been. Now, she uses most of her energy to create with the goal of giving others the strength to find and be themselves too.

Printed in the USA
CPSIA information can be obtained
at www.ICGtesting.com
CBHW031711160724
11470CB00006B/7/J

9 781961 830059